THE SLOW TRAIN TO MILAN

Lisa St Aubin de Terán was born in London in 1953. At the age of sixteen she left James Allen's Girls' School to marry. She and her exiled Venezuelan husband travelled for two years in Italy before returning to his family home in the Andes. During her seven years in South America she managed her husband's sugar plantation and avocado farm and she based her first novel, *Keepers of the House* (Penguin, 1983), on this experience. After this she returned to England with her daughter and she now lives in Norfolk.

Keepers of the House, which won a Somerset Maugham Award for 1983, received widespread critical acclaim: the *Observer* called it an 'exceptional first novel, richly evocative and cunningly crafted'; *The Times Literary Supplement* thought it 'a remarkably good first novel . . . In effect, this is an account – particularly gripping because of the quality of the writing and the esoteric setting – of a strong-willed young woman's education by experience'; and Paul Bailey in the *Standard* wrote 'a genuine and haunting and unforgettable work of art. It is this novel's triumph to be consistently exhilarating, never less than a pleasure to read.'

The Slow Train to Milan was awarded the John Llewelyn Rhys Memorial Prize for 1983.

LISA ST AUBIN DE TERÁN

———

THE SLOW TRAIN
TO MILAN

A KING PENGUIN
PUBLISHED BY PENGUIN BOOKS

Penguin Books Ltd, Harmondsworth, Middlesex, England
Viking Penguin Inc., 40 West 23rd Street, New York, New York 10010, U.S.A.
Penguin Books Australia Ltd, Ringwood, Victoria, Australia
Penguin Books Canada Ltd, 2801 John Street, Markham, Ontario, Canada L3R 1B4
Penguin Books (N.Z.) Ltd, 182–190 Wairau Road, Auckland 10, New Zealand

First published in Great Britain by Jonathan Cape Ltd 1983
First published in the United States of America by Harper & Row, Publishers, Inc., 1983
Published in Penguin Books in the United States of America by arrangement
with Harper & Row, Publishers, Inc.
Published in Penguin Books 1984

—

Made and printed in Great Britain by
Richard Clay (The Chaucer Press) Ltd,
Bungay, Suffolk

—

To O.B.M.

Chapter I

It's nearly ten years now since I left Italy, and three full years since I left the Andes, but strangers still come up to me sometimes, in Paris, or London, or Caracas. And they say, 'You were one of the four, weren't you?'

And I know what they mean, and sometimes I nod, and sometimes I don't any more, but inside, I always think, 'We weren't really four, there were five of us: César, Otto, Elías and me, and the slow train to Milan.' And the slow train was the slide rule of our existence, often our raison d'être. Our exile was aimless without it. I wonder if we would have survived the waiting, the tension and the failure, but for the luxury of moving on.

I met César when I was sixteen. Like so many others, I was fascinated by him. I suppose that I could claim to know him better than anyone else does, and yet he is still the same stranger of our first days, has still the same shy, cruel smile. Later people asked me why I did it. When I think it over, I can only come up with a kind of restlessness. I joined them out of boredom, and then just stayed on. It all began in London, and then we drifted to Italy, later travelling from Paris to Milan and back, and sometimes to Bologna.

I met César first, although I didn't really meet him as such, I just came upon him in my tracks. I had been doing some quick shopping for the weekend, and I was making my way home, carrying my mother's round wicker basket clutched to me with both hands as an improvised shield from the wind. As I went to turn the corner into my street César loomed up in front of me, immensely tall, and directly in my path. I looked up, ready to dismiss any explanation that might be proffered, but before I could fully collect my thoughts, César, who was then a total stranger, said,

'South America', and I said, 'Yes', and I still don't know exactly what he meant.

He took my basket and walked beside me. I waited for him to say something else, and it took me some minutes to grasp that that was all. I was living with my mother in a rambling flat in south London. She was away for the weekend, and I was preparing for my Cambridge entrance, traipsing from Clapham to Eccleston Square to my crammer's. I stopped in front of the row of bare pollarded limes, hoping to disguise my home. But it was early January and very cold so I moved back to the entrance to the flats. I tried to dismiss César at the outer gates, at the door, on the stairs, and finally at my door. But each time he nodded and followed me on. I realised that despite his appearance, he wasn't English, and his 'South America' made more sense. When all my farewells failed, I gave up and shut the door in his face, only to find that he had his foot wedged in the frame.

He forced his way into the flat without a word. I was physically blocking the way to the sitting-room, so he made his way into the kitchen and sat down. Once there, he stayed very still and silent with his arms crossed. I made a few jokey attempts to get him to explain himself, and then asked him to leave. César took no more notice of me than he did of the specks of dust drifting over the stove. He would neither talk nor move.

I was secretly rather pleased with this course of events. I had just returned from a tour of Canada and the Caribbean with my father, and I was bored with London. There was something about the nervous greetings of academics that weighed me down. The highlight of our tour had been one evening in Barbados. There was a kind of reception party held in our honour, with the usual bustle of dresses and champagne and the endless questions and introductions. Then out of the blue my father. Serge, came up behind me, and whispered to me to make for the bay window at the back of the room. I did, and we slipped out and on to the crumpled beach that flanked the campus, and walked along the sand and through the moonlight into Bridgetown, with its pirate masts and its Mount Misery. After that, I decided that I would like to step out through more windows. And here, in the kitchen, there was a tall stranger unlike anyone I had ever known.

I dismissed the idea of calling the police, and even of calling in one of the neighbours, because although he was uninvited, César wasn't bothering me. It was this last factor that really decided me to let matters take their own course, since I was (and still am) very nervous of Jack the Ripper characters. It seemed to be perfectly natural that César should be sitting in the kitchen, and that I should be alone, and that I should have no idea who he was.

I walked around him, as one might at a gallery. I viewed him from different angles. He was very beautiful in a strange passive way. I was reminded of Buster Keaton, or of a Greek statue. His eyes were the golden brown of an eagle, and the line of his nose was perfectly straight. Later, I learnt that he was very proud of that line and of his pride itself which he carried like a Siamese twin. I began to want him to speak. But he was silent. I tried tempting him with other languages, with French and Dutch and Russian, I even exposed my faulty Latin. He showed his good-will, he smiled indulgently. He was like a mountain towering over my table. I offered him food. He shook his head, then he pointed to himself, like Tarzan in corduroy, and said,

'C'est ça.'

I was delighted. I didn't realise that that was his name: César. He was silent again, and I left him so I could have a bath. I locked myself in, poured an extravagant quantity of my mother's bath salts into the water and lay back to day-dream and think, in that order.

The next time I went back to the kitchen, he had gone. I hadn't heard the front door, which meant that he was probably still in the flat. I wasn't keen on looking for him. It occurred to me that he might be carrying a knife. I realised that

I should have done something about him sooner. If I tried to get out and run away, I'd have to come back some time, and he could be waiting for me; anyway, I argued, he could be on the stairs. I decided that my position was hopeless and I'd take a risk. Maybe he was just stretching his legs.

I found him in the sitting-room with a battered atlas on his lap. He was tracing around Italy. I sat down with relief, and wondered why I hadn't noticed how debauched he looked. He tried again,

'C'est ça, c'est ça.'

He looked sad and there were dark rings under his eyes. I lit a fire and shut the door. César sprang up and opened it, and then sat down again, almost apologetically. It seemed an odd thing to have done. I had told him my name before, but he hadn't seemed to take it in. So I too tried again. This time he shook his head. It seemed that he didn't like the name. There didn't seem to be much that I could do about it, so I repeated it. This time he said, 'No', firmly.

I laughed. 'What do you mean, "No"? My name just happens to be Lisaveta.'

However, it obviously wasn't so for him, because he shook his head again and turned back to the atlas. It was getting dark and I was wondering what to do about him, when he stood up and left the room. Making his way back across the hall as confidently as he had come in, he left, and disappeared down the stairs. I sat staring into the fire without even attempting to make head or tail of what had happened and I was still in this position of toasted reverie when someone knocked on the door.

It was César, carrying a large cardboard box which he thrust into my arms. I staggered under the weight of it. It contained a collection of books and records, none of which I appreciated at the time, but which I later learnt were his most treasured possessions. With the box came a note in spidery italics and in French. It had been written to me by a friend of his. From this letter I learnt that César was a Venezuelan newly come to London, that he wished me to have all the books, etc., that he spoke no English, and that he would like to call on me. The last seemed an odd request, under the circumstances.

We had no sooner sat down than César began to tell me something. It was the first of our many frustrating attempts to understand each other.

'Wigo pop?' he asked, and looked at me, obviously requiring some reply. I repeated his words incredulously, and he repeated them again, insistently. He looked at me with a faint hint of disappointment in his gaze. It was a look that I was to see rather often. It was as though I had committed some indiscretion that he hardly liked to mention further. He was carrying a small dictionary in his pocket, which he drew like a gun, and pointed at me. Then he took it back and flicked through the Spanish–English section until he came to, we go.

'Veta,' he said, for such, it seemed, he had decided was my true name, 'Veta, we go pop.'

I took his dictionary and looked up, in turn, what was to be the most useful phrase in the whole language; 'What does it mean?'

'What does "pop" mean?' I asked.

After a long and exhausting battle of signs, and cross references, I discovered that I was invited for a drink in a pub, and we spent the remainder of the evening sitting in a noisy, mock-Edwardian bar. Neither of us said much, and what we did say wasn't understood. César asked me to sing to him. I was getting used to his odd requests, and I sang a few bars, rather quietly, aware of the people at the next table. He walked me home, and kissed me lightly on the forehead and left me outside the flats. I had braced myself for a struggle, and felt a little disappointed at not having to show my puritanical flag.

César returned the next day with a bunch of carnations. He was wearing a three-piece suit, and he made straight for the sitting-room and stationed himself beside the fire, where he remained for the rest of the day. I was most intrigued by his not eating. He turned down all my offers of tea and coffee and food, and yet stayed for the entire day. My mother would be returning from Loughborough on the following morning, and I couldn't quite make up my mind who to tell first, her or him. I decided that, in all decency, she should be the first to know that a strange man was keeping up some mysterious vigil in her sitting-room, so I telephoned her at my sister's.

We exchanged our news and were about to ring off when I found a way of telling her about César. She seemed more alarmed than I had predicted. I couldn't keep up with her questions:

'What does he look like?'

'Old.'

'How old?'

'Very old.'

'Oh.' The last very disappointed but still keeping a brave face on it.

'And who is he, darling?'

'Well, I don't know.'

'But where did you meet him?'

'Just on the street.'

'Oh God. What do you mean just on the street, where on the street?'

'In Abbeville Road.'

'In Abbeville Road!' This last was too much for her and her voice rose. Why that road should seem worse than any other I don't know.

'Well, never mind, darling.' She was brave again, in control. 'I'll be back tomorrow. Just wait until I get there, all right? Where is he now, anyway?'

'He's here.'

'What do you mean, here?'

'He's here, at the flat, in the room.'

'Oh my God. Why did you let him in?'

'Well, he just forced his way in, actually.'

'I see, you're alone in the flat with a very old Venezuelan man whom you have never seen before and who forced his way into the flat and has been there for two days and he doesn't eat anything and he's got rings under his eyes and he's changed your name to Veta but he doesn't say anything else, is that about right?'

'Yes, that's more or less it.'

'I see, now, do you think', my mother weighed her words very carefully, 'that he is going to attack you? I mean, I think that I should call the police.'

'Oh no, he's all right, he's very old-fashioned.'

'So was Jack the Ripper.'

'Why don't you come and take a look at him and then see what you think. He's not doing anything, he's just here.'

We agreed that I was scarcely to breathe until her return, which would be in a matter of hours, and that things would then be settled. Things seemed ominous for César in his armchair. My mother was the headmistress of a remand home in south London and her voice had gained authority over the years. Sometimes she gave people the impression that they were all maladjusted teenagers in disgrace. César sat through the remainder of the evening oblivious to the storm that was about to break over his head. It was not just my person, but my mother's territorial rights that were at stake here. He was in her room.

I decided to weather the row by ignoring it, like an earthquake that you cannot avoid, except by sitting still, since to go outside means death, and to stay inside means death as well. César always claimed that it was destiny that brought us together. Whatever it was, it was a very strong force that bowled over all the obstacles in our way. When my mother arrived home, cold and tired from her journey, and put out by having to come home a day early, she was in a mood for no nonsense.

She was visibly relieved to see me in one piece, and the furniture still holding together. She was inside, the door hadn't been barricaded, I was not a hostage, all these things soothed her rage. She swept into the sitting-room like a dragon with its claws drawn for a fight. César had moved towards the window when he heard the knock at the door, and he'd peered into the street to reassure himself. My mother stared at him for a moment and then said,

'But he's beautiful, darling,' and they shook hands. César clicked his heels like a Prussian officer, and they smiled as though at the signing of some treaty.

'Sit down, sit down,' she said, 'you must be tired.' All her own tiredness had fled. My mother has always had a passion for lame ducks, and a great respect for genuine sadness, and as a very beautiful woman herself, she admires the quality in others. César came like a sacrament to her house, both sad and beautiful. He was her world as it should be, the aesthete's dream.

On the third day after I met César he asked me to marry him. We were standing at a bus stop on the edge of Clapham Common. I shook my head. His face was always very pale, but sometimes it became quite expressionless, almost ghostly. It did then.

'Why, no?' he asked me.

'I don't know you.' I laboured with his pocket dictionary and brought out a 'Maybe later, tal vez luego.' He said some words in Spanish that I didn't understand but that I remembered later. He said, 'You will never know me,' and then again, 'Marry me, vamanos a Italia.'

I was saved by the arrival of our bus.

After the first week, we went out with Otto as well. César introduced Otto as 'a brother'. But I soon realised that by brother, he meant that they were best friends, inseparable, but not related. Unlike César, who had a decidedly Germanic air about him, Otto looked like every gringo's idea of a South American, a sort of ageing Zapata, or a slightly jaded Mexican ranchero from a 1940s film. He had dark penetrating eyes that turned easily from melancholy to anger, and he was short and slight of build, and against the pallor of his face, his copious moustache stood out. That and a kind of neatness about him, almost French in its meticulous care.

In direct contrast to César's lazy calm, Otto was jumpy. He was nervous with a kind of electric spark that made him almost frightening to talk to in his aggressive brilliance. From the very earliest days, Otto tried to draw me into the intellectual side of their group, and my constant dismal failures to live up to his plans were the source of many hours of scornful banter. At first, he was very kind to me, translating and explaining César's oddities. But my shyness infuriated him. On the second evening that I met him, he asked me to read aloud a poem of Lorca's in English to see what it sounded like in translation, so I read,

14

'Green, how much I want you green . . .' blushing all the while until Otto took the book from me mid-verse, and asked testily,

'What *can* you read?'

The next six months were a downhill run in Otto's estimation. Notwithstanding, we began to operate as a group. They visited me together, and together we made plans to travel. I had travelled a lot, and I have always liked it. We traced a route across the Alps and down to Milan and Bologna. I asked, 'Why Bologna?'

'We have friends there.'

'When will this be?' I used to ask Otto, and he would say, 'First we must wait for Elías.'

'Who is Elías?' I would ask him, and he would always answer the same thing,

'Elías is a very serious man.'

Weeks went by, and then a month. César was growing thin and pale, and Otto looked positively ill.

César moved less than any person I have ever known. His passivity was the only truly unnatural thing about him. He would come to the flat early in the morning and wait for me to be ready and then sit in the same room as I, all day, staring vacantly at things I couldn't see. We set aside a room for him to sleep in during the afternoon, a kind of winter siesta that gradually prolonged itself as his confidence in our friendship grew, until he would sleep for the best part of the day and then read a little and then fall asleep over the television and then go home. We continued in this laconic sexless style until early March, when Otto announced that they had to go to Amsterdam 'on business'. 'On business' became a catch-phrase. I discovered that 'on business' meant merely 'to do something that is none of your business', and would be applied, on principle, to anything and everything from buying a loaf of bread to finding a new house.

I was sorry to see César go when he left for Holland. He was only away for a week, but it was enough to make me realise that I wanted to go with him the next time that he went anywhere. I had grown strangely fond of having him around. Much later, in court, when the judge asked me why I married him, it occurred to me that it was simply because he was there. He sent me a postcard,

'Amsterdam is beautiful, I love you always, César.' He had never said that he loved me before, and I was glad to see him admit it.

With his usual cryptic calm, César had given me a brown-paper parcel to look after while he was away.

'It's money,' he had said.

I thought he was joking. I found it hard to follow what they did, and didn't do, and found it far easier not to bother with the details of our life. So apart from switching to South American History for one of my 'A' Level papers, I made no concessions to their unorthodox ways.

'Don't lose it,' Otto had called out from the taxi, and I had meant to put the paper bag away with the trays of faded letters and documents that we kept at the bottom of Aunt Connie's battered bookcase in the sitting-room. But I forgot in the end, thus beginning a career of nonchalance in money matters. César and Otto returned at three o'clock in the morning, a week later. For some reason, they usually arrived in the small hours, and always telephoned at ungodly times. They were both very drunk, and they came sheepishly, laden with presents and apologies, and then César collapsed on the carpet.

I gave them back their paper bag. It contained sixteen hundred pounds in bundles of two hundred. They divided it and then César gave me his half for safe keeping, and I became his cashier for ever after. After Amsterdam, we discovered the Embankment Gardens with its concerts and quiet benches and the statue to the Camel Corps. And we began what promised to be a blissful summer. I fitted in my six hours a week at the crammer's while César waited for me at Charing Cross; he would sleep through the brass bands, and sleep on the benches, on buses, and in bed. I would read a book, and catch him between siestas, and Otto would come and go, and then he too began to lie down a lot.

Tidying up their flat one day, I discovered a wallet full of passports, each with the same photo and fingerprints, but with a different name. Since I spent virtually every minute with them, I knew that they couldn't be doing much in London, but

I began to wonder what they did elsewhere. Otto's behaviour, I realised, was not just eccentric, he was actually hiding, and not just paranoid, as I tended to be. And then, one day Otto was taken away. We were all drinking at their flat, something we did rather a lot, when there was a knock at the door. It was the police. César and Otto were both very calm, almost resigned. I noticed first how César's actions seemed to slip into a kind of slow motion that I came to know as being so characteristic of him. It was Otto who answered the door, while César stayed where he was, sitting on a low-slung sofa under the window.

'Good evening, sir,' one of the policemen said, and then, immediately, as though programmed to say his whole piece and unable to stop, 'I believe that a Mr Orlando García Rodriguez lives here.' Otto was about to answer, but the police constable continued, almost breathless in his haste, 'I'm afraid we've got some bad news for you, sir.' The two of them towered a good head and shoulders above Otto, as they moved slowly through the door.

'I wonder if we might come in a moment?' they said, looking round the room at César and myself. 'I suppose you know why we have come,' the first one suggested, and there was a hint of reluctance in his voice, as though he didn't really want to do what he knew he had to.

'Perhaps', he added, 'you would rather discuss this alone', and he eyed us.

Otto too had grown slow to answer, but he said, 'Yes', and looked at César with real pleading; here was his chance to act alone, for César to go free. I didn't understand what was happening, but I sensed that in some way this would be final. César didn't move.

'You'll have a chance to see your friend before we take him away,' one of them said.

And then César rose to go, pulling me gently by the sleeve. As we left the room, I heard one of them say to Otto,

'We traced you through one of the mobile units, your case has been given top priority, we shall escort you as far as Oxford, and then hand you over to the authorities there.' Throughout the interview, Otto was silent. It was a small flat, and even after we left the room, César and I could still hear the chewed south London voice drifting through the walls.

'We realise this must be a shock for you, though of course you will have been expecting it from day to day. I believe this isn't the first time . . . Paris, Caracas, Maracay, it's a wonder you're still going,' he mused.

This was followed by a long silence.

'I'm afraid you'll have to come with us now,' the voice droned on, 'just collect a few of your things together and say goodbye, we'll wait downstairs for you. Of course,' he added from halfway down the stairs, 'you'll have to go into the isolation block.'

I had listened until then in a stunned and resentful state, ashamed that it should be so near to my own home that Otto should be dragged away. I was shocked by this voice that offered sympathy but no rights, no caution, no hope. But when I heard him mention the isolation block with his offhand throwaway calm, I rallied, and went out into the hall. I was very angry. 'What do you mean by an isolation block?' I demanded.

'Well they can't deal with a case like his without it,' one of the policemen explained.

'And what right have you to take him?' I asked.

'It's the law of the land,' he shrugged. 'Nobody is allowed to wander around with an infectious disease. I tell you, it's a wonder your friend can stay on his feet, he's riddled with T.B.'

'T.B.?'

'Yes,' he said, 'there's a hospital in Oxford will admit him tonight. You had better have an X-ray yourselves as soon as possible.'

Otto had grasped the word hospital, and he was piecing together the rest of their words, not wanting to believe his luck. He began to pack, César refused to move. I asked him in French if he had been to a mobile unit for a chest X-ray, and he said that both he and César had gone in to see how they worked. Then he relayed the news to César, who relaxed and lit a cigarette and smiled. It all seemed unlikely, but it was better to believe in it than in nothing so we did, and Otto left, reprieved from the arrest he had feared, and, looking positively jubilant, was escorted to a police car. We were left with a hospital address on the outskirts of Oxford and the exhaustion of the anticlimax as we picked our way through the irises and the fallen laburnum flowers to the front door and the stairs and the cases full of Otto's things, including the one with the bundle of passports that was now one short, since Orlando García Rodriguez had gone.

'That isn't his real name is it?' I asked César. And he said, 'No', and closed the door and fell asleep.

Chapter II

César grew restless with Otto away. After our initial relief at his illness, the outlook seemed more bleak. The attack was serious. It turned out that Otto had had T.B. before, as the police had said, three times, in Paris, Caracas and Maracay. Once, very badly while he was studying at the Sorbonne. He had spent a whole year in a French clinic then. He even had a theory that the best men in France could all form a league of tubercular patients.

'We were the centre of France,' he claimed, when speaking about his year in the clinic. And indeed, the list of names of his fellow patients read like a literary roll-call. But this time his lungs were almost too scarred to bear the extent of the infection. Everything was overshadowed by his being ill.

César moved in with me at my mother's flat, but it seemed like an unimportant step, since we were already together. April passed, and May came, and Elías didn't come and didn't come, and there was a general restlessness in the air. César's whole attitude to life was one of doom. It was a meticulous doom. He seemed not to care much whether he lived or died, he could not bear to mention his country. He was deeply hurt by his exile, and shunned his compatriots like the plague. But his socks had to come from a particular shop in Edinburgh. When I asked him why, he said:

'My socks have always come from there.'

'Even in Venezuela?'

'Oh yes, and my father's socks as well.'

And then César's shirts had to be of a certain length on the tails, longer, in fact, that any shop-bought shirt. He was very difficult to buy presents for. One of the things he liked best of those I bought for him was a box of five hundred mother-of-pearl buttons. He couldn't abide any other kind. He also had a fetish about boots. Shoe-shop assistants in London and Oxford threw up their arms in despair. They were showing him exactly what he asked for, but he would always cross his arms, and utter his, by now characteristic, 'No', and we would be back to square one. Then, worst of all, there was his watchstrap. He wore a very lovely Longines watch with what appeared to be a perfectly fitting strap. However, César claimed that, by a fraction of a millimetre, the strap was out of true. He tried every watchmaker in every town we travelled through from England to the Adriatic, and still none of them was right. It often became a question of pride for a jeweller to produce the very one, to file one down, to have one made. But each time, César would take it or leave it, and toss it into a box that he kept for the purpose. They were never right.

Otto ended every letter from the hospital with a 'By the way, have you found your watchstrap yet?' It was a standing joke. In César's life everything had to be just so. Otto used to say, 'He's like a prince you see, he has a kind of royal itch in his blood. This exile is harder on him than on any of us. We have lost our country, but César has lost his kingdom.'

In June I went to Ireland with my mother and a friend. I had planned the holiday the previous year, and it seemed uncivil to change my plans. I couldn't tell if César minded or not, he seemed quite emotionless. He said that he would be all right anyway because he had the washing to do. He had just discovered the automatic washing-machine, and it was giving him endless pleasure. He often stood over my mother while she did the weekly wash, and sometimes he would ask if he could have a go. He himself had a habit of changing his clothes from head to foot twice a day and then having everything laundered at a proper laundry. But he began to experiment with the machine, and would then spend several hours a day recycling the suds and the rinsing water over his clothes. From there he progressed to washing all the clothes for everyone, and then to 'doing' the linen, blankets and bedcovers as well. Sometimes, he would just empty out the airing cupboard and rewash everything before it had even been used, just for the sake of 'doing' a wash. The kitchen became a den of drying clothes and towels, but it all appeased his restlessness.

So I went to Ireland, and César stayed behind. I began to miss him in Ireland, and I toyed with the idea of breaking off our relationship before it became any more involved. It was months since I had been to Yale to visit my father, and my own university plans were getting lost in the tumult of events.

Otto came out of the clinic in July. He was still being given injections night and morning by a visiting nurse, or nursery, as he insisted on calling her. César and I moved to Oxford to be near him. We took a suite on the top floor of a heavily dormered hotel with Gothic windows in the dressing-rooms and turrets in unexpected places. Someone had written 'William Butterfield woz 'ere' on the sloping wall of our lavatory, and the hotel was a fair hotch-potched copy of that man's designs. We began our rather embattled stay there, quartered inside its marzipan layers of brickwork. It was embattled for several reasons. Firstly, César had changed a little, he slept less and talked more, and Otto was jealous of our friendship in his absence. While it had grown under his care and protection, he had taken a gardener's pride in the affair, but now that we were managing without him, he felt ousted. Also, he had learnt enough English in the hospital to carry on fluent conversations with me, and I had in turn perfected my French. These conversations developed more and more into embittered arguments.

Every time a car splashed him in the street, then it was my fault: it had been an English car, I was English, therefore I was to blame. Otto had a mind like a fish-filleter's knife, he would curve his blade up under your arguments and discard them like a stray bone. He was one of the most brilliant men I have ever met, and I admired him. I knew that I was nearly always on weak ground when arguing with him. But for some reason he had taken exception to me, and he picked fights over every tiny detail of our lives. He set himself to undermining me with the same determination with which he had planned and executed his campaigns when he rose against the government of Rómulo Betancourt. I fought back for the sake of not giving in, but I never did much more than fend off the brunt of his wrath.

On one occasion I mentioned to César that Otto didn't like me any more. He waited before he answered, an ominous sign, and then he said,

'Otto *adores* you.'

For some reason, it was impossible to argue with César once he had decided something. Sometimes he didn't say things, he told you them. For all his gentleness, and he was a very gentle man, there was a constant undertow of tyranny. He had the kindness of a dictator. So Otto and I continued our guerrilla 'adoration'. Once, visiting my elder sister in Loughborough, César carried his firmness too far. Wherever we went, people would be bowled over by his unassuming manner: tea ladies and bus conductors, immigration officials and friends were all enchanted by him. Everyone thought he was 'charming'. I often looked at him with new eyes after these bouts of praise. It was only when he said 'No' that the forcefulness of his character became apparent. He had a special way of saying no, accompanied by a rapid uncrossing of his hands like the flash of an invisible garotte.

We were sitting down to Sunday lunch in Loughborough and we had just finished a very good first course of roast lamb, when my sister took the joint around the long refectory table to serve any second helpings. When she reached the end where César was sitting, she asked him if he would like some more. And César gave his usual 'No', accompanied by the swift movement of his hands. My sister was so frightened by his answer that she leapt backwards thinking that he was actually going to attack her, and she teetered through the open french windows, into the garden. Poor César couldn't understand what the matter was. Gale, my sister, had been the first person in the family to see full-on his terrifying expression when his thoughts were negative. She had caught his fanaticism unawares.

César once explained this fanaticism on religious grounds. He told me that he was an atheist, but that he had been brought up a Catholic, educated in a Jesuit college.

He said, 'I've never known a man who has been with the Jesuits who didn't live by extremes.'

César certainly lived by extremes. In company with them, I became the shy spectator of his and Otto's Bacchanalian excesses. My embarrassment on these occasions was so acute, my loathing of a scene so intense, that I would shrivel into some corner while restaurants became scenes of chaos. I hoped beyond all hope as I picked my way over broken glass and over upturned tables that nobody would notice that I was with them. I can't even remember all the occasions when I wished I could die rather than have to face the stares.

Otto had a mistress, Elba, who was also living in Oxford with us. Their relationship had reached that point of no return when everything turns sour, but they were still very much involved with each other, and they clung on for dear life. There wasn't a day went by when they didn't have a fight or something. Otto is a very difficult man to live with. He lives in the stratosphere of neurasthenia. His mind is exacting, exhausting. In short, he has many sins; but compared to his mistress, he was an innocent. It was becoming more and more difficult to conceal the number of breakages from the hotel management. We would play our gramophone at full volume in an attempt to drown the shrieks and abuse as the two of them chased through all the rooms of our apartment. The furniture was mostly Victorian, and heavily built in such woods as mahogany and walnut, but Elba was no respecter of veneers. Everything became scratched by her long, pared nails. César and I would lie as low as possible, creeping about our room on tiptoe in the hope of not being noticed. But in Elba's eyes we were as guilty as Otto. Some days were worse than others. Luckily, she gave us some warning of these, because she would dress in a certain way when she was hellbent on revenge.

She had a very colourful cotton bedspread, woven by the Guaojira Indians of Venezuela, and in this she had cut a slit. Whenever she felt in a bitter mood, she would put this garment over her head, and tie it around with a rope. For this reason, Elba was known as the Guaojira behind her back. Otto was devoted to her, and she to him, but they were impossible together.

I wasn't sure at this stage whether César was 'legal' or not, but I knew that Otto was on the run, and in constant fear of apprehension. He was still not recovered from his recent bout of T.B. and he had gone up to London on a day trip, and bumped into an old friend and compatriot of his who worked at the B.B.C. This man, Luis, had been knocked down by a car on a zebra crossing and had broken his leg in three places. He was swathed in plaster, and virtually unable to cope with everyday chores like shopping. In a fit of generosity, Otto invited this friend to share our suite and take a few weeks' rest in Oxford.

When Otto returned, with his friend in tow, our problems really began. It was not his fault, but the poor man couldn't get downstairs on his own, so he stayed in, all day, every day, in a temper so foul that it matched only Elba's. The added strain of an extra person in our group brought everything to a crisis.

One day, Elba pulled out a fistful of Otto's hair, and Otto, in revenge, put her gramophone records into a huge pot of borsch, then Elba proceeded to burn Otto's books and papers in the gas fire in the sitting-room. The carpet caught fire, and our chairbound guest had his foot and plaster singed. Then Elba, in her wrath, added César's Prescott's *Conquest of Peru* to her blaze, and César was so angry that he tipped all Elba's expensive scents into a half-empty bottle of bleach in the bathroom.

After the damages had been signed for, and the hotel staff appeased, and everyone had had a drink, it became clear that Otto was no longer speaking to Elba, who was no longer speaking to us, or to Otto, who was desperately trying to unruffle Luis, who refused to speak to anyone at all thereafter, but banged his charred, plastered foot in sheer rage on the floor. Arrangements were being made to find somewhere else for him to go, when a call from the reception announced that Elías had arrived.

Elías was the only one of the three whom I had known as a legend before I met the man. I was expecting someone very different, someone almost superhuman, so I was surprised and disappointed when I saw a shy, quiet man with clear-cut features and pale suede shoes. Only his car, a brand-new Mercedes, lived up to the image of him that had grown in my mind. He took one look at the number of people in our suite and ordered two rooms for himself on another floor. The coming of Elías relieved the general feeling of restlessness and tension at the hotel. For those first two weeks of August there was an air of festivity. César had taken to pacing the rooms and staring gloomily out of the window cracking his knuckles, but he livened up when Elías came.

I began to sink into the background. I was drifting away from them. César, Otto and Elías seemed to make a perfect unit. They were at their best together. I could follow much of what was said in Spanish, although I pretended to be as in the dark as before. They would talk until late into the night in Elías's rooms. I wanted to learn more about their politics and their past, about what they were up to and what they were running away from, but, surprisingly, they never discussed these things, or at least, not in any way that made sense to me. I started to go out and sightsee around Oxford each day, or just to walk along the edge of the river. The town was deserted without the students, held only by invading bands of tourists. Lying down under the dying cow-parsley, and watching the sun fragmented through its spikes, I thought about what I was doing for the first time, and it seemed like a pointless mix up. I was still only sixteen, I had time to leave them to it. I could have gone home to my mother, but I would have felt embarrassed to return with nothing achieved. On the other hand, I had enough money from my father to go anywhere and make a start. Even Cambridge was still on the cards. I thought about it for hours and hours until the heat and pollen lulled me to sleep. Then I would go back to the hotel and watch Elías, trying to fathom his personality as I had begun to with the others. He worked like a catalyst on Otto and César, and I noticed that he worked like a catalyst on my feelings. It is virtually impossible to know Elías, and almost as impossible to describe him. Perhaps his most striking quality is that he eludes all description. His face has the passive stoniness of a Mayan statue, the perfect Indian features of an Atahualpa as seen in the clay models that fill case after case in the British Museum under the general heading of South America. There was a kind of chiselled beauty about Elías's face, so anonymous that he could easily be just anybody. Despite his bronzed skin and his hair that gleamed like Welsh anthracite, he managed to look anonymous even in Oxford. Maybe it was just the calm he exuded that put people at their ease, but whenever anyone asked,

'What does Elías look like?'
I always heard the answer,
'He just looks like Elías',
and it wasn't intentionally evasive. I never knew his exact age, but I think it was about halfway between mine and César's. He always dressed informally, except for his pale suede shoes which were, he said, de rigueur.

I began to tug away from the group. It felt as though they had all proved themselves, while I had done nothing but travel and go to school. My qualifications seemed inadequate, and I wanted to tempt fate, to see if we could just drift apart. It seemed that they needed each other but they didn't need me. I was determined not to come to need them. I was just there for the ride. In that, at least, we were equals.

It began to turn cold, and the new wind brought with it a feeling of time passing. One evening I told César that I was going back to London. He said, immediately, that he would come too. I had been prepared to ask him not to, but at the last moment I realised that it didn't make much difference to me either way. I was going, I didn't mind what anyone else did.

We spent the next morning drinking coffee at the hotel bar, and playing one of Otto's strange word games. My Spanish wasn't nearly good enough to even pretend to play these games, and I didn't find it entertaining just to watch, and get landed with all the forfeits that seemed to ensue, so I went and sat in the window by a bowl of dead anemones, pretended to write a letter to my mother and watched an old man playing patience by the door. I was extremely glad to be leaving. I began to feel drawn towards the man by the door. It was nearly time to go, and I stood up to fetch my coat. Our cases were in the hall. I knew that 'they' didn't believe in time. I decided not to care that day whether we missed our train or not.

As I passed him, the old man by the door spoke to me.

'You are very beautiful,' he said.

I couldn't help but like him more, and I waited to see what else he would say.

He said, 'I need you', or 'I can't believe you', I didn't catch his exact words. He was a foreigner. He sounded so intense that I didn't like to ask him to repeat it and left instead with a sense of vagueness.

César and I had lunch on the train. As the wheels began to turn, I realised that it was not the people that I was tired of or bored with, it was the place. I wanted to move from one place to another. I had always moved, from home to hospital and back, and then abroad. I enjoyed the mere act of travelling. I didn't want to go anywhere in particular, I was just restless, and I didn't want to stay anywhere either. It occurred to me that maybe that was what was wrong with Otto. Perhaps he just needed to move on as well. It must have been worse for them, in their exile. I was very pleased with myself. I had discovered not only the key to their safety, but the key to our sanity. Apart from Otto's illness, I felt that they were tied to England because of me. No wonder Otto cursed my very existence, I was holding them back. From now on we would travel abroad. Despite all their precautionary speeches about never saying anything over the phone, or even using it at all, I telephoned Otto from Clapham that night and told him that I was ready to go.

I had imagined that my willingness would have meant our immediate upheaval. However, nothing happened, except that César suggested that he and I went to Paris for a holiday. I had never left the country with César, and I was a little apprehensive as to what might happen on the other side of the

Channel. I suppose I imagined that there might be some kind of Jekyll and Hyde transformation. But since I was, by now, intrigued to know who he was, and what he was really like, I agreed, and we made ready for our trip.

Chapter III

It was just before this trip to Paris that César and I had our first real disagreement. Looking back on it, it seems rather arbitrary, but at the time, it was very real. I think that it was first and foremost the impression of unreality that I was trying to combat, and not César himself. I had come to accept that if we got on a train, we had always to jump off at the last minute, as though escaping from some invisible pursuer. And visiting anywhere automatically meant walking around the block and then diving in through the doorway. Telephone calls were out. There was an air of mystery so thick that I was suffocating, and I couldn't see any danger. So when César said that we were postponing going to Paris so that we could carry two guns across the Channel, I couldn't understand why.

César didn't want the guns. Not even Otto and Elías wanted the guns, since they were both staying in England. I went to collect the first one with a bad grace. It was in Richmond, and that was the last straw. Why one had to go to Richmond of all places, I could not understand; through Balham and Tooting and the interminable car dealers, it was one of the dreariest roads in London. Otto could see that I was upset, and he interpreted this as meaning that I was afraid.

'It'll be all right,' he tried to reassure me.

'Why us?' I demanded.

'It's just a little favour,' Otto said. 'They would do the same for me.'

The others were very relaxed. I let them stay that way, all afternoon and all evening. I was waiting for my best moment. I kept thinking about the boat train sliding through the night: it was my train, and I'd missed it for their hare-brained ideas. From Richmond to the West End I regarded César and his friends with rising distaste. It was as though they were scratching each other's backs over the contents of my suitcase. I was carrying the Smith and Wesson wrapped in cotton wool in my bag, and it felt to me like a dead weight buried in dandruff.

Otto had found a new place to eat. We had a list of restaurants which he compiled for each city in Europe. But all the best ones in London, the ones with the little asterisks beside them for excellence, were crossed out, or pencilled in with special warnings like 'impossible for a while'. These were the places where Elba had had a fight and broken all the rows of waiting bottles, or attacked a waiter, or merely smashed a glass and held the jagged edge over the hand of a white-faced customer until he would agree that he was the only one who could understand her. We were still in favour at Simpson's, at Fortnum's, and this new place of Otto's near the Strand. It was one of those places where you paid a flat rate which entitled you to an unlimited quantity of food. We had gone there mainly for César's sake, because he could eat more pork than anyone I know. There was a kind of eighteenth-century splendour about César's appetite. He didn't fuss around with garnishes and vegetables; 'I'm not a rabbit,' he would say at the mere sight of greenery, or else he would tip jam on it and pretend it was a pudding. I was waiting to spring the news on him, that I would leave him if he didn't come to France as planned, on that night of 3rd September, not the 4th or 5th. But there didn't seem a moment to tell him this, with all the others there. So I watched dispassionately while he waded into plate after plate of his roast meat.

After his first three trips to the centre table I stopped hoping that he'd choke on every mouthful, and began to calm down. Otto was particularly nice that evening, attentive and kind. It made a welcome change from his usual banter. As we left the restaurant, much later, one of the astonished waitresses

31

prophesied that César would 'have a turn, eating all that meat'. I thought, 'Let's hope so', and we walked arm in arm down the Strand, and past the railings of the Embankment Gardens with the beginnings of its green holly berries, to the Underground. On the train back to Clapham South and my mother's flat, I sat opposite the three of them, examining their habits with the detachment of a sociologist. I decided that I liked the three of them, but I didn't love any of them. César loved me, and that was all.

I felt that I had done a lot of sitting in the background, and waiting off-stage, and I wanted what I was going to say to have its maximum effect, so I waited until the others had gone to bed, and then I told César on his own. He said,

'Nonsense, Veta, you're tired.'

I wasn't tired, just determined. I wasn't even angry any more.

'I mean it, César, either we go first thing in the morning, or I'm leaving you.'

'What do you mean,' he asked me in Spanish, 'leaving me?'

'I mean that I am going on my own, and I'm not coming back.'

We were exchanging more consecutive words and views than ever before. It was my moment of triumph. And then, César turned slowly green. The dark rings under his eyes turned darker, and beads of sweat stood out on his long upper lip. He began to run his hands through his hair, making it stand out in a wavy frame around his head. He stared at me, and I thought, 'He's looking for the door.' There was a trapped expression on his face. He staggered out of the room, and down the long corridor to the lavatory. I half-sat on the coal stove in my room and listened to him being sick. He didn't call to me, and I could tell that he had shut the door by the muffled sounds that emerged. I had never heard anyone being quite so sick. His convulsed spluttering was interspersed by heavy thuds as he fell against the door and walls and struggled up again.

Otto came, he spoke to César who couldn't speak, and then to me.

'What's the matter?' he virtually demanded.

32

'It's the pork,' I answered.

'César never gets sick on pork. He can eat pork until it runs out of his ears.'

'Well, it's running out of his ears now.'

We stared at each other for a while. And then Otto went back to César with a parting, 'Don't you make him ill.'

I went to bed, ignoring all the commotion. Joanna, my mother, came in to me.

'César's very ill,' she said.

'I know, it's all right.'

'You don't understand, he's collapsed, he's gone cold.'

'I expect he'll live, we've just had an argument, that's all.'

'Don't you make him ill,' she told me. And I began to wonder if he was a protected species. I lay in bed listening to the coals twitching in the fire, and I was growing uneasy about the whole business. I could hear my mother insisting on a doctor, and Otto's voice saying, 'Joanna, no ambulance, no police.'

César came round before either of them had won, and he came and lay down and said that he was all right. He said it was the pork that made him ill. Otto protested, but César denied any other cause.

His skin was very cold to touch, and he smelt of Old Spice aftershave. He had scrubbed and doused himself in it in his passion for cleanliness. Joanna came in and asked what to do with his clothes. He said to throw them away. We lay for a long time, in silence, looking out at the jagged backs of the rambling Victorian houses across the way. Some of the lights stayed on all night, and on three pillows I could just see them without moving my head. I stroked César's hair out of his eyes, and asked him, 'Are you all right?' It was an unhelpful question, but it broke the silence, and I was tired. César spoke to me slowly, in Spanish. I could understand him pretty well by then.

'I want you to stay. Only leave me when I die. My friends are waiting for a bullet. Maybe they haven't got long now to wait. But it is different for me. My family is of the élite, I have the power and the protection of my family's name. For hundreds of years we have ruled Venezuela – I am almost the

33

last of the line, they don't shoot people like me, but I am very old inside. You are my life now. I thought you understood.'

'I'll stay with you,' I said, to reassure him as much as anything. 'You sleep now.'

'But how can I know?' he asked.

It seemed like a very reasonable point, and I thought about it and didn't really know what to say. It was clear to me that I might decide any day, or even every day, on some new ultimatum. My feelings were volatile. I wanted to travel. I didn't much want anything else. Other things just came and went.

'I'll tell you how you can know,' I said, 'I'll marry you.'

'You are a child.'

'We'll get a special licence.'

'You are a child,' he repeated, dully.

'That's never bothered you before,' I reminded him.

César was exhausted by all the talk. He was ludicrously extravagant with money, but economical with words.

'It is Paris in the morning!' was all he said.

We caught the train at Victoria, and I suppose that it was the last train that I ever really caught, as opposed to missing. After that, time, as such, began to matter less and less. Once we began travelling for the sake of not staying still, any train would do. We always travelled by train or car, there was less risk of anyone being recognised and arrested that way.

As it turned out, we were ill-prepared for our travels on this first occasion. For one thing, I was used to taking vast quantities of luggage with me. César warned me that this could hamper us, but I insisted. I couldn't conceive of travelling without my books and papers around me. One especially tough leather suitcase was set aside entirely for these books. It needed a strong porter in a good mood at the best of times. In another case, I took my dresses. These were no ordinary dresses, they were made of yards and yards of trailing velvets. My clothes were as extreme as César's philosophy. They were either so short that even other girls stared, or so exaggeratedly Edwardian that people assumed I had just stepped off some film set and would be returning soon. The minis were all made of suede, and the boots and trappings and bags and hats all squeezed together to make up the dead weight that we lugged across the Channel.

It was an ill-fated voyage, but the idea of it pleased me. We couldn't afford the trip to Paris, not until the end of the month. I had boasted to César,

'Don't worry, we won't need to pay a hotel, just our food and outings. I know a lot of people there. I used to live there.'

It was going to be my turn to be the host. I cabled to America for my next cheque to come directly to Paris. But when we arrived, the flat that I always stayed at, and where I had once lived, had actually been demolished since my last visit. In contrast to the windy autumn that we had left in London, it was hot late summer in Paris and the streets had the air of a ghost town given over to a film crew, as they often do when the tourists are there, roaming, but the citizens have locked up and gone. César was threatening to throw my suitcases under a tram. And I was listening to him, practising his English with such perfectionism that he still hardly spoke a word, but those he did speak, he spoke very well. He was trying out 'Vegetable'. Vedgetable, Vedgetibble, vegetibble, vechtubble, vechetebull. The word rang through my head. It had come all the way from Victoria. It was spoken at intervals of about one minute. It was driving me mad.

We picked our way over the rubble that was all that was left of the Square Charles Laurent on one side. César just looked at me over a haze of red brick dust.

'It was here,' I shouted over the droning of the cranes. 'It was on the fourth floor. I'll see if I can find the concierge.'

'Don't bother,' he shrugged, walking away with the back of his neck straining under the weight of my cases. I followed him, confident that one of my other friends would charm away César's anger.

We took a taxi, and went to see the pop singer, the nuclear physicist, the professor, the actor from the Gramont, and the man from Agence France Presse who always ate on the corner where the Mafia ate. This trip to Paris was my first chance to throw in a little colour, but all these friends were out. Most of them were away for the summer. I searched through my address book, and found one more friend in Versailles.

'Don't bother,' César shrugged, bowed now under my books. We took a taxi, and César sat brooding, rubbing the crease marks from his stiff fingers. The driver had asked, 'Where to?'

'Anywhere,' César had said, and the driver had stood to attention and was now doing his bidding, driving aimlessly around the fourteenth arrondissement.

'Tell me a hotel,' César told me.

I thought desperately. I rummaged in the back of my head. I didn't know a hotel. The names had all gone. I once visited a girl near the Luxembourg. I was stalling.

'Rue de Vaugirard,' that would keep him going. He liked the sound of French, he had been learning it in prison.

'Trianon Palace,' I remembered, hoping it would be all right, and wishing it could have been somewhere better.

We could have really done without the trouble we got at the reception. I don't think we had ever really noticed the great difference in our ages. The receptionist, however, noticed at once. I was under-age. Back in London, we had sacked our housekeeper so as to avoid any possible unpleasantness; and I had kept César out of sight whenever Denis, my Latin tutor, came to cajole me through my exams. But we hadn't thought how much trouble we could get into abroad. César was actually only thirty-five, but he looked at least fifty, and his two years in prison and ill-treatment there had given him an air of distinct debauchery. To add to this, I looked even younger than my age.

César disliked the French intensely. He considered them a race of traitors. No amount of intercession by me, or Otto, who greatly admires them, ever swayed his opinion.

'They deserted you in the war,' he used to say bitterly. He felt very strongly about the war. It distressed him deeply that London showed so few signs of remembering it too. I was thankful that his French was not sufficiently good to understand the abuse that was being hurled at us as we beat a retreat through the swing doors with our baggage. We sat on a bench in the Luxembourg, and began to enjoy the sheer perversity of our situation. César refused to go into a restaurant with my cases. So we sat and watched the evening gather over the peeling plane trees.

Eventually César got up and walked away; I wondered whether it was for ever. But he returned with a bottle of milk and a baguette. Through all the bother of that day, I had managed to preserve an unruffled appearance in a new long white linen dress, smocked and embroidered most laboriously to the waist. It had been a labour of love by my mother, and I knew it had taken her over a year to do. This was my first day of wearing it. I took the bottle and drank, forgetting that French milk bottles are made of soft plastic. The bottle gave way in the middle. I just sat there, as it spilled and dripped down me, and I knew that it was going to be some holiday.

We stayed at a very cheap hotel with clean sheets and no bath. It was about the only one that would take us. We delivered the offending gun to a place off the Boulevard St Michel. 'Just take it in and ask for Juancho, say you've come from London and if he says "Machette" give him the gun and go.'

'And if he doesn't?' I asked.

'Then don't,' César said. He was irritated.

'Why me?' I asked, this time to annoy him.

'Because they want two,' he said, 'and you know why there's only one.'

César carried a wartime toll of all the defeats and ignominies of the French. He would accost taxi-drivers and demand to know why they had no sense of honour. We went to the Arc de Triomphe, at his instigation. He said that he had something to do there. It turned out that it had always been his ambition to put out the eternal flame as a mark of protest against the treachery of the nation. His bitterness grew with every day that we stayed cooped up in the heat and the emptiness of our threadbare hotel on the Rue Cambronne. After ten days I decided that we should go back to London, marry and then move on. We left more noisily than we had come: César was incensed that the man in the street didn't understand his French. He was, in fact, reasonably fluent.

'I just want to know', he'd say, 'why they don't understand me. They have always been very quick at languages. I have seen films of them, during the war. Any word that the Nazis said, they understand like a flash. They obviously have a natural flair. I have German blood,' he would say, 'why won't they understand me?'

We took a train from the Gare du Nord, and César was still haranguing a porter who had been particularly rude to me, long after the train pulled out of its long platform and into the night.

I was glad to get back to Oxford in one piece. This time we all made plans to leave for Italy. For some reason, Italy had become our Mecca.

Chapter IV

I had been meaning to tell my father, Serge, about César for some months, but the right moment never seemed to come. Serge was going to Japan for his next Yale tour, and, as usual, he invited me to go with him. We had been travelling together on these lecture tours since I was ten, and I felt very uncomfortable about refusing. It was bad enough to tell him that no, I wasn't going that time, without adding that I probably wouldn't be going with him again. The actual formality of the marriage meant very little to me at the time. Perhaps that was why I had offered to bind myself to César quite so readily. As far as I was concerned, I was already bound to him, and to all three of them, since the night of César's sickness at my mother's flat.

As it happened I didn't need Serge's signature or permission to marry, since Joanna was my legal guardian by the terms of their divorce. And somehow I didn't get round to telling him about the wedding, and then it became more and more difficult to tell him at all. It wasn't until he himself came over in the following spring that I even mentioned it.

We were married at the Lambeth Registry Office on 2nd October. I remember that we had some difficulty filling in the forms. Firstly, the registrar took down our names. He asked me first, and then César. I gave César's name. I had come to speak for him on most occasions, owing to his lack of English combined with his natural reticence.

'Is that your full name?' the registrar asked. César looked at him for a while, and then he said, 'No, but it is enough.'

'Oh, I'm sorry,' said the offended registrar, 'but we must have your full name. All your names.'

César shrugged, and then took a long breath, and began, 'César Alejandro Diego Rodrigo . . .' and the names unfurled in a dull litany of Spanish vowels, repeating themselves over and over again until they came to a halt with a final '. . . de Labastida' and César took his breath.

The registrar looked at him very hard, and then from him to me and back again. 'Is he serious?' he asked.

I nodded, and we began to decipher the string of names that had just been reeled off. It was a revelation to me, as I had never heard them all before.

When we reached the column marked 'profession' we were held up again.

It occurred to me then, for the first time, that I had no idea what profession César had. I knew that his passport said 'businessman'. But previously, when I had asked him why, he had just looked away in his usual manner and said, 'Life is easier like that.'

'Shall we just put "businessman" then?' I asked him.

'No!' Short and sharp with the unleashing of his hands.

'It is very simple,' the registrar explained. 'Just put down your work.'

'He doesn't work, as such,' I volunteered.

'Well then, that's easy, he's unemployed.' The registrar prepared to write 'unemployed' in his careful copperplate.

'No!' César said. 'Unemployed' conjured up a layabout to him and he maintained that layabouts should be lined up against a wall and shot, preferably by him personally. The fact that he spent most of his time literally lying about, sleeping, was somehow different.

'I see,' the registrar said, humouring him. 'What *do* you do then, sir?'

'I don't do,' César said, 'I am.'

'But what are you?'

'I am an hacendado.'

We looked up the word in my by now very frayed pocket

dictionary; he was a landowner. This was news to me too, and I was strangely reassured by it. I didn't know exactly what my three friends did, but I was pretty sure that it was illegal. Now I would be able to tell my grandmother, and Bridie, our housekeeper who was coming back, and Jonah, my English tutor, what César was. People would be satisfied with the answer. For once, it wouldn't sound like an evasion.

Joanna came as one witness, and David, my brother-in-law, came as the other. The wedding photographs drifted into the family album, and but for the carnations on our lapels, and the fact that I was wearing a fur coat and Russian hat on what was obviously a sunny day, they didn't look at all special, following all the other photos of my mother's four marriages. It didn't really feel like a wedding, not like my sister's had been. There was no Bishop of Dover to officiate, no lace or orange blossom, and no gathering at Westminster for the reception. César had a loathing of the Church, and I didn't feel strongly either way, so we stuck to the registry, and a glass of champagne, and then went to a cinema in the evening.

Everything felt unreal that day. The weather had changed and become strangely warm. César had eaten his usual breakfast: a plate of fried eggs and half a pound of strawberry jam, and then he had insisted that we take a walk. We walked past the murderer's house, where at the turn of the century an Indian prince had been stuffed in a mattress and left to rot, and outside which I had first met César, and we walked on through the winding backwaters of Clapham. It was eleven o'clock, and our wedding was fixed for one.

'We're not getting married,' he said, solemnly.

I stared into the window of the Indian shop on the corner, and said nothing.

'It's better that way,' he added, and then walked on. I could see that he was going to tell me something, and I thought that I'd do best just to let him get on with it. So I hurried to keep up with him, and waited for what was to come. I had a feeling that he was going to tell me something about himself that I wouldn't like. We were walking past the tall railings of the South London Hospital for Women.

'Estuve preso,' César told me, 'I have been in prison.'

I nodded. It had been easy enough to guess, over the months. His phobia about closed doors, the scars from bullet wounds in his neck and leg, his restlessness, his pacing, the way he groaned and shuddered in his sleep, gave him away.

'You don't mind?' he asked.

'I mind,' I said, 'but it doesn't matter.'

'Otto, Elías, and me, we believe.'

I didn't know what they believed in, but I was glad to hear that they believed in something. So I nodded again, encouragingly.

'We rob banks,' he said.

I nodded again. 'And what else?' I asked, casually.

'Nothing else,' he said simply. 'There was the guerrilla, Otto was like our general, our speaker; Elías was the commando. I robbed the banks.'

Put like that, it all sounded very straightforward. They were all more scrupulous than I had thought.

'I am a rich man,' César continued, obviously determined to say his whole piece. 'All the money from the banks was for the guerrilla. You understand.'

I was understanding very clearly now, and I could feel a great wave of relief sweeping over me. I liked a man of principle. Even the grey stained windows of the hospital looked less menacing as we walked along.

'We are an army of three now. We are defeated. There is a price on Otto's and Elías's head and I am exiled. There is no reason why you should stay with us. You are young, Veta. If you marry me, you might never be safe again.'

'I would like to stay,' I told him, and he stared at me dully, as though in pain.

We walked along in silence for a while, past the scarred bunkers on the edge of the common, and the gaping mouth of the Underground. Then César said, 'My father is dead.'

Everything else had been like some unburdening of his mind. He was offloading his conscience. I didn't feel that he really wanted to tell me the things he did, it was just that he didn't want me not to know them. What he had said last was what mattered to him most.

'My father would have liked you.'

Such high praise made me uneasy, and I tried to change the subject. 'How long were you in prison?' I asked him.

He didn't seem interested any more, he was looking out across the common.

'Two years,' he replied, and then, 'Where was the spy murdered?'

There was a spot on the common, a corner near the edge of the road, where the body of a German spy had been found during the war. He had had SS carved into his cheeks. This last detail had fascinated César, and he would stand on the spot in wonder and ask for the whole story over and over again. He was always deeply moved by anything about the war.

'How did you get out?' I asked.

'I was somewhere else.'

'What do you mean, "somewhere else"?'

'I waited two years for my trial, and then, when it came, my alibi was right, I had been somewhere else. I have friends with the military police. They told me, "Now you are free, but this country is upside-down, they are going to kill you. Go into hiding for a bit, and then everything will be all right with you. They must not kill a man of the élite, they know it is crazy. When they cool down, you can go back to your estates." I hid for two months on my uncle's estate, and then I came to London.'

'Was that how you got the bullet wound in your neck?' I asked.

He looked surprised.

'No, that was a hunting accident.'

I felt rather cheated over this and so I asked a question that I wouldn't usually have asked.

'Were you tortured?'

César looked at me slowly, and then he said,

'Tortured!' with a twist of disdain. 'They take you out in the middle of the night, they tie you up in the yard, they bring a priest. There is a firing squad, they take aim and shoot you with dummy bullets, and then they take you back to your cell. They call that torture,' he said, vehemently. 'But my uncle died. My father's only brother. I was not with him, not even at his funeral. That is torture, to let a good man die alone.'

'My uncle,' he repeated vaguely.

We walked on in the direction of the spy corner. We split up to get through the traffic. On the other side, César said,

'I don't like people who whine. War is war. When they arrested me, I didn't expect a party.'

He had grown stern again, every trace of his confessional mood had left him.

'If they arrest you,' he said fiercely, 'don't you come out complaining.'

It was twenty to one. We had to rush to get home in time. A taxi was waiting at the door with my flustered mother inside.

'I've got your coat, darling,' she said. 'Just get in. I've brought your furs in case you are cold.'

During the ceremony, rather than give a full translation, I had instructed César to simply say, 'Yes, yes, no, no', and 'I do', in answer to the registrar's questions. But he lost track of his replies, and said 'Yes' when the man asked him his name, and the 'No' when he was asked if that were his correct name, and then 'Yes' he was sure and 'No' when the registrar asked if he understood, and then continued to reel off a mindless procession of yesses and nos until the marriage was stopped. The office had, on call, interpreters for every conceivable language from Swahili to Gaelic and Bengali to Luxembourgeoise; however there seemed to be no one who spoke Spanish. The registrar himself felt convinced that there was some kind of swindle going on, with César as the dupe, and he flatly refused to let me translate for him. So we waited for nearly two hours while an elderly gentleman was dredged out of Pimlico to officiate. Meanwhile we discovered that we had no ring.

'Never mind,' César said, 'one day you shall have lovely rings.'

But it seemed that we specifically needed one then and there. Luckily my mother came to the rescue. She said that she had a stock of wedding rings in her bag that she carried round for sentimental reasons.

'If I were you,' she said, pointing to a platinum and white-gold one, 'I would have that one. Andrew gave it to me in 1947, and it was easily my best marriage.'

I took it gratefully and showed it to César, who was relieved to see that I didn't mind having this impromptu hand-me-down.

The day after our wedding we sat all afternoon in the Embankment Gardens with the sparrows and the wind and the falling leaves, and then we walked to Piccadilly for dinner. Otto had some business in the morning, so we met outside the Chandos by the Strand. We often met there, and Otto was often late. On this occasion, I suspected his 'business' of being a visit to the National Portrait Gallery across the road. César and I particularly disliked waiting, so we would join the queue for the poste restante in William IV Street. César hadn't written a single letter in all the months that I had known him, and yet he went regularly to this and all the other postes restantes in all the other towns we stayed in. This central post office showed London at its worst, and it took all César's patience and ingenuity to explain away the jostling and pushing and the blatant rudeness of the employees, and he could only say that the good manners he believed to be the birthright of every Englishman were tarnished in that place by their constant exposure to foreigners. There were no letters for César, there never were, and Otto still hadn't come. We stood outside the pub, stamping our feet against imaginary cold, and becoming more and more enraged.

'I should have known,' César kept saying, shaking his head. 'I should have known.'

He paced now, from the alleyway and the cinema back to the Chandos pub on a great wave of impatience.

'It's no good,' he said, taking up his position outside the mullioned windows again, 'You can't live with a man like Otto. He's impossible. He's got Third World manners.' César was growing pale with anger.

'There is something positively French about his behaviour tonight,' he said. 'He's not a man, he's a common prostitute!'

César seemed suddenly embarrassed by his own rage, and explained,

'The only reason why I am waiting for that swine is to give him a piece of my mind.'

At that moment Otto appeared in person, but César was so deep in his diatribe that he didn't notice.

'When I lay my hands on that scrawny, tubercular great-grandson of an indecent woman I'll . . .'

'Loyalty, that's what I like in my friends,' Otto laughed, 'loyalty.'

We dined at Simpson's, where someone took exception to Otto's casual dress and wouldn't let him in without a tie. This time, Otto was truly offended.

'Can't you recognise good clothes when you see them?' he asked in a ruffled voice. One of the staff slipped something into his hand. It was a drab brown tie.

'I don't want that tie,' he said, almost speechless with indignation. 'Do you think I am going to wear that dreadful tie with this?' he said, preening the sleeve of his expensive open-neck shirt.

Otto was the most meticulous of all of us in his dress. He lavished time and money on looking 'just so'. César, Elías and I were all eyeing the door, calculating what our best chance would be once the inevitable fight broke out, when quite suddenly Otto said,

'All right. You have no aesthetic values, no taste, I despise you, but you win. Give me your tie, and I hope that the service stands up to your own rules.'

He smiled at me. 'You see,' he said, 'we have a truce today: I'll be less cross, and you be less idiotic.'

We had a pleasant, rather silly dinner, and drank champagne and pledged our friendship, and toasted our marriage. Otto said that most people would think that I was mad to marry César, but that he thought César was mad to have married me.

'He's trying to say he likes you,' Elías butted in.

Otto insisted on having a pot of tea after dinner. He always drank tea instead of coffee, China for preference. Our waiter disappeared and returned shortly with the head waiter who listened to the request with a pained expression on his face. He approved the order with obvious disdain and then looked at us from time to time, not as a table that had ordered something bizarre, but with the scorn of those who have denied the ordinary.

'You never really love something until it hurts you,' Otto said laconically, 'and I love my liver.'

However, when the liqueurs came, he drank so many that the glasses lined up like toy soldiers around his saucer.

'Are those good for your liver?' I asked.

'Love is fickle,' he laughed, and ordered three more Benedictines.

On the way out, he dropped his tie into an ashtray. He had been holding it between his fingers like an unfresh eel. Otto went back to Oxford that same night, while César and I and Elías returned later the following day.

Otto's parting words had been, 'Any day now, we'll be moving on.' He was looking better despite his drinking.

The last three weeks that we spent in Oxford were by far the quietest I had known. The worst of the summer tourists had gone, and although the term had just begun, we saw little of the students. Otto and Elba were very wrapped up in each other. The hotel no longer echoed to the sound of a radio disguising their fights, and most of the other rooms were empty. Some mornings we had the dinning-room entirely to ourselves, which pleased César as he could have as much jam as he wanted without having to ask. It was turning cold again and most of the leaves had fallen and soaked into a mottled sponge underfoot. I spent a lot of time in the garden.

Otto was absorbed in his study of linguistics, and in long conversations with Elba; Elías was studying aviation, he intended to take a flying certificate in Italy; César was deep in a mound of leather-bound volumes of sixteenth-century history that he had found in Blackwell's.

I had climbed considerably in status since my marriage. I now went out 'on business'. Every morning at ten o'clock, Otto and I walked to a phone box, and made a long-distance call to the Midland Bank in Gracechurch Street in the City.

'It is easier for you, you speak English,' he explained. 'Ask for a cable in my name. It is for $340,000 U.S. Nothing else, just ask if it has arrived yet.'

47

I dutifully telephoned each day, and each day I was told that there was no such cable.

By the end of the first week, I made them check, and double-check. Nothing came, and we waited after that and telephoned only on alternate days. Finally, after it had begun to seem like an entirely mythical sum, the mere routine of asking and nothing more, a young man said: 'Yes, there is a cable here.'

When I told Otto, he kissed me, and we bought a whole cardboard-boxful of cream pastries to take back to the hotel, and everyone got very drunk on aquavit mixed with whisky, rum and vodka.

'It's a Molotov cocktail,' they said, 'you'll love it.'

I could hardly move for the hangover the next morning. My head had become icily heavy. 'We're going to London,' Otto said. César was virtually unconscious in bed. I knew from experience that it took him several days to recover from a hangover. His kidneys didn't function properly and every time he drank, he got a kind of alcoholic poisoning which literally crippled him. On the first day he would lie in a state of near-coma, on the second he would vow never to drink again, on the third he would muster his forces, and on the fourth he would claim that it was a man's social duty to learn to drink and that he was a martyr to the cause of good manners, and begin again.

'César can't travel the way he is,' I said, hoping to be let off the hook as well.

'Then we'll have to leave him. It's only for the day, anyway.' Otto left the room, and came back shortly with a mug of cold beer.

'Here,' he said, 'drink that, it'll put you back into first gear.'

I felt very sick all day but I had been commissioned to go into the bank and see about the money. I didn't see why Otto shouldn't have gone himself.

'Why can't you go?' I asked him.

Otto glared at me, in a way that he had when he thought that I was being purposely idiotic, as he put it. We had a roast-chicken lunch on the train, and when the wheels started moving, I began to enjoy the trip.

'Just remember,' Otto kept saying. 'Don't let them follow you out.'

We took a taxi to the city and Otto dropped me off in Gracechurch Street outside the bank. We had arranged to meet up not far away. I was feeling rather grand, wearing a great fox-fur hat. I asked by name for the young man I had last spoken to on the telephone. He came towards me, saying something as he walked.

'You're not listening,' he whispered.

I apologised.

'Have you spoken to anyone else at the bank?' he asked. I shook my head, and he seemed relieved.

'I've spoken to you on the phone,' he said. 'I could tell you were a child by your voice.'

'Thank *you*,' I thought, and wished I could look a bit older.

'I don't know what part you play in all this,' he continued, 'and I don't want to. But I'd like to give you a chance. I shouldn't tell you this, but whoever touches that money is in trouble. Do you understand me?'

I was beginning to but I wasn't prepared to believe him.

'I just don't like to think of you getting involved,' he said, and then he looked slowly around the bank and then back to me. 'I'm afraid your husband's money is frozen – ' he paused. 'No one knows who you are here. Please go now, and if you're wise, don't come back. There's a special instruction with that cable, and your husband is mentioned by name. I'm sorry,' he added.

I felt as though I was going to cry. I didn't really know why, except that what I was being told seemed to imply some kind of betrayal. I can't remember how I left the bank, I don't think I even thanked the man, and I had forgotten all about not being followed.

I wondered how I was going to break the news to Otto. It was my first assignment, and I felt personally responsible for its failure. Otto listened very carefully when I told him the news, and then he asked me to repeat what I had said, and then to repeat it again.

'What does it mean?' I asked.

'It doesn't matter,' he said, and we walked towards the

Underground staring grimly at each other. After a few minutes Otto burst out laughing.

'Why are you laughing?' I asked.

'Sometimes things are that bad,' he said.

Chapter V

The freezing of the money signalled the beginning of virtual penury. I still had my allowance from Serge. But what had been lavish for one was quite inadequate for four people with extravagant tastes.

Elba and Otto had begun to fight again. These fights were always one-sided by the time they came to blows. Otto would stand his ground, firmly but gently, with his hands cupped over his head to ward off the more lethal punches.

'Elba,' he would say, coaxingly, 'you don't need to do this. Think of our position.'

But every word that he spoke seemed to make things worse, and her handbag of tooled leather would swivel around on its shoulder strap, slapping him across the face or chest each time.

'But of course I love you, Elba. You know I do,' he would say soothingly, dodging her fists and bag like an experienced boxer.

'But, Elba,' he would argue as reasonably as his position allowed, 'remember last night. But remember, and tell me I don't love you.' And then Elba would deliver a sharp kick to the groin, from which Otto would stagger to his feet.

César and I looked on in anguished horror. We couldn't understand why Otto didn't defend himself. We had seen these one-sided, almost ritualistic fights many times before. Both Elba and Otto would be very drunk, and the fights usually ended at about this stage, and the two of them would help each other home, and Elba would fall asleep, and Otto would say: 'I've had enough. I am not going to have anything more to do with that woman.' Then he would walk around the room, adjusting his shoulders as though to shrug off any stray traces of her touch, and then he would pour himself a double aquavit, and say, 'I suppose I had better go and see that she hasn't taken an overdose.'

And he would go into their room and close the door, and we often wouldn't see him again for anything up to two days.

So, when Elba attacked him outside the Mitre Hotel one night on our way home, we thought that they were just going to have one of their usual bouts when we were startled by a series of shrill piercing cries. Elba was screaming, and Otto was reeling back against a wall, his head covered in blood.

Before we could decide what to do, a police car pulled up to the kerb beside us and two policemen jumped out. One of them took Otto roughly by the shoulders. The constable had obviously decided that Otto was the dangerous one, while the other one put an arm round Elba and spoke to her soothingly.

'There, there, Miss,' he said, 'you'll be all right now. We won't let him get you.'

He accompanied this statement by glaring ferociously in Otto's direction.

'You should be ashamed of yourself,' the other one said to Otto as he manhandled him into the car. 'And it serves you right,' he said, referring to the streaked wounds on his face, from which the blood was gushing. 'Picking on a girl on her own.'

They were both seated in the police car, when one of the officers turned his attention to César and myself.

'Are you anything to do with this?' he asked.

César trod on my foot, purposefully.

'No,' I said, 'we're just on our way home.'

'Well, hurry up then,' he said, wanting to have the last word.

'He didn't touch her,' I added, trying to help.

'That's what they all say,' he said stiffly, and walked away.

Elías had been out on a date, but he was waiting for us at the hotel. We told him what had happened, and he rolled his eyes in a characteristic way he had of mock horror. We decided that our best course of action would be to find out where they had been taken, and then try and pick them up in the morning. After three abortive phone calls I found the right station, and asked after them both as my aunt and uncle. There was an unpleasantly long silence at the other end, during which I heard someone say, 'There's someone here asking about that sod who attacked his girl.'

'They won't get much joy out of him tonight,' another voice jeered back. 'We had a hell of a job getting him into his cell.'

'He will be appearing in court tomorrow, drunk and disorderly, causing a disturbance, using foul language in a public place, and resisting arrest.'

We all went next morning, to see what happened. Otto was standing pitifully in the dock. His face had been cleaned and we could see long gashes in his cheeks. He also had a vivid black eye, and his clothes were ripped and torn.

'What do you think happened in his cell?' Elías nudged.

The magistrate took a very poor view of Otto's behaviour. He fined him fifteen pounds for his offences, and said that he would have liked to have sent him down for hard labour for having so vilely accosted and mistreated his wife.

'. . . and from the facts, and the loyalty of this dear lady,' he smiled across the room at Elba. It was clear that he found her attractive. 'She is your common-law wife, and it is for you to treat and respect her with all the dues of a legal spouse. I don't know what you do in your own country,' he said with great disdain, 'but here, in England, we will not stand for this kind of shoddy behaviour. You just cannot get away with attacking a defenceless woman, and therefore – ' he paused for effect. Otto was looking very ill again, holding on to the railings for support. I don't think he could even hear what the magistrate was saying, he certainly couldn't see through his swollen eyes. 'And therefore,' he insisted, 'I hold you up to shame and ridicule.' The members of the court all looked around at Otto, with his newly mutilated face making him look scarcely human.

Elba was released without any charges being brought against her, and the magistrate hoped that the whole 'ordeal' hadn't upset her too much.

The costs went to Otto. As soon as we got him away from the court, we took him to a doctor. Elba was amazed at what she had done. She kept rubbing her long, shaped fingernails and saying in admiring disbelief: 'I never thought they were so strong. It must be all the gelatine I've been eating.'

Otto's slashed face took two weeks to heal, and then left scars furrowing his cheeks for years to come. During those two weeks he was unspeakably angry. We used to joke about it, and whenever we wanted anything from him, we would ask someone else so that they could say, 'Ask the tiger', and Otto would snarl and glare with his great mane of greying hair and tawny stripes on his skin. Elba's behaviour was regarded with indulgence, since, unlike myself, irredeemably ranked with the idiotic, Elba was among those few who were said to have 'behaved well' on the field of combat. This good behaviour in her past gave her a special dispensation for more recent eccentricities. It was no good asking why Elba was so unreasonable, or why she got away with never doing any shopping or chores. Elba was 'serious', everyone said so, and Otto, especially, was always more inclined to see the heroine than the headache.

But, one day when we were playing Monopoly in our rooms, Otto came through with a handful of postcards.

'I'm going to post a letter,' he said, and walked out.

We went on playing all afternoon, and then Elba commented that Otto hadn't returned. He didn't come back that night; and by the afternoon of the second day, we feared the worst. Our rooms became littered with the international press. Every newspaper that we could lay our hands on was somewhere on the floor. We hunted through them, but there was no reference to Otto under any of his names or guises, no arrests, no deaths, no murders. He was not in any local or London hospital. He had vanished.

On the fourth day we received a postcard from Berlin. It said, 'I couldn't stand it any more. I'll write again, Otto.'

From then on, whenever we needed to extricate ourselves

from some situation, or whenever we just needed to move on, one of us would say, 'I think we should post a letter.'

Elba was the least surprised of us all at this new turn of events. They had already decided to split up, the only question had been when. This occasion seemed as good as any, and we prepared to leave.

About two days after this, Elías came in looking unusually pensive. We had arranged to leave at the weekend. It was only Wednesday, but Elías said, 'Let's go tonight.'

I had observed that, unlike his two compatriots, Elías didn't make eccentric remarks and suggestions out of the blue. He had an entirely rational mind. If he said, 'Let's go tonight', it was because he had a good reason, even if that reason were only his unfailing instinct of self-preservation. Elías survived by a kind of ruthless efficiency. He never relaxed, even when he appeared to be drunk and half-asleep, he was alert to every sound and movement. He himself moved almost silently in his pale suede shoes with his large hands swinging by his sides like a toy soldier.

I had discovered that there were different degrees of being wanted, in the sense of wanted by the law. And the categories criss-crossed in a complicated tartan. Roughly speaking, there were those who were wanted by Interpol, and those who were not. For instance, César was free to roam Europe, but not to return home, while Otto and Elías were actively 'on the run'. Otto, however, was 'wanted for questioning' and in the event of his surviving this 'questioning' could have looked forward to an indefinite term of imprisonment. But Elías, on the other hand, had a category almost to himself. We knew a fat man in London who did the washing-up at a German wine bar, and who, I had been told, was wanted dead or alive. But Elías was just wanted dead. Much later, when a peace was made in Venezuela, and all the guerrillas were pardoned, the price was never lifted from Elías's head. He alone of the living remained on the other side of the law.

During our weeks together in Oxford, I had discovered that Elías had what Americans call an old world charm about him. He inspired confidence. Old ladies in the street trusted him, and they would often ask him to help them across the street, or with their shopping.

'What a nice man,' was the general verdict of outsiders. But, more even than César, he kept himself to himself. He moved at a slow, steady pace, feeding in all the events around him and reissuing them as part of his master plan.

César knew, when Elías changed his plan then, in Oxford, that something had happened, and he asked him what it was.

Elías shrugged. 'I've taken against the city,' he said.

'Why?' I asked.

Elías gave me one of his long, incredulous stares, which meant, 'You just asked a question'.

I hardly ever asked questions, and they liked that; it was considered inelegant to ask the reason why. Elías smiled at me.

'You are like my doctor, just like my doctor', and he shook his head indulgently as though this doctor were a cross he had to bear. He often told me that I was like his doctor. It didn't make any sense to me, but it always softened him, and it seemed to bind us together in a sort of private way.

'There are rats here,' he said, finally, and began to pack.

Later that night, César told me that Elías had been recognised in the town. It had happened quite by chance, he had been browsing in Blackwell's bookshop when he had seen a face he knew over a shelf. He had instantly recognised the man and the danger, and left the shop, but the other, who was an informer, had followed Elías out into the street, tried to catch up with him, and lost him in the crowd.

'A lot of people will know he is in Oxford now,' César said, gloomily.

Elba arranged to go to London, she said she would like to stay there for a while and learn English. I asked her if she would go back to Venezuela now that she had split up with Otto. 'I wish I could,' she said, 'but when I took up with Otto I was already up to my neck in the guerrilla. I had nothing to lose by coming with him. It's just a matter of time before they get us. I bet you you'll see the Andes before I do.' She kissed me, and left in a taxi jammed full of her suitcases and boxes of belongings.

As it turned out, I did get to Venezuela before her, and it was there that I saw one day on the front page of the newspaper that they had 'got' her, and sent her to the ravaged prison by the sea where even the seagulls stay away – at Catia la Mar.

Elías finished his packing and then told us what we ought to do.

'I'll leave the hotel tonight, you two leave tomorrow,' he said. 'Make everything natural. César, you get yourself to Paris, I'll make my own way. I'll wait a while, they'll expect me to make a dash for it.'

'And what then?' César asked.

'We'll take the slow train to Milan.'

He wasn't one for saying goodbye, and when I called him for dinner, he was already gone.

I asked César: 'Do you think he'll be all right?'

César didn't seem worried about him. It was roast pork for that night.

'Elías is a very serious man,' he said.

I was still uneasy after our trifle, and César looked across at me. I could see that he was worried now, that I might be going to cry. He had a horror of any show of emotion. The mere sight of his alarm cheered me up, and he brightened and said, 'And now,' as though about to introduce something sensational, 'for television!'

César was inordinately fond of television. He would watch it regardless of the subject matter. From programmes in Welsh to Closedown it could hold his attention in a way that I couldn't hope to rival. When I first asked him why he watched so much, he told me simply, 'I used to watch it in the castle.'

It was hard to deal with César's answers, so I usually just left them alone. One day, I tried Otto: 'Why does César watch so much television?'

He pouted a little, in a way that he had, pursing his black moustache. 'I think he used to watch it in the castle,' he said.

I came to regard César's viewing as an integral part of his life. It attained an almost mythical status, and I listened out for any further news of this mysterious castle.

When César passed out in the hotel lobby and it took four

57

men to carry him upstairs, and the sweat ran from his upper lip in rivulets, Otto shook his head and said, 'The castle.'

And again, 'the castle' when a high-pitched whirr fixed itself in César's ear, and no specialist could fault his hearing, but he sat up at night, and paced our room harder and harder.

So, on our last night in Oxford, we watched television at one end of the long sitting-room while someone played the piano at the other end. César had a very low opinion of any television set that gave trouble. It didn't make him stop watching, but he spoke to it, menacingly, under his breath, while adjusting his own position to whatever imperfection on the screen. At Joanna's flat in Clapham, he had developed a regulated twitch, to compensate for the looseness of the horizontal hold. That night in Oxford the picture was good and we were subjected only to the usual outbursts of alternate disgust and anger, notably at any lack of action, or at kissing in public.

'You fool, you fool,' César would say, grinding his fingers together, 'get on with it!'

César was always more affronted by what happened on the television than what happened at the cinema. The fact of it all happening in his home, however temporarily, gave him a sense of personal involvement. I remember when we watched the funeral of General de Gaulle, César was particularly angered by the sight of the mourning French, and when the cannons began to fire, he stood up and left the room, and stood stubbornly in the hotel garden with his arms crossed until it was all over.

'Common decency', he said, 'does not allow me to stay in the same room as those cowardly baboons,' and resumed his seat, close by the screen, and promptly fell asleep.

We left early the next morning. The proprietor seemed distressed at our going.

'You were beginning to feel like family,' he said. The bill was astronomical. Nearly a fifth of it was for breakages, and much of it was for drinks.

'I don't suppose you'd consider staying,' the proprietor said, as he ferried our cases to the stripped forsythia near the road.

'I beg your pardon?' I asked, looking round the hall for a last time, remembering the positions of things and their heavy faded colours.

He cleared his throat and shuffled his feet on the tiles with some embarrassment.

'I haven't liked to mention it before,' he said. There was a touch of Yorkshire about his voice, and an assumed intimacy. 'But I've had a spot of trouble.' He paused and looked down at the floor, rubbing a graze in the wax polish with his foot, as though it were the spot of trouble he was talking about.

'I was hoping that we could come to some arrangement,' he said.

The thought of blackmail crossed my mind, and I listened to what he had to say with a little more attention.

'I'll come right to the point,' he said, rubbing at the tarnished floor with new vigour. 'I need a bodyguard.'

César turned away, it was a word he knew, and he was relieved to hear that that was all he wanted. 'I had a spot of trouble, last spring,' he insisted. 'I went out to my car, and it blew up.'

He was shorter than I, and he looked up to see if I was listening. 'The police said it was a bomb. I know who put it there, mind, and they know that I know, but I'm getting a bit old for this lark and, the fact of the matter is . . .'

He cleared his throat again and then continued, 'They've stopped bothering me since your lot moved in. I know it's ridiculous, but they think I've hired you, and I don't mind telling you, I haven't denied it.'

I looked at him with new eyes. I couldn't conceive of anyone wanting to do him any harm, he looked so inoffensive as he stood there rubbing the floor nervously with his toe.

I couldn't make up my mind whether to smile or say something. I thought that I should, under the circumstances, sound a little sympathetic, humour him. However, I couldn't quite decide, so I just made my way slowly to the front door.

'They killed my collie before you came,' he volunteered, sadly after me, as I walked down the mosaic steps. 'They left his corpse on the back doormat,' he added, almost to himself. I turned to say goodbye. He had followed me.

'Don't go,' he said, 'please don't go.'

I looked back at him apologetically.

'I'm sorry', I said, 'about the dog.'

'I used to be in the betting business,' he explained, 'but I'm getting too old for that lark. I bought this hotel for my retirement.' He smiled bitterly. 'Suppose they'll be back any day now. Once you get mixed up in something, there's no getting out of it.'

Our taxi had drawn up to the kerb and César was piling in our coats and bags.

'I could manage with just one of you,' the proprietor said, 'you could take it in turns.'

I asked the driver to take us to the station.

The old man wouldn't give up, he put his hand on the door and held it open.

'I'd make it very worth your while, of course,' he said.

'Look, I'm sorry,' I told him, 'but we have to go.'

'I was just hoping,' he said, 'you see, I need protection.'

I was feeling sorry for him by now, but also impatient to get away.

'Have you tried the police?' I asked him.

'The police,' he said, scornfully, rubbing a stray oak leaf into the kerb, 'they'd make a meal of me once I was down, but up till then, they don't care.'

'I hope you find someone, anyway,' I said politely, and taking the door from him I pulled it shut. César leaned back against the seat and sighed,

'Now we're all mad,' he said.

The taxi-driver slid back his window.

'What'll you 'ave then?' he asked.

'A plain full of silences,' César said.

'You what?'

'We'll have the railway station proper, please,' I said, hastily.

'What's 'e finking about then?' the driver asked, jerking his thumb towards César.

'I think he's thinking about the castle,' I said.

'Well, good luck to 'im,' he said, winking, and drove on.

Chapter VI

Back in London there was a telegram waiting for me. Serge would be arriving within the week. I telephoned him at Yale, where he worked, and told him that I was married.

He was more than unpleasantly surprised, and nothing I said seemed to reassure him in the least. We had a bad line, which didn't help.

'Don't throw yourself away,' he warned me, as though no step had yet been taken.

'I'm on my way to Italy,' I said, 'but I'll wait for you now.'

'What about Cambridge?'

'That'll be all right,' I lied.

'How old are you?'

'I was seventeen last month,' I said. I knew he knew that already.

'What have you done?' he said twice, flatly, in a broken voice.

There was some further crackling on the line, and then he said, more brightly,

'Meet me at Heathrow, I'll cable the time.'

And then the telephone clicked, I didn't know whether he had finished or if the line had just gone dead. I stood at the window holding the silenced receiver in my hand for a long time, staring out at the pollarded limes, and feeling uneasy.

I remember it was early November and the arrivals hall was already full of Christmas decorations. I met Serge at the airport; he was late as usual, but as glamorous as ever. He is six foot six, and he arrived swathed in furs and with his usual entourage in tow. César shook hands with him and called him Sir, and we travelled squashed into two taxis to the London Hilton where he had decided to stay. We spent two rather silent days driving round London behind a grey-uniformed chauffeur, and filling in our time shopping so as to avoid having to talk. On the second day, my sister, Lalage, met us all for lunch, and then we had tea together in Serge's rooms at the hotel. We ordered twenty-three teas between the four of us, and Lalage, who is endowed with a kind of infectious gaiety, filled the room with her laughter, and we ate our way through the cakes and sandwiches with some of our former pleasure. César, however, was silent. The sight of Lalage and myself seemed to sadden him, and all our efforts couldn't make him smile. He and I were the first to leave.

On the last day, Serge bought César a black musquash coat, and for me, a brown leather one down to the ground. He gave us a great many other presents, and the atmosphere was one of strained good-will. Then, after a round of diplomatic dinners and literary receptions, and his usual whirlwind visits to 'old flames' as he called them, Serge left with a parting: 'I'll meet you in Rome.'

As soon as Serge had left, César and I took the boat train to France. We would be meeting him in Rome, at the Hotel Continental, in three weeks, and we began to make our way south via some Venezuelans in Paris who were staying near the Bastille. We arrived at nearly midnight with strict instructions to avoid being seen by the concierge, who had forbidden any more visitors to come into the building.

There were, apparently, so many people already staying in the top flat that the sight of any more suitcases would have resulted in them all getting turned out.

Despite the crowd, Elías wasn't there, and if I had any illusions about leisurely travel, they ended during the week that we spent in Paris waiting for him. To begin with, the flat we stayed in belonged to a man who practised black magic and collected voodoo objets d'art. These he had pinned and hung in the most obscure places. There were bats' skulls in the egg rack on the door of the fridge, and there were strips of yellowing skin dangling from the lampshades. There were spears and javelins criss-crossed over the hall, and strange black drapes on the walls. The spice jars ranged from nutmeg to belladonna and some of the jars were labelled, and some were not. I noticed that the one marked root ginger had what appeared to be little claws in it. Against this sinister backdrop, there was the constant hilarity of our hosts.

César and I arrived very tired. César claimed that there came a point where he would rather die than stay awake any longer and that he had reached it, and he went to bed. I was about to follow him when someone said to me, 'You can't both go to bed. You stay here and have a drink.'

Not to drink with Venezuelans was social disaster. As it happened I was fond of drinking but I lacked the stamina for their marathon three-day runs. I knew better than to refuse, though, whatever the hour, however inappropriate the place, so I accepted and sat down, forcing myself to smile.

César claimed that whenever I forced a smile it gave me the expression of a donkey on a boat. I became aware of this expression, whatever it was, and tried to compensate for it by drinking down two tumblers of whisky. It was only a matter of minutes before I felt violently sick.

'If you're going to have a pee,' someone said, 'let's play a joke on Vitaliano.'

My heart sank. I didn't even know Vitaliano. I was swathed in a torn white sheet, and a voodoo mask was pinned over my face. They gave me a spear to hold, and stationed me outside the lavatory door in a dark corridor. I hadn't liked to mention my own fears of the dark so I waited in silence for this strange man to appear. My first urge to vomit was still as urgent as ever, but there seemed no way out of this silly vigil.

Vitaliano was also ill. I could hear him in the lavatory. I waited for two, five, eight minutes, until my legs ached. The others forgot about me and closed their door. I could hear laughter through the darkness. I leaned against the wall, half-asleep, and when Vitaliano finally did emerge, I was so startled that I jumped and gasped. He took one look at me and then drew back, kicked me, found I was real, and proceeded to attack me with all the vigour of a trapped man.

My reflexes were so slowed that I scarcely defended myself. Vitaliano was in a frenzy. I fell from his punches on to my spear and then the others came.

'It's Lisaveta from London,' they explained.

I took the mask off my face. Vitaliano was furious. My shins and elbows ached. I sat in the lavatory nursing my cut hand with paper and wishing that I had had the courage to reject their ill-timed joke.

I put as good a face on the matter as I could. The donkey in the boat face.

Next morning I woke up with streaks of bruises down one side. I showed them to César and explained what had happened.

'You'll live,' he said, and then, 'You be nice to Vitaliano, he's having a hard time.'

I hoped that Vitaliano would be receiving similar instructions about me, and then dressed and braved the crowds. The mornings were always hung-over. I drank my coffee to the sound of gargling and the fizzing of Alka-Seltzers. Melina, our hostess, was sitting in the kitchen in a silk kimono. She was very beautiful. She looked about twenty-three but her hair was entirely white.

'I married at your age,' she said, nodding towards me. I smiled. 'Do you regret it yet?' she asked me. 'They're all bonkers, you know. Let's dump them one night and go out on the town.'

I liked Melina. I liked walking through the streets with her because so many people stopped to admire her. She was very short-sighted and reputedly going blind although I never heard her say so herself. She bumped into virtually everything there was. In the local market she stopped in front of the cheese stall, enthusing over the camemberts and the bries.

'What I really want, though,' she said, 'is some of that. Have you got any money?'

'I've got travellers' cheques,' I said.

'Forget it,' she told me, flicking her fingers over the cheese counter like a lizard's tongue. Before I could think, she had taken a cheese as large as her fist and put it skilfully into her pocket.

'Why did you do that?' I asked.

'Because I wanted it, silly,' she said.

'Feel it,' I suggested.

She slipped her hand into her pocket and shuddered. She had taken the wrong cheese, and her pocket was full now of a wet creamy mess. We walked back quietly. After a while Melina interrupted the silence, to shout after a passing gendarme who had stopped to stare, 'Who do you think you are, Casanova?' Then she turned back to me.

'These French!' she said angrily. 'They're all the same. All stares and no action.'

We walked on for another block and then she asked me, 'Do I stink?'

'A bit,' I said, tactfully, trying not to think about the heady cheese that was beginning to ooze through her new camel-hair. Melina became suddenly as depressed as she had been cheerful and didn't speak again until we reached the Bastille, and then it was just to say 'Ciao' as she left me on my own.

That night we all went out to dinner.

'We may as well spend the money while it's there, and then we can be poor in style,' César had said.

While we were changing I asked him why Melina's hair was white. I'd been meaning to ask her all day but hadn't wanted to sound rude.

'Why does she bleach it?' I asked.

'She doesn't,' he said, 'it's just like that.'

'But why?' I was determined to know.

'Why do they all laugh hysterically and why do they play Monopoly all day, and why are they so afraid,' he said.

He was combing back his own light-brown hair with his fingers and looking at himself in a mahogany-framed cheval-glass. He made a stern face into the glass and drew himself to attention.

'Were you a soldier?' I asked. 'I mean, a regular soldier.'

César clicked his heels together in a way he had, and said, slowly, 'After the Jesuits I went to the military academy. But I used to run away,' he added.

'Was it near your home, then?' I asked.

'It was six hundred miles away,' he said, 'but I didn't like it!'

I spent as much time as I could away from that ghostly flat. César and I went every day to the Tuileries and then wove our way in and out of the mesh of Paris. It was turning colder and we stopped often for cups of coffee to warm us up. Every time we went into a bar or café, César would ask for water first, and then for coffee. If the water was refused, he would say, 'You see,' triumphantly, 'the meanest country in Europe!'

Wrapped in our furs we would sit on park benches and watch the handfuls of Parisians drift by. César was impressed by the architecture. He used to stare up in wonder, and every time someone passed us he would say, 'Imagine Paris, without the people.'

Otto telephoned on the third day and arranged to meet us at Domodossola, just inside the Italian border.

'Take the slow train from Paris on Tuesday,' he said, 'and I'll pick it up along the line.'

'What if you miss it?' I asked.

'Then we'll miss each other,' he said and rang off.

We didn't have much to pack in Paris; César had insisted on travelling light. I even left some suede things at the flat near the Bastille, and filled their place with books. César was amused at Otto's wanting to meet us on the train. He said, 'Otto loves a mystery. If he didn't have anywhere to go he would hide in a broom cupboard for the sake of coming out again.'

I sometimes thought that César would too, given half a chance.

Despite our meagre luggage, we were laden anyway, with final presents of French wine, marrons glacés and chocolates. Melina had invited us to return for Christmas but César was set on Italy and we turned her offer down. 'Watch out for the Lambrusco,' Melina shouted as she jogged beside the train.

'What does she mean?' I asked César.

'Wait and see,' he said. 'Once you've drunk it, you'll never forget.'

All the fluster of finding the right platform was gone as soon as we stepped on the train. We had a compartment to ourselves with working blinds and hot-air grids at our feet.

I had hardly taken off my coat when César said: 'Tell me, Veta, do you like the train?'

I thought about it for a moment and then nodded. I couldn't explain why I liked it so much. I had just begun to gather my thoughts together enough to tell them to César when I noticed that he was asleep. The steady purring of the train kept him that way for most of the journey. I read my book, and thought about all the trains I had known, and watched César breathing heavily through his mouth.

I remembered Serge bundling us into the train from Moscow to Hoek van Holland when I was ten, with our suite in the first class, in the end carriage. Serge himself had returned by ship with the Daimler; it was too long a drive for him over days of cobbled roads. Only Joanna and I went by rail. Dinner on the first night had come like a feast on Queen Alexandra's private coach. We had watched the people piling into second- and third-class compartments with their bags of food, cooked chickens and melons, and crates of soft drinks. Even the corridors reeked of fish and garlic. We were alone in the first-class wagon except for an old man with a samovar who sold tea for a dollar a cup. It seemed that the whole train knew that the restaurant car unlinked and left us at Brest Litovsk. Only my mother and I had come without our three days' picnic.

Also at Brest Litovsk we had climbed down from that beautiful train, they called it the Western Express, and frontier guards had changed our currency into Russian travellers' cheques. Not even the scheming tea-man with his samovar would touch these cheques.

'It is two dollars in rubles, or one dollar in dollars,' he explained.

By the end of the second day we had no dollars left. I made journey after journey to his tiny room, bartering socks and pens and gloves for his bitter mugs of lemon tea. Our train slid through the heat wave, pausing at Warsaw where I bought two Polish doughnuts on the platform from my box of foreign coins; and at Berlin, where grey-uniformed guards came in and rammed their bayonets through the mattresses on our beds. And where they lined us up on the platform while they searched our bags.

A ticket collector was standing in front of me. I rummaged for our tickets, and found them, in my passport. The collector marked them and moved away in that slightly bored way Parisians have, implying that their hearts aren't really in what they do, but saved up for some future work of art. I followed him out into the corridor, and stood propped against the window, looking out into the night. The train was worn like a seaside hotel past its prime. It rattled along in a sort of bronchitic wheeze, lurching from time to time as it swung its long tail over the winding tracks. Occasionally an express train would burst past us and its smug efficiency seemed to shriek 'rush of art, rush of art' as it sped out of sight.

Our train spoke in a different voice. It had a confident whisper as it rolled along, like a drunkard with money to spend. Everywhere there was a station, it gasped into it and waited with its iron feet hunched up under the platform, and clouds of steam drifting along its sides. A handful of passengers got in or out. Soldiers on leave, a few tourists, a few teenagers and a few quiet people on their own. Some of them drifted out into the corridor to smoke, or, like me, just to watch the night. Whenever the train jolted or braked everyone fell back a little. Only the ticket collector swung his way up and down the corridors as sure-footed as before. I began to practise, incorporating the train's lurching into a rhythm of my own.

It nosed its way through Melun and Fontainebleau, through a maze of SNCF signs and signal boxes and hooded, disused sidings. By Dijon I was getting the hang of its movements, grafting them into my system, studying them like a new creed. In fact, it took many journeys to perfect that seaman's sway, to be able to stroll down the corridors from one carriage to another, to open the doors with one hand and a shoulder and never trip or lurch, or touch the doors and windows like a walking pattercake from link to link. It took months of practice to cross the black flaps that connected the carriages with the wheels gnashing visibly underneath my feet, without showing fear. And it took a year of practice to be able to tell our exact position in Europe by the gush of cold air that came up through the scaled basin of the ladies' lavatory. But later, it was possible to calculate our whereabouts by taking into account the altitude and the time of year as we rattled through the Alps.

Even the boys who sold coffee and rock-hard rolls were not perfect at riding the train. Sudden halts could make them slop and spill their fizzy drinks, and drop their apples to bruise along the floor. Riding the slow train needed skill and concentration. Mâcon, Lyon, Annecy, it wound its way through all the grey towns of Champagne and Burgundy, past their scarred fields and timeless waiting-rooms and past the grey slates of their town halls.

One country distinguished itself from the next by the magazines and fizzy drinks that were offered through the windows in different languages and dialects, and in different flavours according to where we were. César slept and woke and slept, and he seemed brighter and younger after each bout. The food got worse as we went along. The rolls became even harder, the ham drier, and the apples and bananas more bruised. It was as though all the bread had been cut a week before our departure and carefully distributed to all the stations on our route. So that the nearer we came to Italy, the staler the rolls became. We had our own hard rations of chocolate and wine, and César had several jars of strawberry jam, which he ate with a teaspoon. Once a day we trekked along the train to the restaurant. It would take thirty hours to reach Milan and the best part of another day to get to Rome. César was unmoved at the thought of Rome. 'The best place in Italy', he said, 'is Bologna.'

Chapter VII

At Domodossola I looked out for Otto. When I couldn't see him, I wanted to get down on to the platform and look around.

César said, 'Don't bother.'

He was reading a history of Peru and his lack of interest in our rendezvous infuriated me.

'Don't you care about Otto?' I asked him.

'But of course I care,' he said, looking up from his book for a moment. 'It's just that he won't come; so don't bother.'

'How do you know he won't come?' I asked.

'He never comes,' he said, without this time looking up from his book.

I had, in fact, noticed this myself, but had never formulated it quite so clearly. It took me some time to fully accept it, but I sensed that it was the key to Otto's character. Or, at least, it was the key to being able to live with him.

We passed through Milan with its network of converging tracks, and grimy shelters leading up to the Stazione Centrale. On every available wire or fence, and on every wall and telegraph pole, there were notices: 'è vietato . . . è pericoloso . . .' Smoking, talking, sitting, stopping, loitering, looking, everything seemed to be forbidden, everything was said to be dangerous. César nodded at the different notices as we shunted past them.

'You see,' he said, gleefully.

'See what?'

'All the notices,' he said. He slammed his book closed and smiled knowingly. 'They're afraid.'

We had a long stop at Milan and we bought coffee and replenished our food supplies with freshly made sandwiches and cakes.

The city of Milan itself looked grim and ugly, straggling on for endless miles of purpose-built flats and drab, spreading factories.

'Tell me if you see a tree,' César said.

'Why?' I asked.

'Because there aren't any.'

I looked out at the littered suburbs, with all their unsightly blocks, draped from balcony to balcony with streamers of washing, and there really didn't seem to be any trees.

'Why aren't there any?' I asked César.

We had three other people in our compartment by now, two women and a priest. César noticed the priest for the first time. He stared very hard at him before answering me and then he said, mockingly,

'They were probably "dangerous".'

I had never seen him look quite so unpleasantly at anyone before. The priest shifted uncomfortably in his seat, and then smiled politely and left the compartment.

'I thought you liked Italians,' I said.

'I do,' he replied, smiling sweetly at the two women opposite him, 'but I can't sit in the same compartment as a priest.' He nodded indulgently at the two women and then continued, 'Besides, liking Italians doesn't mean that I like their faults.'

The two women were very taken with César.

'Molto gentile,' they said to each other and to me, nodding their heads sagely, as though I could take their word for it, and pointing towards César.

'Molto gentile,' they repeated, smiling at him encouragingly. César had some magic appeal for old ladies in Italy. I think they would have had him beatified if they could have. Even when he was angry and looking quite murderous, old ladies would nod their heads at him approvingly and still find

71

him 'molto gentile'.

I found that César regarded Italy in a special indulgent way: he was actually prepared to tolerate its faults. People or places either had no faults at all, or they had no good points. The French fell firmly into the latter category. Any individual who seemed to qualify for a measure of respect became 'not really' French, according to César. Otto and the English, on the other hand, were faultless. Hence Otto 'adored' me, despite the fact that we spent half our time together bickering and glaring and getting in each other's hair. And his not turning up with such meticulous regularity was taken as yet another sign of his strength of character. Everything about him contributed to César's high opinion. And in vain did I point out to César that many of the things he admired about the English were obsolete. To him they were real, and always there.

'What about the war?' he would say, no matter what subject I had been speaking about, and he would wait to see if I dared reply, and then interpret an answer as disloyalty.

Italy, César claimed, had no faults but the Italians had a lot to answer for. Over the two years that we spent in Italy I discovered that he was prepared to turn a blind eye to their peccadilloes, but that still left them guilty of four grievous faults. These were, firstly, that they were 'silly', secondly, that they had 'behaved badly during the war, and were cowards anyway', thirdly, that they hated and massacred trees, and fourthly, that they shot down ospreys. Intermingled with these four loathings was a great deal of admiration and affection.

For instance, César had a theory that food tasted better in Italy. Even camembert, which he loved, he claimed tasted better in Italy.

'Why can't the French get it right,' he would say whenever we bought it. 'It is so good here!'

Sometimes it feels as though that first train journey really lasted for the whole two years. We went from town to town so many times that it is hard to remember the first time as an isolated event. Our train stopped at Prato and Florence and at a string of other places with names like introductions. Orvieto was the last stop before Rome. The train had become increasingly crowded.

'When we get to Rome,' César said, leaning across to me, 'let everyone get out first. Do you understand. We must not rush.' I would have liked to have got out and seen the city quickly but I didn't feel as strongly about it as César seemed to, so I nodded, and sat back.

'The first thing we'll do,' he said, 'when we get to Rome, is visit the tomb of Pope Alexander the Sixth.'

I couldn't believe my ears. César, the atheist, making such an announcement. He looked across at me and saw my disbelief.

'Alexander Borgia was a serious Pope,' he said firmly. 'The only Spanish Pope,' he added. 'I might still be a Catholic', he said, 'if there was such a Borgia on the papal throne.'

'I thought you didn't believe,' I said.

'I don't, but when I was at the Jesuits I used to wear a supplice *and* sackcloth, even at football.'

Not being a Catholic myself, I didn't really see the relevance of the football, so I asked him what he meant. He explained that a supplice was a belt with iron spikes on the inside that dug into your flesh. It was worn as a penance by the more ardent believers. Some of the boys had used it occasionally, but he himself had kept his on all day, and when he played football, it drew blood. I thought that if I had to imagine César as religious it was actually easier to imagine him as a religious maniac than as just an ordinary churchgoer.

It was night when we finally reached Rome. César insisted on trying to find the tomb. He asked several people in the street, and was depressed to find that not only did they not know where it was, but they had never heard of it.

'I don't want to go there in a bad mood,' he said. So we gave up our quest until the next day, and went to find the Hotel Continental.

Our finances were becoming more and more precarious. César had been penniless for the last two months. Once or twice I had asked him if he was expecting any funds to arrive.

'Some will come,' he assured me, but he didn't know when, and he obviously found the subject distasteful since he brooded for hours afterwards whenever I brought it up. I had a generous allowance from Serge which I had calculated would be just enough to pay for a cheap hotel, meals, travel and César's cigarettes. As soon as we went into the Continental, I realised that we couldn't afford to stay there for the eight days until Serge arrived.

I explained this to César with some embarrassment, but he didn't seem to mind in the least, and taking our cases from the hands of a protesting doorman he led the way back to the street.

'It doesn't matter,' he said, 'it's still early. We'll find somewhere else.'

We were doomed to be unlucky with our hotels. We found one not far from the Continental. The front door was closed so we rang the bell. A small grid in the door opened and a woman's face stared into César's.

'What do you want?' she snapped.

'Is this a hotel?' César retaliated.

The face relaxed a little and then asked more kindly, 'How many are you?'

'Two,' César told her.

'Let me see,' she demanded, hostile again.

César stood back and the face peered at me. It relaxed once more.

'E bellina,' she commented, and opened the door. She led the way up a worn oak staircase and along a tiled corridor to her registration desk on the first floor, which was festooned with coloured paper-chains and dusty paper lanterns. We discussed a price at half board. César did the talking since he spoke Italian.

Then she took us back down the corridor jangling an enormous bundle of keys. She showed us a single room and standing back as flat against the single door as her obesity would permit, she said: 'This is for the gentleman,' and smiled at César.

It looked ridiculously cramped but we were so tired we decided to take it for that night anyway. Then she asked us to follow her again, this time to another floor. We thought she was going to show us the bathroom. But she unlocked the door of another single room, and said, 'And this is for his daughter,' and she smiled at me.

César smiled indulgently, although I knew he hated people thinking I was his daughter.

'You don't understand,' he explained, 'she is my wife.'

The woman stayed very still with her hand on the door. She was staring at us with narrowed eyes. After a while she dedicated her glare entirely to César, and then quite suddenly began to scream.

'Sadico, sadico!' she shrieked.

We looked at her with amazement.

'Help, help,' she shouted, 'un sadico!'

The corridor began to fill with half-dressed angry people. A small man with a moustache stepped up to her and another woman was holding her hand.

'What's the matter?' they asked; she began to tell them.

'The moment I set eyes on him,' she said, pointing an accusing finger, 'I knew he was no good. And now,' she cried hysterically, 'this child,' she said, 'this bambina! He's a monster.'

'But we're married,' César protested. 'Look.' He pointed to the magic word in his passport, and to the Mrs in mine. The apparent stamp of legality on the crime only incensed her more. 'Call the police,' she demanded. 'Call the police.'

'Basta,' César said firmly. 'Come on, Veta.'

We moved in the direction of the stairs and the door. But our path was barred by a mixture of guests and staff, and we were obliged to wait until they would let us go. The police were very quick to come, rushing up the stairs with their weapons drawn. One of them understood enough English to see that our marriage certificate and passports were in good order, and they apologised and left, ogling me unpleasantly all the while. Our accuser was in no way mollified by this news. She continued to mutter 'sadico' and 'fuori' under her breath, and insisted on carrying the lighter of our cases which she held at arm's length from herself, and with great disdain, as though the whole thing were crawling with vermin. On her way down she knocked on every door that we passed and called out, 'Look at this monster, è un sadico.'

Many of the doors opened behind us, and we were jostled along by a mob of spiteful faces. Once in the doorway, the woman hurled our bag into the street, she had obviously been carrying it for that sole purpose, and slammed the door, only to open the little grid again and shout abuse at us.

We tried another four small hotels and, although they were less violent about it, they all turned us down because I was still, legally, a minor.

'But we're married,' César insisted.

'I know,' they would say uneasily, 'but she looks like a child.'

'We could go back to the Continental,' I suggested.

'No,' César said, and I knew that was final.

'We could take two singles,' I argued, 'just for tonight.'

'No,' he said again. He thought for a while, and then said, 'I know, we'll follow a prostitute.'

I had visions of a kind of ménage à trois with this unknown figure, and I didn't like the sound of it. At the same time, I didn't like to seem prudish.

'She might have V.D.,' I said.

'So what,' César said, 'she'll still have to stay somewhere, and wherever she can stay, so can we.'

It sounded like an ingenious solution, and we set out in search of our prey. For some reason, it took a long time to find anyone suitable. I've never been able to understand why, considering how many there are in Rome. Perhaps it's just that, like buses, they are never there when you want one. Having located a likely lady, we had to wait while she found herself a customer. We were rather conspicuous with our fur coats and our cases, but we managed to keep a watch on her, and finally to tail her back to a narrow alleyway and on into a very cheap hotel.

I was glad that César was as large as he was. It looked like the sort of place where a mugging came included in the price of the room. We were both exhausted and we didn't even notice how cramped and seedy the room looked. César had insisted on a clean sheet, and he made up the bed, while I sat slumped half-asleep on the floor. 'I hope we get our passports back,' he said. We had been obliged to leave them downstairs. I was too tired to care whether we did or not. I crawled into bed and was on the verge of sleep when someone came pounding at our door. César sprang up and demanded who it was.

'It's the portinaio from downstairs.'

'What do you want?' César asked fiercely.

'You have to go,' the man said firmly. 'She is under-age; if the police come, I lose my licence.'

César unlocked the door. 'She's my wife,' he shouted in the man's face. He looked at our passports, at the names and the line where it said casado, married, in Spanish.

'Oh,' he beamed, 'you are the first married couple I ever had.' He clasped his hands together and said, 'A real hotel, mamma, a real hotel,' and went away.

Next day there was a little bunch of freesias in my room, and I learnt my first Italian leaning over the yellowed counter in his downstairs hall.

'I always wanted a real hotel,' he told me.

His hotel may not have been 'real' as he put it, but it was certainly busy. There was a constant shuffling of coming and going at all hours of the night and day, and the walls of our room resounded to grunts and groans and the bouncing of springs on three sides.

We divided our days into mornings, siestas, cinemas and meals. In the mornings we did sightseeing, beginning with the tomb and chapel of Alexander the Sixth. Our man from the hotel directed us to the chapel where he was buried. I could see him climbing in César's estimation when he said that he knew it well. When we finally found it, however, it was closed for three months. César was bitterly disappointed.

'I have to see it,' he said.

By asking around, we found out that the chapel was in the care of an order of monks who lived near it. We went to their address and knocked on the door. An elderly friar answered. César explained that we had come 'all the way from Venezuela' to visit the tomb.

'I can't go without seeing it,' he said.

'Does it matter so much to you, son?' the friar asked him.

César nodded, he was pale and tense, with a strange watery look in his eyes.

'It is a long time since I have seen such faith,' the friar said. 'I shall fetch the keys and take you to the chapel. In these days of hardship we must nurture our fold.'

César stood very still on the pavement and then we both followed the friar in his brown cassock and sandals. He unlocked the door and led the way to a vault in the far wall in which the tomb and effigy of Pope Alexander had been placed. César didn't go up to it at first, but stood transfixed at a distance. The friar stepped respectfully back and then waited at the other end of the church by the great door.

I walked about, admiring the architecture and keeping myself warm.

As I passed him César said: 'Go and talk to that friar.'

I tiptoed towards the door.

'Parla italiano?' he asked me.

I shook my head and said, 'Inglese.'

'Oh,' he said gravely. 'It is wonderful to see such faith,' he said in clipped English.

'Yes,' I answered, feeling the chill and wishing that César would hurry up. The old friar noticed my restlessness and asked suddenly:

'Are you a Catholic, child?'

'Yes,' I lied. It seemed inappropriate to bring up atheism, but it also seemed wrong to lie in such a place, so I added: 'My mother's family are Catholic,' and left it at that. It was, at least, true, although my mother had lost her faith long before I was born. I was hoping that he wouldn't ask me something that I didn't know. I looked around to see if César was coming, and saw, to my horror, that he was in the process of pocketing a silver chalice. I began to blush a deep beetroot blush of fear and embarrassment.

The friar looked at me with concern.

'What is it?' he asked.

'It's, er, very moving,' I said, fanning myself with my tourist map.

'I am glad,' the old friar said, 'you too feel the religious experience.' Then he lapsed back into Italian and his words were lost on me. César came up and collected me from him, thanked him, and we were gone.

For once, I was really angry with César.

'Why did you do that?' I demanded.

He stopped, and we sat down on a stone parapet. 'It was Alexander the Sixth,' he said.

'But why take a silver chalice; what good can one chalice be to you?' I said crossly.

'But Veta,' he said, 'one chalice is no use, that is why I have two.' Here he pulled out the pair of them one after the other, to illustrate his point. 'And two are beautiful.' He stood them side by side on the stone.

'Do you do that kind of thing in Venezuela?' I insisted.

'Of course not,' he said, as though the mere idea was ludicrous.

'Then why here?'

He didn't answer, he wasn't listening, he was running his finger over the filigree silverwork as he rubbed one up on the silk lining of his coat.

Chapter VIII

We met Serge at the Hotel Continental, as arranged, on 5th December. He had come with a group of Yale professors. We met in the main bar, and ended up spending most of the evening there. One of Serge's colleagues kept wanting me to show him how much Italian I had learned. I explained that I was still at virtually one sentence, but he protested, 'Your daddy says you're good at languages', and I had to keep saying my one sentence over and over again so as not to let the side down. It was 'Waiter, please bring me another pear juice', and one of the three waiters who hovered attendance on us would slip away and come back with yet another whisky-glass of pear juice, until I became tired of drinking them, and they began to clutter up our table and get knocked over in a syrupy mess.

It was awkward because I knew that César couldn't follow the conversation in English and he sat silently in one corner, watching the collection of pear juices grow around me and saying: 'Why do you do that?' from time to time under his breath, as I had about the chalices.

Serge booked us a suite in the Continental and we arranged to move in on the following day. He stayed in Rome for three days, and then had to leave unexpectedly. I spent a couple of hours with him on my own, while he packed. Far from travelling light, Serge had a series of brand-new leather cases, which were virtually unmanageable when empty and quite impossible by the time he had filled them with his books and papers and innumerable changes of clothes. We discussed going to Japan, and I told him that I wouldn't be going, because of staying on in Italy. He seemed very tired, and opposed to my plans. 'What are you going to *do* in Italy?' he asked.

'Nothing,' I told him.

'What about Cambridge?' he asked me.

'I think I'd rather go somewhere here,' I said, and changed the subject. I didn't want to tell him that I'd decided not to go to University, on our last evening together and while he was so tired.

'And what are César's plans?' he asked, trying not to be too depressing.

'I don't really know,' I admitted, 'he doesn't talk a lot.' We phoned down to room service for a drink for me. Serge never drank much.

'I've got you a new medical insurance,' he said, 'it's international. It'll cover you here, remind me to give it to you before I go.'

I thanked him and drank my drink and then another, and grew sad at all the things we hadn't said.

When he left, early the next morning, he thrust a roll of dollar notes into my hand.

'Buy yourself some more boots,' he said, 'for Christmas.'

I had a fetish for expensive leather boots.

I put the money away, there were five hundred dollars, and kept it until such time as I should run out. I had no idea we were going to need it so soon.

The day that Serge left, César and I went to the Colosseum. I was feeling sad about Serge and I think that César was missing Otto and Elías, because he talked to me about them a lot.

He told me how Otto's uncle had been a famous guerrilla commander, and how he had been ambushed and killed. And he told me how Otto's mother had gone to the dentist, months later, and reading a magazine in the waiting-room she had read about the death of her own brother whom she had believed was still alive, and how she had gone in and had her tooth drawn all the same.

'You should try to like him more,' César told me, 'he is my best friend.'

He told me how Melina, from Paris, had been in and out of prison since she was a child, and how the last time they had hung her from a helicopter by the wrists, and her hair had turned white, and she had come to Europe now as well and how he and Otto and virtually everyone else we had met had been in prison.

'But not Elías,' he said. 'Nobody has ever caught Elías.'

We had been walking all the while between the inner walls of the Colosseum, and with every step we took, cats scattered before us, and reassembled behind. They were thin and mangey in varying degrees. Some of them were scarred from fighting and some had twisted limbs. One kitten in particular was following us around. It was a rumpled grey made clumsy by its rib-cage, which fanned out like a broken corset about its head. Each time we tried to lose it, it scampered up behind us and trotted along. César knelt to stroke it and it came up and nudged itself against his hand.

'Mis, mis,' he coaxed, which is Spanish for puss puss. We stayed until long past lunch-time, not wanting to leave the kitten or the solemn grandeur of the place, and then we jumped over a wall and stole away.

We ate in a quiet trattoria about ten minutes' walk away from the Colosseum. César seemed very talkative and he told me odd scraps of stories about the Romans while we waited for our late lunch. We had ordered tagliatelli con maiale. It took so long that the waiting irritated me.

'It'll all be worth it,' César sighed, 'when you get that plateful of pork in front of you.'

When the food finally arrived it was hot, home-made pasta, peppered with minute dots of fat bacon fried crisp. César was speechless. He let his plate grow cold, staring at it, and then he called the waiter back.

'What about the pork?' he asked.

The waiter pointed a greasy finger at César's congealing plate.

'It is all there, bacon is pork,' he said in a hurt voice.

After he had gone, César drank his wine, and pushed his plate away from him.

'Pork is pork,' he said vehemently, and then, 'No wonder the fascists took over.'

When the waiter returned, César asked for a paper bag to take his uneaten food. He was given one with a bad grace. We took the food back to the Colosseum and tipped it out on the ground.

'Mis, mis,' he called, and cats leapt out from every hole and corner and from behind every stone. It had all gone by the time most of them got there, and among the last was the silvery kitten we had seen before. Gradually, the edges of the arena began to fill with ragged rough-haired children. They came towards us with streaked faces and outstretched hands and they came so close that they were clawing at my coat.

'Move back,' César told me.

But I couldn't move. I had never seen so many beggars before, and I was riveted. More and more of them came out from between the walls, some lame, and some maimed, but mostly just dirty.

'Soldi, soldi, soldi,' they chanted. They were mixed in with the cats, and looked very like them in some ways, mewing and whining at our feet. César was angry with them, he was shouting something that I couldn't understand. I caught, 'Have you no shame?' a few times. They glared and slunk away, crawling back into the walls, a few of them running across the arena, whooping defiantly. One boy remained, his hair was blond with the kind of colourless tarnish that comes with malnutrition.

'Ho bisogno . . . ' he began, but César cut him short.

'Go away,' he said roughly.

The boy was very young, probably not more than seven.

'But you are kind,' the boy whispered, 'I saw you feeding the cats.'

'Yes,' César said, 'but they were cats.'

'But I am a human being,' the boy choked.

I felt a lump come to my throat.

'Exactly,' César said curtly and swung away. He took my arm, and pulled me towards the gate. I looked round and the boy was still standing there, crying.

I went back to him and gave him a handful of 100–lire coins. He smiled at me and wiped his eyes and nose on his sleeve.

'Grazie,' he called after me.

'Does that make you feel good?' César asked me, scornfully. I was upset, and I didn't answer. 'That's a nice boy, he won't get anywhere by wheedling. Cats don't come to you with excuses. I respect self-respect,' he added and walked away from me.

I couldn't keep up with César sometimes, not when he was walking, and not when he was thinking either. The grey kitten was following me too, demanding some more attention. We went out through the gateway and it trailed behind me, catching playfully at my long skirt. It followed us to the kerb.

'It'll get run over,' I said.

'No it won't,' César tried to persuade me. 'If it has survived this long, it'll survive a little longer.'

'I'm going to take it home,' I said, defiantly.

'You haven't got a home.'

'Well, I'm still going to take it,' I said.

I picked it up and cradled it under the fur collar of my coat. It was incredibly light and bony, and not very pleasant to touch, but it began to purr, and we picked our way across the winding streets to the Continental. I smuggled it past the long mirrored lobby and into the lift and then safely into our rooms. We had a room and a sort of dressing-room, a bathroom and a study that Serge had thoughtfully paid for for another two weeks. The kitten didn't seem to like any of these. It darted from one side to the next, knocking against the skirting boards and then reeling back. It evacuated itself on the carpet in a kind of spasmodic frenzy. It began to yowl pathetically. It was the same heart-rending yowl as one of our cat Ffuphi's kittens had yowled when the housekeeper shut the fridge door on it by mistake. It had lain down on the carpet with its feet in the air and gyrated its lower body in a strange, rigid dance until its spine snapped and it lay limp, but still yowling. Now this new kitten was behaving in the same agonised way. César lay on his bed reading a *Life of Napoleon*. He looked over the top of the book at the kitten and at me. I was entirely helpless.

'Pick it up,' he said, and turned back to his book.

I did, and it was instantly quiet.

I made a home for it in the dressing-room. Partly because it was small and dark, and partly because I could lock it away from the prying eyes of room service. We called it Coliseo. It ate voraciously, and then sicked up most of its meal. Over the next few days it began to fill out and grow sleek and sleepy. It had fleas and ring worm and what seemed like a constantly open bowel. It purred whenever I held it and fretted whenever I put it down.

I could see that César disapproved of Coliseo, and after he or she, it was difficult to tell, had been with us for a week, I began to agree. It was clear that Coliseo hated the dressing-room, and it hated the other rooms even more. It even began to lose interest in its food; smuggled scraps that were difficult enough to keep, and sardines whose empty tins had to be carried out into the street, and milk kept in a carton outside the cloudy bathroom window.

Coliseo was pining. I decided it was a he. Twice there had been complaints about his yowls. The maid began to look around our room suspiciously. There was an overwhelming smell of disinfectant to douse the other more noisome ones. The fleas kept us awake at night. Our whole suite was jumping with them. I began to stay in with Coliseo, leaving César to wander off on his own. Trying to keep the kitten quiet was a losing battle. He wanted to be constantly petted but his vomiting and ring worms were getting me down. 'What's the matter with him?' I asked César one night when Coliseo's yowling passed all proportion.

'He wants to go back,' César said.

The telephone rang. It was the reception with yet another complaint about the noise. I knew that César was right although I didn't want to admit it. I tried to console myself with the thought that I had meant well. I could imagine him saying, 'Meaning well is never enough.' I put Coliseo in my Gladstone bag and we took him back to the Colosseum. It was nearly midnight and cold and the gates were closed, so I slipped him through a railing and hoped for the best.

'I'm sorry,' I said to César, after a long, silent walk.

'I'm not God,' he said.

I walked behind him and stared at the back of his neck with intense dislike, hoping that a car would run him down.

I awoke relieved, and ready to resume my sightseeing. César ran my bath for me and tipped a whole bottle of bath oils in the water.

'The last of Coliseo,' he explained. It was true that the rooms were slightly fetid. He opened the main window and leaned out to smoke his first cigarette of the day. He always smoked before breakfast. Sometimes people would tell him how they had given up smoking and he would ask them, 'When did you have your first cigarette?'

If they said any time later than first thing in the morning, he would announce, 'Ah, then you were not a real smoker. I'm serious about smoking,' thumping his fist down. And he was.

After breakfast we went to the Vatican and stood in the Piazza di San Pietro.

'I want to go back to Milan,' César announced.

'When?' I asked.

'Soon,' he said.

'How soon?'

'Tonight.'

'Has anything happened?' I asked.

'No. I just want to move on.'

We went to the Vatican Museum. There were a lot of people there, despite it being winter, and the tourist season not yet begun. We were obliged to look at all the manuscripts while being jostled along by a winding queue of anxious pilgrims. There was a huge visitors' book at the door, at least a foot thick, and cut off from the guard by a hub of pressing people. As we walked past, César picked it up, staggering slightly under the weight, and would have pulled it out with him had it not been chained to the wall.

'Hijos de puta,' he said angrily, putting it back, and tripping up half the queue like a pack of cards in the process.

'What did you want that for?' I asked him once we were outside.

'For Otto,' he said.

86

By the time we had packed and eaten there wasn't a direct train to Milan, so we settled for one via Florence. The Hotel Reception had been reluctant to let us go.

. 'You still have eight days in credit. Eight more dinners,' they said incredulously. 'Christmas dinner, you know.'

It took some time to make them see that it would actually be to their advantage if we left. Once on the train, César said: 'I've got a feeling I'll find my watchstrap in Milan.'

He often had 'a feeling' about this strap. He had been having 'feelings' all over Rome about it, to no avail, and I was less hopeful than he about the outcome in Milan. But in searching for this Longines strap, César was an eternal optimist. Every shop looked promising, and every jeweller's was 'bound to be the one'. We retraced our tracks: Orvieto, Arezzo, Firenze, and then changed and continued crawling through the night to Prato, Pistoia and finally Milan. The names began to engrave themselves on my mind. And the more we travelled, the more I proved César wrong. We were not refugees as he had claimed in the Colosseum: this slow train was our home.

Chapter IX

Both Otto and Elías were in Milan. César found them at a prearranged address by the Naviglio Grande. Milan was crowded and dirty and downtrodden, but I liked it. We had left our luggage at the station, and arrived just in time for breakfast. Otto nodded to us to take a seat, and Elías reshuffled the food on the table, dealing it on to four rather than two plates. Nothing was said about our having been away. We ate, and took up our conversation where we had left it over a month before, in Oxford. Every time any of us went away, we rejoined the group in the same manner, as though we had just run downstairs for another packet of cigarettes, or left the room to fetch some matches. Elías had acquired a car, a Fiat this time, and not his usual Mercedes.

'There's a recession on,' he laughed.

Elías's driving had struck me as extravagant in England, but now, unleashed on the less law-abiding roads of northern Italy, he lost all restraint. To do him justice, he was not the only driver I saw who always drove on the pavements, but he was the only one I ever knew who always parked by shoving the car in front and behind out of his way and then squeezing in between them. Despite all his malpractices at the wheel, he was never fined for a traffic offence. He would rattle over the cobbles, chasing pedestrians with his car as a child might chase pigeons. He would drive down steps and through markets shouting, 'Geronimo!' as the little car rattled and bounced, but always just managed to scrape through. Elías liked Italy. It pleased him like a new train set or a toy aeroplane, and he played with what it had to offer, making the most of every hour.

We spent the days together, visiting friends of Otto's and browsing around the bookshops and just sitting in cafés talking and drinking wine. Every day seemed colder than the last, and César was suffering from it more than any of us. He was rheumatic. Even during the summer his hands and legs troubled him and he would carry around aspirins and liniments wherever he went. César didn't really approve of either drugs or illness but accepted that there existed varying degrees of discomfort. As a cure for these he believed in aspirin. He had a passionate faith in the power of aspirins to overcome all evil. He himself would take anything up to twenty a day and he couldn't bear to let a day pass when he didn't take at least one. He told me that all the men in his family died at about his age or younger as a result of a congenital heart condition. I think he believed that if he didn't take a daily dose of aspirin this fate would instantly befall him.

In London he had insisted on having his heart examined by a specialist. César claimed that he was already very far gone in this family complaint. But when the cardiologist announced that his heart was as sound as a bell, far from being convinced, César had said: 'You see, that is how good the aspirins are!'

Every pocket of every jacket and waistcoat had at least one paper of salicylic acid with the usual caution about exceeding the stated dose. César ignored this as a typical instance of people not wanting you to have enough of a good thing and sucked his aspirins like lozenges at odd times during the day.

Despite all this, his rheumatism grew worse in the biting cold of Milan. He didn't complain about it, but his face assumed a kind of greyness and his legs moved stiffly, and sometimes even locked.

As our money dwindled, we stayed in more and more. Everything was very expensive and we were at pains to make ends meet. We decided to take a more economical flat and ended up by accepting two rooms that were offered to us free by a friend. On our first wave of enthusiasm, we were blind to the drawbacks of this offer. Firstly, the flat was on the sixth floor of a tenement slum in the Porta Ticinese area of the Grand Canal. We didn't care, we thought it was picturesque, especially since the tenements had once housed all the painters of Milan, over a hundred years before. Secondly, there was no bathroom, just a shared tap and lavatory for the entire floor. We didn't mind, we wanted a taste of Italy as the Italians knew it. Thirdly, the stone steps of the building turned around a dark quadrangle, thus each flight was really four. This too seemed picturesque, but later it made César nearly house-bound with his swollen joints. And then, fourthly, it was a cache for vast supplies of illegal equipment. Again, we argued, we didn't mind, at least it was somewhere to live, and somewhere to ourselves.

The flat had two rooms. The first had a small skylight let into the ceiling and the second had no window at all. They were both dark and dank and the electric lighting was inadequate. It didn't seem to matter that there was no furniture. We bought a large mattress which César, Otto and I shared. Elías was going away 'on business'. And we bought a very ordinary table, a high stool, two chairs and a Calor gas stove. Our friend, Tito, gave us a paraffin heater, blankets and a tin bath.

César was particularly pleased with our new home. The second room had a heavy metal grid dividing off about two-thirds of it, which was always padlocked. Behind this grid there were piles of electronic equipment.

'You're welcome to the flat, for what it's worth,' Tito told us. 'I only keep it for the transmitters and things. You can use any one of the television sets outside the grid, but don't touch the other stuff.' He smiled rather shyly and then added, 'It interrupts the national radio stations and it should transmit to the television as well. We'll only ever be able to use it the once before it gets traced and found, and I don't want it to be by accident.'

César was delighted. Three television sets. He used to put all three of them on at once, often on different channels, but sometimes with two on one, and then swivel around on his stool from screen to screen. He never seemed to tire of watching.

When Elías returned, he took us out on excursions. He knew the area well and would often drive us along the course of the River Ticino around the edge of the Lago Maggiore and up into the Alps. The snow sat like creased damask over everything, and had been shovelled into massive barricades on either side of the winding road. The Fiat bounced and ricocheted against these icy walls as Elías spun around the bends, forcing the car to lurch over the humps in the road. Despite his antics, he was a first-class driver, and we never seriously crashed the car.

At weekends we sometimes drove up the motorway to Como. Elías would always time himself on this stretch of road, accelerating the car and beating his own record time and again. He had a friend with a garage and, gradually, he fitted out the Fiat with a bigger engine and powerbrakes. One day, on this stretch of motorway, we were stopped by a police car.

'Porca Madonna,' one of them said angrily, 'you're flying a bit low.'

Elías gave a winning smile. 'We're getting ready for Monza,' he explained.

There are few Milanese who can resist the glamour of racing driving. The car is more of a status symbol than anywhere else in the world. La macchina rules supreme. For a common policeman to be talking to a real racing driver made any and every offence excusable. We drove away, spouting an impressive cloud of smoke behind us to salute their gullibility.

Otto would sit morosely in the back of the car with me, while César co-piloted in the front. César and Otto came from the Andes, and they had seen snow before, about once every ten years, when a sprinkling of it fell over the Eagle's Peak, and hundreds of people would roller-skate in the streets to celebrate. But Elías came from the plains, from the dry savannas of Venezuela, and he had not seen snow before his coming to Europe. He never ceased to marvel at it. As the roads corkscrewed higher and higher into the Alps, the snow became deeper and crisper in the surrounding fields.

We would stop every half hour or so and rub it into our

faces, and clambering over the roadside stockades, we would wade, thigh-deep, in its powderiness. After the first time César did this, he was in bed for two days with his joints seized up and a fever. So he would just sit in the open car, smoking, or wander up and down the road to keep warm. Otto enjoyed playing in the snow as much as anyone; and Elías used to crouch in it and then spring up and try to chase us, with our slow hampered movements.

Elías was studying photography. He disappeared twice a week for his classes and little by little his cameras and equipment began to infiltrate the flat. One day he told us that he had had enough of his 'business' and that he would move in with us. He already spent most of his time with us at Porta Ticinese, using our televised grid-room as a dark room for his photographs. He took literally hundreds of these a day and then soaked and developed them and hung them from metal clips along the grid. Each time we went into the mountains he would return with several reels of film. There would be whole series of César walking up the road, César walking towards the car, and of Otto waist-deep in the snow with only his grizzled mane showing over his coat. There was César asleep. There was César in bed with me, with and without Otto, all swathed in fur on our thin mattress. Then there was a series called 'il dottore' which showed Otto in various poses, thinking, arguing, debating, reading, browsing, anything. Elías had a vast number of cameras, ranging from a four-inch tube that he could conceal in the palm of his hand to great tripod affairs with hieroglyphics circling every lens. Elías had another series, which we dubbed 'il sadico', in which César and I stood outside the Duomo of Milan, César in his furs looking unspeakably debauched, staring down at me with my hair up and a high Edwardian collar, and an icon on a chain, and looking like an angelic twelve-year-old. Elías had about fifty different angles to this shot, all against the backdrop of the white marble, and he enlarged and exposed and darkened them endlessly. There was also one of César and me standing in the snowy garden of a great mansion near Como. This last, César sent to his sister in Venezuela. He scrawled, 'Don't worry about me, as you can see, we have a nice place to stay.'

'They wouldn't understand about Ticinese,' he said.

The coming of Elías to the flat brought home the slum aspects of our accommodation. He arrived one morning while we were having breakfast. Breakfast often dragged itself over half the day, with César reheating his coffee and Otto topping up his tea. Elías brought with him a single mattress, his books, his matching Yves Saint Laurent bags, and his cameras. He had to make three journeys for the cameras. He was the only one of us who was never daunted by the stairs. After he had brought in all his things he said firmly, 'Anyone who calls me a communist lies. Sharing is all very well but this is *my* flannel.' He shook open a pink cloth, 'And *my* toothbrush and *my* soap, and I'll kill anyone who touches them.' He put them down on our makeshift washstand, wheeled round and went out.

It was March and my cheque from Serge had failed to arrive. We had decided to move to a larger place. It was intolerable where we were. With four of us in the flat, queueing for the lavatory had become a real problem. There were about seven other flats on our floor, all sharing the same hole and the same tap, and each one held at least one family, with children and parents and all. Almost every day, we had to buy a new toothbrush for one or other of us; they had a way of slipping out of a pocket and down the dreaded hole during the complicated processes of squatting or taking a shower. Much of the washing took place in our room and at Tito's proper flat, where he had a bath and two boxes of Marlene Dietrich L.P.s in German and a real fire.

Tito knew South America well, he had spent several years there, and had fought in a kind of international brigade in Cuba. He was immensely generous and we all felt unable to repay his kindnesses. One day he asked if we would help him with some documents. Elías said he would happily forge anything, but that although he was good at seals and stamps he was not good on signatures. Tito's face fell.

'But Lisaveta is good at them,' Elías added hastily. 'Aren't you.' He looked at me significantly, and whispered in Spanish 'Piratea'. He was telling me to bluff, so I did, and we spent the next month forging a pile of rather indifferent passports and visas and permits of one kind and another. I had done a lot of botanical drawings and I had an unusually steady hand. Notwithstanding this, nervousness and lack of skill combined to afflict the signatures of all the consuls and under-secretaries for whom I signed that month with what looked like an epidemic of Parkinson's disease. Elías said, 'Never mind, they only have to pass the inspection of some Abruzzi peasant.'

I wasn't convinced, and nor was Otto, because whenever we needed anything like a licence or visa, we went to the proper quarters, and queued up for them.

Actually, I was the one who did the queueing. I would take my own British passport and one of the others that needed restamping, and wait at whatever consulate I needed. I used to sit or stand well away from the desk and appear to be overcome with shyness. I often was, at first, so it wasn't difficult. Eventually, the kindest of the clerks on duty would come over and take pity on me, and ask what I was waiting for. Then I would tell them that I was going to visit an aunt in France or Switzerland or wherever, and that I had come for a visa. They would reassure me, ask for my passport, and I would pretend to want to cry. They would take my passport and smile, 'But you don't need a visa, dear, you're British.'

I would thank them profusely and then ask, innocently, 'What about my uncle?' and produce one of the others' passports, which they would take and I would collect later in the afternoon.

'They can't touch you,' Otto had explained, 'but if they get wise to us, we would be trapped in the consulate.'

In London we had had a different way. We used to go all together to the Home Office building in High Holborn and take a number and wait to be called to the little booths that lined the hall there. The first one to go up would take a wallet bulging with five-pound notes. I would go each time as interpreter. The usual questions would be asked and the usual bank statements required. At this point, I would relay the question to César or Otto or Elías, and they would look blankly at their inquisitor.

'I haven't got any on me,' they would say, 'just a little cash.'

'How much?' they would be asked.

'Not much,' they would say, and produce the wallet, with

five or six hundred pounds in fivers.

There would be a gulp and 'You can stay' and another three months stamped on their passports. It seemed that the only requisite to stay in England was to be rich enough.

To get the Italian visas we would take the train to the French frontier, cross over, and return. Sometimes we stayed on all the way to Paris, just for the ride, and then caught the next train back. Otto had a friend who was a friend of a friend who gave us free tickets for the slow train. Once, when we caught the express by mistake, we had to pay the difference and it nearly bankrupted us. But returns for the slow train were always available although we couldn't change the tickets into ready cash.

With the coming of spring I began to grow tired. It sometimes seemed that even the spring was forbidden in Milan. 'E vietato sporgersi.' César was right. It was as though leaves and grass and flowers were forbidden to lean out. There was just the long walk down the old tow-path of the Naviglio Grande, and the narrow linking bridges that rose in the middle, and from which one could watch the slow, almost stagnant canal forcing its way through the bed-ends and the garbage that made islands in its weeds.

Elías used to stare into the water, he was tired and restless too. 'I want to see my doctor,' he said.

And I would stand on the next bridge down and stare at the debris and a rubber glove caught in the weeds used to wave at me like a drowned man's hand.

It was May and I hadn't heard from Serge for nearly two months. Not even my usual cheque had come, by special order through the Chase Manhattan Bank in New Haven. I had the sensation of being ill, but I didn't like to tell the others. They didn't approve of illness. It would have been inelegant, in our cramped quarters, just to lie down and give way to the gnawing sensation inside me. Serge had forgotten to leave my medical insurance. I had written to remind him, I had even sent a cable. I, too, wanted to see a doctor. One morning in particular, Elías leant over the bridge, scattering stale breadcrumbs to imaginary ducks. 'I'm going to think about my doctor,' he announced, and took his position on the bridge. I had woken up feeling dizzy, and was glad to get away from the flat under any pretext. I had said I was going to model for Elías. So he stood on his bridge and I stood on mine staring into the dirty water. We stayed there all morning, undisturbed except by one solitary wherry, and a slow panic began to take hold of me that I would die in that tenement slum in the Porta Ticinese, and my hands would catch in the weeds and wave to any sad passer-by who took the time to notice.

I was disturbed from this fantasy by the arrival of César. He stood and watched the water with me for a while and then he said, 'Let's go and fetch our mail.'

Having decided that thinking was dangerous, I felt much better and we set off on our daily trek to the poste restante. I had a letter from Joanna but nothing from Serge, and César, as usual, had nothing.

Chapter X

We set off to fetch our mail, anything from every three days to twice a day. I had begun to live through the post, making closer and closer pen friends out of a mixture of friends and family. Especially during that spring, I wrote a battery of long explanatory letters about my feelings and my lack of them, interspersed with controversial statements that I hoped would result in clear but emotional replies. Life at Porta Ticinese had come to seem unreal. Sometimes I would look across at César or Elías and wonder if they weren't still total strangers. I developed a heaviness in the small of my back; it ached and needled me. I wanted a doctor to tell me that it was all right. I was still waiting for my medical insurance, and we had used up my February allowance. The March cheque had never arrived and now April's was overdue as well. We were saved by the boot-money I had brought with me from Rome.

César was waiting for a letter. He believed in this letter absolutely. He assured me that all our problems would be solved when this letter arrived from Venezuela. So whenever we could, we walked and rode in the dislocated tramcar to the Ufficio Centrale and asked for any letters in our name. César used to insist that a check be made under the first three of his names. The clerk would thumb through the Bs and the Cs and the Rs and then return his passport, with an apology.

'Niente per Lei.'

César was determined, he was sure that there was

something. 'Perhaps it's under the L,' he would suggest, and when the employee returned, having leafed through yet another bundle of letters, he would insist, 'It could be under the D', and point to the relevant letter of the de Labistida in his name.

Sometimes the employees at the post office were well disposed to his quest. But sometimes they would see us coming and begin to jostle among themselves as to who should have the chore of dealing with us. Whenever we got a particularly angry reply or a really flat refusal to examine all the Ds and Ls as well as the other letters, we would wait a day or two before returning. César would have liked to have gone every day, but often hostility ran so high at the post office that he had to admit it was better to wait a while.

My mother used to include postscripts to César and once she said that she was going to write to him. However I managed to dissuade her. The letter that César was waiting for, and that never came, seemed so important to him that I didn't think it fair for any other letter to take its place. No matter how many times he was refused, César never lost faith in it. Each time we went, it was not to see if it was there, but to fetch it. Otto gave me a little book by García Márquez, about a colonel obsessed with a letter.

'Your husband is famous,' he said, 'here is a book about him. They'll be buying the film options next.'

César remained calmly determined. Otto used to banter him: 'How can anyone write to you if no one knows your address?' César was adamant. He had faith.

I began to stay behind on some of these forays, reading. I was acquiring a whole new library. All the others in the flat read avidly, working their way through anything from farming to aviation. César had a passion for history, and Elías carried Liddell Hart around with him like an annotated Bible. Otto still argued with me as often as the chance arose, and he was always horrified by my ignorance. I noticed that he had taken it upon himself to educate me by way of anonymous gifts of Tennyson and Rimbaud, histories of France and dissertations by Sartre. I had always read a lot, but Otto regarded me as some alien species, and probed at the gaps in my learning with relentless zeal.

'I have to live with you,' he said.

Secretly, I read most of the books he brought, from Rosa
Luxemburg to Fernando Pessoa, and even the two-volume
Italian edition of Bertrand Russell's autobiography. But I
stayed at home not so much through any thirst for learning as
from the feeling of lethargy that was beginning to take hold of
me. César tried to rouse me into joining him.

'You're a vampire,' he would say. 'The summer is coming,
why hide from the sun?'

But I didn't really like the sun, I didn't like its glare, and I
hadn't the energy to face the stairs. I had a kind of cystitis, and
each day bound me more and more to the proximity of a
lavatory.

César had befriended an old man called Athos who made
shoes in a cupboard-like shop overlooking the Naviglio
Grande. There was just enough room for Athos to sit in the
doorway of his shop and for a thin person still to scrape by him
to the counter, and as soon as the winter lifted, he was the first
to sit out in this way. Every time that we walked to or from
the post, we passed him, and unlike the other Milanese and
Ticinese who would turn away from strangers, and avoid
catching an eye, Athos used to smile.

César had some leather boots that he claimed were
irreplaceable. He was so fond of them that he had worn
through the soles and heels. All of our shoes felt the wear and
tear of the uneven cobbles, but César had refused to part with
his even for repairs. One day, he decided to trust Athos, and he
took him his treasured boots. After the repair was done, he
praised it so highly that Athos invited him in for a cigarette.
'In' meant some five feet further towards the back of the shop
and to sit on a stool in the semi-darkness, while Athos leant on
his counter.

By the time I came to meet Athos, he and César were firm
friends. He was about sixty years old, and a veteran from the
war. His wife and daughters had left him when the girls were
still young, and he had never heard from them again. He
talked slowly, weighing his words, and he shared César's
views and opinions on virtually everything. They would sit

together watching the soiled canal seeping between the Po and the Ticino and discuss campaigns and wars, from Hannibal's victory on the Ticino's banks to Rommel and Mussolini. Athos liked drinking wine and he usually had a large bottle of Merlot under the counter of his shop, shared readily, although he never drank with us on these occasions. I think he was so poor that he rationed himself in everything, and when César and I accepted a glass of his wine, it was his day's ration we were drinking.

Behind a curtain at the back of his 'shop' was what looked like the wall, and about two feet of space to spare. He used sacking for blankets, and he had a washbowl, razors, a primus stove and a billycan as his only other furniture. He accepted his poverty with a kind of enthusiasm and claimed that if he hadn't been so poor, he would never have had all the time to think and reflect, and he would never have got so much enjoyment out of life.

As the cystitis grew worse, I had virtually no control over my bladder. One day, while we were visiting Athos, I asked him if I could use his lavatory.

'I don't have one,' he explained.

'What do you do then?' I asked him, unable to swallow my curiosity.

'I have the best lavatory in Milan,' he said, waving his arms in the direction of the canal. 'I have the Naviglio Grande.'

Inside the clutter of his shop, with its tools and its off-cuts of leather, there was one object that stood out against all others. This was a dome-like sculpture about three feet high and two across. We all went in to look at this work of art, and none of us could quite decide what it was. It was very beautiful, and took up about half of the counter, which it towered over like some hybrid between a tree and a mushroom-cloud of nuclear fall-out. Every time I went to see Athos, I touched this thing that seemed neither entirely dead or alive, but more like some dormant fungus of a rare kind.

One morning César returned beside himself.

'It's grown!' he said in astonishment.

'What has?' I asked.

'Athos's mushroom tree has grown.'

Otto tried to reassure him but he wouldn't be reassured. 'Come and see it for yourself,' he insisted.

I didn't want to go, I couldn't bear the thought of the stairs: six flights, two hundred and sixty-four stone treads. I had counted them, wearily, resting halfway around on each flight, dividing each floor into two laps, pausing to stare down at the dark quadrangle below, where only the portinaia lived, and the portinaia was blind. So Otto went to calm César's fears.

He returned in an even worse state. It had definitely grown.

'Shall we ask him what it is?' I suggested.

But César wouldn't hear of it. He said that it was all that Athos had that was his own. 'You don't ask a prisoner why he keeps stale bread under his bunk, and you don't ask him why he turns his back to the wall for two days and then pretends that he has been to the Mediterranean, and you don't ask Athos what his fungus-tree is.'

'It's funny,' Otto mused, 'it doesn't look stolen.'

'It does look alive though,' César said.

It was Elías who finally discovered the nature of Athos's sculpture. It was made entirely of shoe glue which had hardened into the metallic strands and branches that we saw. Every time that Athos mended a shoe, he put another blob on his fungus-tree, sculpting it into shape.

No more money came and our resources dwindled to the strictest rations; there was barely anything left from the $500 boot-money. We decided not to tell Tito since we knew that he would do something to help and he could ill afford it. I was confused; by the heaviness of my body and by the stuffiness of the rooms. The summer progressed, and the heat increased, but our skylight window would only wedge open a few inches. Elías went to Rome 'on business'. Otto, César and I stayed behind. I telephoned, reversed charges, several times to Yale. Each time, the calls were refused. 'Serge isn't available,' I heard a southern voice drawl to the operator. 'The Professor is away.' I wrote letter after letter but no reply came. I used up the money for César's cigarette ration to pay for the stamps and the express seals on my letters, but there was still no reply, and my anger and paranoia grew in the silence. I felt the pain in my side grow with Serge's neglect, and finally, when a letter came, curt and with no money, I sent it back, and never wrote again. Meanwhile, we were managing without money; surprisingly, it was quite easy to do. It was just a matter of adjusting one's thoughts. But I wanted my medical insurance, I wanted to see a doctor. I hadn't told César how ill I was feeling. I felt shy at first, and then it all seemed too far gone.

After Elías left, Otto took over his single mattress, until such time as he should return. By July Otto spent more and more time away from the flat. I think he believed that I was finding lack of privacy a strain. Apart from baths, which I insisted on taking on my own, I didn't really mind the other aspects of our cohabitation. But even before, when we had shared a bed with him, we had a convention of marital privacy. César and I always waited for Otto to fall asleep, debating in whispers whether or not he was. However, I suspected that he only pretended to be asleep, and that his measured breathing and sleepy turning away was sham, and that he listened to us as we made love. At the same time I realised that half of his anger towards me was sexual frustration, and another part of it was the natural irritability of an insomniac. I had given up my struggle to maintain a simulacrum of well-being in June and stayed permanently at home, making one concession to Otto and César by sitting propped up against a wall while they were in and not lying as I did for the rest of the day, staring at the yellowed ceiling from the bed. The walk to the communal lavatory began to seem too far. It was too much of an effort to go through the motions of locking and padlocking our door to keep Tito's apparatus safe, walk down the narrow corridor and then squat precariously over the hole. I had once fainted in that tiny lavatory and come round on the mouldy green floor, and thrown away the skirt I had been wearing.

We had a long, low cupboard and I crawled into it and used a chamber pot. Thanks to this, I was able to observe the blood in my water turn from a mere pink to a thick cloying haemorrhage. Otto went to Paris to raise some money while César and I stayed at home at Porta Ticinese. I draped a cloth over the skylight to keep out the sun, but even so, the room gathered heat and held it, defying me to sweat it out. César began to bring home fruits from the market as they came into season. But I had no appetite and he ate alone. I could feel the flat getting dirtier and dirtier. There was hardly room on the mattress for me to sleep any more, there were so many clothes that needed laundering.

I had been ill before, and even spent years in bed as a child with glandular T.B. The fever and the pain were nothing new, but I had never felt so entirely helpless. I could feel my life draining away, like hot sand through my side. I flexed my muscles to monitor the pain. At the stage where even the movement of my fingers brought on waves of nausea, I stopped caring. César didn't know what to do.

'When you get a bit better,' he said, 'I'll take you to a doctor.'

I didn't care any more, not even about a doctor telling me that it was all right. My mattress was like a sponge, soaking up the blood as it trickled out of me from my kidney. I could hear laughter in the next room, there were always voices talking together. Sometimes I remembered that they came from César's three television sets, and sometimes I forgot that they were films and chat shows, and I imagined that they were crows waiting for me to die, lured by the smell of blood.

'You'll be all right,' César told me, as he made himself snacks to pick at while he watched television. 'Very few people bleed to death.'

The floor grew wet and stained, fresh and stale blood was seeping out of the mattress, and the jugs of tea and water that César made for me I spilt as often as not. There was no air and no escape from the smell. I imagined that I was decomposing and I wondered how much a person had to decompose before she died. I worried about what to tell my mother. I knew that César didn't have enough English to explain that one of my kidneys had just gone off. Sometimes, between sleeping and waking, I could feel the swollen mass on one side of me through the cotton dress I had worn when I last stood up and which I hadn't the energy to change. I could escape from any thoughts and any discomfort by touching this swollen side at a certain point and losing consciousness.

I hadn't done any of the things I wanted to do with my life. I hadn't even washed César's shirts, with their mother-of-pearl buttons and their long tails. I wondered what he would regret most, my loss or the dirtiness of his shirts. His face was turning to stone. He showed no emotion but I knew that apart from anything else he must hate the chaos and the stench. He was pretending that it wasn't happening, ignoring it all like a bad dream, turning up the volume of his three sets, watching right through to the late film, sleeping on the single mattress dragged into the other room. I wondered if one day he would throw out my mattress and me as I had thrown out my skirt when I fell on to the filthy lavatory floor. Whether later he came and sat by me I don't know. I never asked him.

When I came round though, I was struck by the tidiness of the room; there were even some flowers and little things like a shrine by my head. I was on the single mattress and the other one had gone. I was wearing different clothes and my hair was brushed and arranged over the clean white sheet that covered me. César smiled at me and made some tea. I asked him what day it was.

'You've been out for five days,' he said.

Another week passed before I left the flat, and then we had to sit down on the stairs halfway to the ground floor and César brought me a bar of chocolate, and we went back again. None of my clothes fitted me and none of my rings.

'We'll go, as soon as you can,' César told me.

I asked him how much money we had left and he told me.

'None.'

'But how do you buy all this food?'

'Tito brings it,' he said.

'But how can he afford it?' I asked.

'He doesn't pay for it,' he said simply. 'He can get anything you want, except for a toothbrush.'

I thought about this for some time and then I asked him: 'Why can't he get a toothbrush?' I wondered if he had some special scruple.

'They're always kept behind the counter,' he said, 'under glass.'

Tito came, bringing with him a chocolate cake for a treat and some cigarettes for César. It seemed that these were two other things that could not be shoplifted; the cigarettes not at all, and the cake only by the most expert hands, so he bought them. He was worried because he hadn't brought any more food. He said that there was a lot of vigilance in the supermarkets nowadays. Tito was hurt that we hadn't told him about my illness. He promised to find us somewhere else to live. He stayed with us for a few hours and when César left the room he said: 'Why didn't you let me know? You could have died.'

'It was all right,' I said stoically.

'No it wasn't,' he said. 'We don't want any heroes. If you had died in this flat we would have been charged with terrorism and if we had tried to get you out we could have risked a murder rap.'

I knew that he was absolutely right.

'Don't worry,' he said, 'I know you're very thoughtful, but you just don't think.'

Chapter XI

During the early summer Tito kept us well supplied with return tickets to Paris, and we travelled along the slow route across the Alps, week after week, stopping for two or three days at either end before turning round again. It wasn't until July that we finally made our way to the Porta Ticinese, back to our picturesque slum. Sometimes, in Paris, we had rejoined Otto and Elías, and sometimes they travelled with us for a few days, but on the whole we travelled alone – if it were possible to be alone in the increasing swell of holiday-makers. For that last journey, before the summer took its final grip, Otto had insisted on staying in Paris, so it was only César and myself who took the rumbling tram from the Stazione Centrale to the Naviglio Grande. Back on the top floor of our tenement, nothing seemed to have changed.

César emptied out our Gladstone bag on the bed; he always carried our passports, rings, his penknives and razors, my papers, our toothbrushes, Rusé's *Life of Napoleon*, and some spare pants and socks as well as a change of clothes each. But this time the latter seemed to be missing.

'What about our clothes?' I asked.

He didn't answer, and I could see that he thought it disloyal of me even to ask about such trifles. He had guided me through cattle wagons of tourists, and brought me back safely to the southernmost exit of the city to this squalid haven that was like our home, what more could I want? By evening we discovered that not only had he left our clothes, but our money, a parting gift from Otto, as well.

We walked through the hot stagnant evening. I would have liked to have walked arm in arm, but César despised public shows of affection. We went into a restaurant near the Duomo on the opposite corner from where the gangsters meet. We had no money in our pockets but we were very hungry. A waiter came, and I spoke to César in English. We studied the menu and chose the duck with orange, minimum wait forty minutes. He told me to be ready to leave. I asked him why we couldn't eat half the duck and then find fault and leave. But César claimed that this didn't work, and that waiters invariably called the police if you did that. We had a bowl of fresh, closely grained bread on the table, and olive oil, salt and vinegar. We sat looking out at the monument of Victor Emmanuel II and ate our way through most of the bread and César cursed the restaurant for not bringing butter before the meal. We had staunchly refused the antipasta and the pasta, and pretended to hold out for the duck with orange, minimum wait forty minutes. After about ten minutes we stood up, César claimed that the atmosphere in the restaurant was insufferable, and we left, complaining vociferously. César made a note of the name and address. We had a long list of all the restaurants and cafés where we couldn't go again. There were hardly any left where we could go.

Otto and Elías joined us from Paris, and the day after they arrived, we telephoned Tito. He said that his line was now tapped, and arranged to meet us by the Teatro alla Scala. We had only wanted to ask him where to pawn our rings and watches, and we were embarrassed to have called him out for so little. Tito was very busy all summer planning what he called 'un golpe'. He told us to go to Piemonte, and invited us to dinner for the following night. He reminded us to avoid the portinaia, who actually took your passport number if she got half a chance and reported you to the local inspectorate.

'What happens then?' I asked.

'Nothing,' Tito said, 'they just watch and watch you, and then one day you might all link up. They watch everyone. It's like buying cheap paintings in the hopes that they will become valuable with time. There's so much chaos here, nobody knows what to do, but their surveillance is an investment.'

César said that he didn't like dinner parties and he refused to go, so Otto, Elías and I went on our own.

We slipped past the portinaia and up the galleried staircase to Tito's flat. I liked this flat, with its wide hallway and arched doors. There was virtually no furniture, but what there was fitted so well into the room that it made up for the absence of more. Best of all were the dark floorboards, over a foot wide and of beautifully knotted wood.

Tito knew that we were short of baths and he invited me to have one as soon as he opened the door. I thanked him, and was in the water before I realised that there wasn't a towel. There wasn't even a bath mat, and my own dress was silk and couldn't have dried me even if I had wanted to use it.

I finally crawled out of the tepid water and looked for a towel in the row of cupboards set into the wall behind the tub. The first two were empty but the third spilled over me when I pulled at its door.

It contained a mass of huge coiled cables that sprang out when I opened it; they were wound around pieces of equipment similar to ones behind the cage at Porta Ticinese. They hit me as they came, and I started back in a panic. I was always frightened of cupboards, ever since the day in Cornwall at Granny Mabel's when a leg sprang out and hit me, and it was her leg, with her thick stocking and built-up shoe, and I screamed and dropped it, and Granny Mabel laughed. I had been seven at the time, and I had never realised that Granny Mabel had only one leg. Mabel Lethbridge O.B.E., who didn't like you to miss out the letters after her name, and who had worked in a munitions factory during the First World War when she was sixteen. The factory had been bombed, and a whole wing of the nearest hospital had been cleared for survivors, but Mabel alone had survived with one leg blown away, and the other ruined. She had received her O.B.E. in hospital from the King. Granny Mabel, who had been everywhere, and married a millionaire and who could swear more than any sailor on the quay at St Ives. I had no idea about her stump and somehow finding her leg in the cupboard had seemed like my fault. Granny Mabel was lying in bed and I had thought, 'What will she say if she sees that her leg has dropped off?' I couldn't bear it, and I screamed, and she had laughed.

But then, in Milan, in Tito's bathroom, what looked like very unusual equipment had snaked its way on to my chest. I pushed it off me, and it crashed to the floor.

'Va bene?' Tito's voice queried from the far side of the door.

'Si, va bene,' I lied, struggling with the sheer weight of the coil. When eventually I got it back, I couldn't shut the door unless I stood it up. I hoped that Tito wouldn't notice the difference. I was beset by a strange paranoia, I feared that Tito or one of his friends would accuse me of snooping, mistrust my motives, find me ungrateful and I knew not what else. By the time I had finished with the coil, I was dry anyway, so I dressed and went out and sat on a Persian rug on the floor and listened to Dietrich's 'Drummer Boy' over and over again. Otto and Tito had gone out, and as the hours slipped by, no dinner came, nor did they reappear. Elías made some coffee and we found the remains of a loaf of bread and a tin of fig jam. Later, Elías dropped me at the door of Porta Ticinese and I made my way up the long quadrangles in the dark. I was saved from having to explain Otto's absence though, because César was asleep.

We woke up so hungry the next morning that we resigned ourselves to finally pawning our rings. We took a tramcar to Piemonte and then went reluctantly into the building itself. It was a massive hall with a domed ceiling and panelled walls. César was to part with his Longines and his signet ring, and I was to part with my five rings but not my icon. The hall was a strange place, surrounded by guards. Around two curving sides of it there were barred windows with grids, through which packages could be pushed and evaluated. Between parting with their belongings and receiving the money they had bartered for, the supplicants were sent from one desk to another, in a series of slow queues, to the cashier. And then the money came like an unreal handout in return for numbered slips of paper, and not for the amber and cameo, moonstone, garnets and jade. I willed myself not to think about the antique settings of my rings, not even the filigree Florentine one that Andrew, my stepfather, had brought back from Venice after the war. People were herded from one queue to the next, like refugees.

One woman was weeping by the steps, trying to haul an old mattress through the doorway, past a guard who was barring her way. She was shouting, 'Everything is worth something.' They wouldn't let her through. She began to appeal to all the rows of serious faces that lined the hard benches in the middle of the hall.

'Aiuto!' she called, but no one would help her, they were all absorbed by what they were doing. Most people were pawning their wedding rings and their crucifixes, handing over all they had for a few paltry lire. César went up to the grids alone, and returned with a fraction of the value of our things, but still enough money to buy two tickets to Bologna, and to tide us over for at least two weeks. It took us the best part of a morning to complete our transactions in Piemonte. We left that strange vaulted pawnbroker's palace with its menace of dungeons at each clink of the small grids. The woman with the mattress was sitting on the steps outside. César was very subdued, he asked me if it felt wrong to have pawned our rings. I said that it was all right, so long as we tried to redeem them.

'I hope I don't find my watchstrap now,' he said, 'not yet anyway.'

We went to a proper trattoria for lunch and ate our way through more than half of my amber ring. César told me that Tito had offered to include him in a robbery but that he had declined. 'I've never done one for myself,' he said. 'It wouldn't feel right.' We drank our caffè corretto out of a sense of formality, since neither of us really liked the bitter taste of grappa in it.

We had arranged to meet Elías at the public baths. I went in through the women's side and left César to go into the men's. We arranged to meet outside twenty minutes later. The public baths were very nice so long as you didn't even think about who had been in the bathtub before you or what they had done. I always took a whole box of bath cubes with me which Elías replenished as I ran low and the combined smells of freesia, honeysuckle and gardenia helped to disguise the carbolic and the creosote of the cubicles.

It was a big day, we were going to meet Elías's doctor. I was intrigued to meet this person who held such power over him, who could soften his speech and his hardest looks and who could cause him to stare lovelorn into the filthy canal for days on end. We travelled into the most fashionable part of Milan, pausing for Elías to buy a bunch of mimosa and a box of chocolate truffles. We stopped outside a tall grey building and Elías pressed the brass intercom.

'It's me,' he said in German, 'with César and Lisaveta.'

He was answered by a woman's voice, also in German. We went through the hall with its black and white zig-zags of marble and into the lift.

'You'll see,' Elías said to me, 'that you are just like her.'

We were shown into an ultra-modern flat sparsely furnished with grey glass, zebra skins and abstract paintings framed by fish nets draped around them. The door was open and a tall woman was sitting on a zebra chair. Elías whispered to me that this was his one-time wife. 'She doesn't really talk to me any more,' he added.

'Chuss,' she said, 'she is waiting.' I looked around me but she seemed to be alone. She called out something that I didn't catch, and an inner door opened as though from the bottom. A very small child with olive skin and fair hair walked into the room.

'This is my doctor,' Elías said shyly, 'La Margherita.' I stared at the child, half-Mayan Indian and half-German and realised that this doctor or Tochter *was* like me, with my own mixture of South American and Jersey, the darker skin and the fair hair. La Margherita, as she was called, spoke only German, which silenced me and limited César to asking her if she wanted a glass of mineral water. The idea of Elías as a family man was hard to grasp, but then I supposed that this child, La Margherita, would find it hard to grasp the idea of Elías, the monster of crime. We went back to Ticinese, sobered by these thoughts. That afternoon Elías asked me,

'What did you think of my doctor?' He pronounced the word in a middle language somewhere between English and German, and it sounded strange in the context of the Spanish that surrounded it.

'She's very sweet,' I said.

'I don't want her to be very sweet,' Elías told me, 'sweetness is a dangerous way to be. Look at you, you're sweet, and if you're not careful you'll get sucked away like a piece of barley sugar.'

'What do you want then?' I asked.

'Reinforcement,' he said.

'Reinforced barley sugar?' I said.

'Well, even an aniseed ball has an aniseed inside it. What have you got, Lisaveta, when the sugar has all melted away, one day it'll be down to that. I'd like to feel that there was something there; and I want to with La Margherita.'

'Well, genetically speaking she's got a good chance of having something there,' I laughed.

'On both sides,' Elías said bitterly; and then added, 'anyway, my mother says I was a nice child.'

'I didn't know you had a mother,' I said.

'No, most people don't, they think I'm some kind of cell mutation.'

Chapter XII

We bought our tickets to Bologna, second-class; they cost as much as my cameo, and César's signet ring. César's Italian visa had expired but we decided to wait until we had contacted Otto in Bologna before we did anything about it. César disliked first days, and last days, and birthdays, he claimed that days just happened, and presents were just given, and he wouldn't be tied to the more conventional ideas of special occasions. However, it happened that our last day in Milan coincided with a visit to the Certosa di Pavia.

I didn't know where Elías was staying, but he still had the keys to Ticinese and he turned up there at eight in the morning and flicked cold water over us until we got out of bed. I had never managed to explain to him that I loathed waking up like that. My sense of humour abandoned me the moment anyone tried to pull off my blankets or wet my face. Once, in Oxford, I had pushed Elías into the water at St John's College while punting after a game of croquet, with all his clothes on and a mass of money and documents in his wallet. We were alone on the punt, and he had been telling me how pretty I looked against the willow leaves in the sun, and I had just pushed him, suddenly determined to get my own back for all the early mornings that he had inflicted on me in his manic enthusiasm. He had emerged like a sea monster, with his eyes flashing, and shunned our punt, preferring to struggle through the weeds to the edge. Otto had run down the steps to the water and helped him out.

'You shouldn't have done that,' he said to me. I knew I shouldn't have, but I didn't care.

'I think Elías really likes you,' Otto had said, 'or he wouldn't have swum away.' I thought about that incident from time to time, and I realised Otto was right.

So when Elías flicked water on us, I didn't swear at him or pull his hair as I would have liked to have done, but just remembered the man with the three chances, and that I had had one.

'I've got a new macchina,' he announced.

He didn't really want us to say anything, he wanted us to go and see it, so we dressed and washed and cleaned our teeth over our pink plastic bowl and followed him down two hundred and sixty-four treads, around the edge of the dank air that seemed to hang over the inner quadrangle like mildewed sheets, to the street. We had three cappuccini in the café halfway along the street, and said a quick buongiorno to Athos who seemed to get smaller as his glue statue grew, then we walked along the edge of the Naviglio Grande to the main road, where, illegally parked, was a beautiful new Mercedes. No wonder Elías was pleased. It was wonderful.

We climbed in and he joked, 'Will passengers please fasten their belts, this is your captain, Elías, hoping you enjoy your flight.' And then we were gone, clattering over the discarded crates of the fruit market, and bouncing on the cobbles of the one-way lanes. The guardia were mostly too surprised to blow their whistles and when they did we were out of earshot before they could do any more.

Elías made up for all his days of walking, making a point of climbing verges with the car, and passing between lorries. It wasn't just the speed, it was the acrobatics of it that he liked. We stopped en route for some 'black wine' at a café in a village off the road, and I noticed all the scratches and dents that the car had acquired in the last hour. Elías didn't seem to care.

'I'm breaking it in,' he said, 'you can't be a good driver and worry about your paintwork. It's one or the other.'

We went into Pavia and then out again to visit the Certosa; Elías stopped the car on a field far away from the buildings and suggested that we walk the last bit. I assumed, wrongly, that he didn't want to be seen with the car. But, in fact, it was so as to admire the view of the old Carthusian monastery from its best point.

Despite it being late July, there was a slight chill in the air, and there had been rain in the night. The monastery was surrounded by open fields dotted with ancient poplars. We had come along the course of the River Ticino and crossed by its stone bridge. Otto used to claim that we were in love with this river, since we could never drag ourselves far away from it. 'Lombardy Lombardy Lombardy,' he had written in his last letter, 'why can't you leave it alone? We belong to Emilia, in Bologna, or on the train. Milan isn't a place, it's a station. You're not meant to live there if you can get away.' Our pilgrimage to Pavia was the last of our love affair with Milan. In future, we too would just pass through on our way to less gloomy towns.

The Certosa had a strange effect on all three of us. It made me feel unusually sad. While César walked around the courtyard staring at the amazing Renaissance façade, and out into the monks' cells, he uttered one solitary 'Qué vaina!' and sat down in one of these low stone rooms that had no space for more than a slab for a bed, and a slot in the wall for food to be passed through, and a door with a grid on to a grassed-over field surrounded on four distant sides by these same low lines of solitary cells. César sat on the cold bunk and stared around at the thick grey stone. The longer he sat there, with the door like a stable door almost closed on him, the more stone-like he himself became.

I spoke to him, but I knew that he couldn't hear me; there was a sort of transparency around his face like that of a newly opened lily or the skin of a dying man.

Elías pulled at me to leave César alone. I went, I had nothing to do with him and the cell, nothing to do with the merging of stone; for the first time, I was the stranger. On the other hand, Elías needed me. He needed me to admire the detail of the ceilings in the main part of the monastery, he needed me to see the vaults and tombs, he needed me to stand by him as the architecture overcame him.

Elías had brought his camera with him and a leather bag with spare rolls of film. He took reel after reel of the roofs and ceilings. There was a kind of religious zeal in his work. I left him now and then, and walked around the rambling outbuildings to the cells. César had not moved from one time to the next. I was frightened by his intensity. The way he had been at Pope Alexander's tomb was nothing to the way he was now. It was as though the feel of the stone in that tiny room – a mere six feet by four – had brought home to him all that mattered in his life, that he had somehow managed to bury or forget until that moment.

Elías didn't want me to be preoccupied, he wanted me to feel as exhilarated as he did. 'Don't worry about César,' he said. 'He's just struck by this place because it's like the castle.'

We were photographing the tomb of Lodovico Moro with its splendid sculpture and I wondered which aspect of the Certosa was like the castle, the profusely decorated church, or the plain stone cells.

'Why did César go to the castle?' I asked Elías. I didn't know if he would know, but he felt like the best person to ask, and I couldn't understand the mystic side of César. I didn't know for sure why he had gone to the weird Kafkan castle, or why he had left.

'What do you mean?' Elías asked me.

'Well, where was it?' I said.

'It was in Trujillo.'

'Have you been there?'

'Not likely,' he said, and then, 'I thought you knew that.'

'I don't know what I know,' I told him.

'Do you know what the castle is?' he asked me, with some concern.

'Not really,' I admitted. I had looked for the meaning of this Spanish word in my dictionaries, but I could never find it.

'You sound as though you wanted to go there yourself,' he said accusing me.

I did. I wanted to desperately, but I didn't want to tell him, so I shrugged and shook my head.

I waited, and I felt that this was going to be another one of Elías's doctors, but he was quickly bored with talking, and turned back to his photographs while the light was still good. I went behind a stone pillar in the hall; Elías came up to me after a while and pulled my ear-lobe affectionately. 'The castle is the prison,' he told me. I went away on my own and stood by a Borgognone painting. I didn't even want to think. When I went back to César he had closed the door, against all his principles, and fallen asleep on the stone bed. We left him there for over an hour, while Elías took his photographs and I explored all the flagged paths and the carvings, and spoke to a monk in a brown cassock who seemed eager to tell me about his bees. Then Elías woke César. 'Come on, viejo,' he called from the door. César turned and smiled rather shyly.

'It was too much of a home from home,' he said, 'I couldn't resist it.'

I was glad that he chose to joke away his depression, I was in no state to cope with it then. One of my aims in life had been shattered. I had nowhere to go now, nothing to strive for. I had hoped that one day I would get to the castle, and now there was nothing left but their company and the reassurance of the train.

Under the arcade, by the main entrance to the Certosa, there was a stand with gradated postcards of the monastery in all its glory, and of the outlying fields, and the barns, and the details on its walls and ceilings, its friezes, and even its beehives.

Elías instructed César and me to talk to the monk who was selling all these wares, while he pocketed as many cards as he could carry.

'What shall I say?' I pleaded, as I always pleaded.

Elías answered as he always answered: 'Nobody is asking you to be one of the great train robbers, just go and talk to the man behind the counter.'

To me this 'just talking' was as much a part of the theft as all the rest of it. It produced a sort of panic in me. My mind would go blank, my mouth dry, and I would blush so much that my blushing would usually become the topic of conversation with whomever I was meant to decoy.

At first, I had believed that it was the voice of my puritanical family coming through, but later I realised that it was as much a question of pride. All my family were proud, and I had been brought up to be so, and you couldn't be proud and caught for shoplifting. It had to be one thing or the other. I had tried to explain this to César but he had said, 'You're not as proud as I am', and I knew that I wasn't.

But César was proud and confident, while I was still proud and shy. César didn't care who saw him or what he did. He lived entirely by his own rules, his own code of honour. He had a second skin that protected him, a second eyelid like a bird's that he could draw across and ignore all the little things that made me blush so much. I was terrified of getting caught. I imagined being humiliated, imprisoned, things that for other causes seemed like a worthy martyrdom, but for shoplifting, seemed unbearable. I couldn't bear the shame of being caught for anything so trivial. If I was to live on the far side of the law, it had to be for some major crime, not a petty theft. César himself despised common criminals. He called them 'chusma' and dismissed the whole lot from his mind. I couldn't understand why he stooped so on all the little things. I couldn't understand why they bothered to steal these postcards.

I had asked Elías in private why they did it, and he had bunched up his shoulders and said, 'When you get bronchitis you cough, and when you're exiled you shoplift.'

'But why?'

'You just do,' he said.

'But don't you do it in Venezuela?' I asked.

'Of course not,' he said, 'we have better things to do.'

'Then it's a waste of time to do it here.'

'But this *is* a waste of time,' he had said.

The old monk told us of Giovanni Galeazzo Visconti, Duke of Milan and founder of the Certosa. He told us how it was a National Monument, and how the bees had had a hard winter, and how if it rained now it would make them ill. The sun was beginning to climb over the roofs of the Certosa. The day had remained a little cold, despite its being late July. We walked back along the grass verge by the poplars to the car. Elías had a prodigious quantity of postcards on his person. He wore a Harpo Marx jacket with pockets that went right round the inside of the lining, and he could, if he wanted to, carry a whole week's shopping in this way. We went for a long drive and for lunch. Elías told us that we were driving around in circles to say goodbye to Lombardy. It dawned on me that we had been cooped up in the staleness of the city for months, and the best months of the summer had passed in a coming of flies and dust, when they might have been spent in the fresh air, with the gorse and the rosemary, and the river as a real river as we saw it that day, and not just a train of tangled rubbish edging its way down the city's canals. I asked Elías what he liked best, the plains or the mountains. He said that he liked the mountains, but that he liked them best when they were craggy and wild; 'I like the high Alps,' he said, 'and the high Andes.' I asked him whether he had lived in the Andes like César and Otto but he said no, he came from the savannas, the llanos of the Orinoco, where there was drought initialled into the bark of every tree, and the grass was so coarse that the cattle spurned it, and they died of thirst and the flies settled like black rain on their backs. They were a mixture of Ceibu and Holstein, which was the only kind with a chance to survive. He told me that his family held lands there, and that he had grown up surrounded by the apathy of the people who were too tired even to turn away from the sun, and who sat and rotted on the parched land where the amoeba was king.

'When I was fourteen,' he said, 'I ran away to the guerrilla, rather than be swallowed up by the lethargy of it all. I want to do something,' he said, 'I don't want to wait for the buzzards to decide when I'm dead.'

'But where did you get all the ideas from?'

'The ideas came later,' he said, 'I just wanted the action.'

Later that same afternoon, we went back to the Certosa and just stood under its great roof for a while. Nobody talked, it seemed enough just to stand with our backs against the wall under one of the richest examples of Renaissance work in Italy, watching the sky reddening around us. We stayed for a long time under that arcade, and then Elías moved towards the gatehouse. He had a way of walking rather jerkily, despite the fact that he made no noise when he moved. We caught up with him and he said, 'I'd rather die in a place like this than on a dung heap.'

This time we walked through the hall of the gatehouse. There were three monks standing behind a high table. They greeted us and invited us to join them in a glass of Chartreuse.

'We make it on the premises,' they explained, 'we like visitors to try our skill.'

We tasted a small glass each of the yellow liqueur offered to us, although none of the monks drank much. When we had finished, the second of the monks asked us to try his green Chartreuse. We were very willing but not ready for his quick, 'Which did you like best?' We tried to hedge our way around a direct answer by saying we didn't know.

'Try mine then,' the third monk suggested. We did, and then we spent the next hour sampling all three in turn, the yellow, the green and the red, rotating the glasses and getting totally drunk. The three monks were very pleasant to talk to; unlike so many priests, they were not the least bit interested in our respective faiths or lack of them. They didn't even ask us if we were Catholics, they seemed to assume that we were Carthusians like themselves.

When we finally left, Elías was bright-eyed and César was virtually unconscious, and I was overcome with laughter.

The Carthusians invited us to come again and we promised we would, knowing that we wouldn't, but not wanting to disappoint them after all their hospitality. We had drained a whole bottle of each of the liqueurs, and really become incapable of deciding which was the best of the three.

That night, we drove around until well after midnight, stopping to drink at bars, and once to eat, and then we all slept in the car, and woke up feeling cold and cramped and irritable. Elías dropped César and me at the end of the Naviglio Grande at about five-thirty in the morning. César leant against the stanchion of the bridge and refused to move. I went back on my own and brought down our luggage. We seemed to have fewer and fewer clothes and more and more books. We took a taxi to the station where we took a train to Bologna. César wanted to get out at Reggio Emilia and sleep on the platform, but I managed to keep him propped up on the train, as far as

Modena, at which point he passed out. At Bologna itself, I pushed him out of our carriage with the help of two square matrons. I had told them that he had a kidney disease, which, in a way, was true, since his kidneys refused to eliminate the alcohol from his body, and kept it in him for days and days. Even with César inert and useless, Bologna looked splendid in its glow of orange sun.

Chapter XIII

Bologna, the basin of flames, secret and proud and neglected. Bologna, the hottest place in northern Europe, where the air blows up from the deserts of Africa and collects in the city. Bologna, smothered by the Apennines, and nowhere, not even along the Orinoco, are there more mosquitoes. Bologna, the only Communist town in Italy, and where the gypsies are not allowed into the city precincts. If the chaos of Milan was for passing through, Bologna was a place to stay.

César arrived like a dying fish in a restaurant tank. He barely moved, he just wanted to be left alone. We sat in the station waiting-room until we were moved on, and then we sat propped against the walls outside.

I watched the sun rise higher and higher over the burnt reds of the city. The roofs and the walls, the bricks and the tiles, were all varying shades of red and orange, and the sun caught up the colours and made a haze of flames on the skyline.

I could see no movement in the town and no noise. I was struck most of all by the silence; after the shrieks and screams of Milan, the screeching of the tramcars and the bickering in the streets, the absence of any noise made me dizzy. A few trains came and went inside the station, mostly goods trains pausing on their way to other parts of Emilia. After a while, there was a lull on top of the silence, a whispering in the air; dozens of mosquitoes were gathering around us.

There were shops with blinds and grids drawn over them, and the broad street was completely deserted. I thought that we must have come on a public holiday or a day of mourning.

We eventually left the station and hailed a taxi.

'Take me to the Via San Salvatore,' César told the driver and he took us to a street of dry, timbered buildings.

'Who lives here?' I asked César.

'We do,' he said, and he produced a large iron key from one of his pockets and opened one side of a double Gothic door. Inside, everything had an air of great age: the warped bannisters and the peeling walls, the sagging flagstones and the dipped treads of the stairs. And at each turn of the stair, worn shrivelled faces peered out at us through the open slits of doors. We went right up to the top-floor landing where it was so low that we had to stoop. There were two flats.

'That one is ours,' César said. I fell in love with it on that very first day.

'How did you get it?' I asked him.

'Well, Otto did, really,' he said.

There wasn't one wall that was true or one ceiling that didn't slope, but it was so pretty that all its defects seemed to add to its charm. The walls were of buckled timbers and plaster and the floors were of great slabs of stone. One room and the kitchen had a fireplace while the other two rooms had none. The kitchen was enormous and lined with fitted dressers; bunches of herbs and onions hung from the beams. Then there were two other rooms, a bathroom, but no bath.

The whole flat was furnished and lavishly carpeted with Persian rugs, the windows had green wooden shutters and there was a single table lamp lighting the sitting-room. A cup of tea was still steaming on one side of the room and one of the Brandenburg Concertos was turning on the gramophone. Everything, in fact, to imply that there was someone in, except the presence of that someone in person.

César took me over the other rooms, each with its ghostly emptiness signalling to me not to say a word.

César pointed to a low room under the eaves which had a jumble of large pieces of furniture stored in it. He moved his hand to intimate that Otto was hiding there, then he banged the small boarded door of it and said in Italian, 'All right, Marie Celeste, you can come out now.' After a long silence, we heard Otto laugh and he emerged on all fours.

'Idiots,' he said, but I could see he wasn't really cross, he so much enjoyed a practical joke that he even liked them when they were played on him. He put all his papers away in an empty drawer, and brought out a bottle of aquavit and told me not to say a word so as not to spoil the evening. César absolutely refused to touch the aquavit, and when Otto insisted he tipped his glass out on the floor and claimed it was poison. Otto then relented towards me, escorted César to bed and we spent the early part of the evening drinking and talking. I asked him why he had the light on by day and he said, 'It's so hot, if I open the windows it's like a fan heater. You're so idle, though, you'll manage in the dark.' I thanked him and we drank some more. I was growing very fond of Otto, his presence did more for me than merely stave off boredom. He asked me about Elías and I told him about the daughter. Otto knew all about this child, but it seemed that he was worried that Elías's feelings for her would one day mar his judgment.

'You know what Elías is like,' he said, 'now you see him, now you don't. It's not like him to keep returning.'

The oppressiveness seemed to be easing and I suggested that we open the windows.

'Not yet,' Otto said, 'wait until after seven.'

'What's so special about seven?'

'It feels human again then. Everyone comes out into the streets and they sidle along the arcades to the steps of the Cathedral in Neptune Square.'

We drank some more aquavit and then he suggested that I change into 'something more sensible' to go and see. I changed, but into an equally draping cotton dress. My clothes always made Otto cross. In winter, he accused me of wanting to be a nun. 'Nobody could ever rape you', he used to say, 'because they could never find a way in through all your layers of cloth and petticoats.' And in summer he said, 'You don't know if you're standing on your arse or your elbow, this is 1970, get out of that Edwardian fancy dress.'

But I liked the silks and the voiles and the mother-of-pearl buttons, and the button hooks for the sleeves, and the lace and the hand-sewn embroidery; I liked the tucks and the chokers and I wasn't going to change. I was unsure about everything in my life, unsure what I was going to do, unsure about my relationship to Otto and Elías, unsure why I had shackled myself to César, whom I still hardly knew, and about whom I felt equivocal. There were only two certainties in my life, two loves, and they were: wearing long dresses and moving on. The extravagance of the clothes and the comfort of the travel.

I went out with Otto, walking under the terracotta arcades to the Cathedral of St Peter with its long stone steps that were cool to sit on, and that filled up like an auditorium as the evening advanced. Alone, and in twos and threes, the people of Bologna came to the square and the steps. They came in their hundreds, wilted and silent, and then gradually they began to pick up the spontaneous mood of the crowd. Everyone came to life as the sun went down. Even the most apathetic were roused from their stupor, and joined in the discussions. They were kind of social mass-meetings at which life in general was discussed, and specific points were debated by total strangers. Should someone's son-in-law contribute so little to the family wealth? Should someone else's second son stay on and take his baccalaureate? Did anyone know why the starlings preferred the Torre Garisenda to nest in?

César and I picked up the habit of going to the Cathedral steps from Otto, and when Otto wasn't there, we still went. César always used to sleep with his head resting on the ridge of the Cathedral wall. I had offered him my lap or shoulder but he preferred hard stone to touching in public. In Milan we had been preoccupied with money, in Bologna we were preoccupied with how to spend our time. The days seemed longer in the heat. César found that he was not rested by sleeping. He slept more and more in obscure places to improve the quality of it. We moved from one room to another in the flat at San Salvatore, and from one bed to another within the room. He slept with his head hanging out of the window over the courtyard until his neck was raw with sunburn and his hair quite bleached from the sun.

'It's no good,' he told me, 'I can't sleep any more, I'm going to have to *do* something.' 'Doing' was always a last resort. The whole concept of doing was anathema to César. Things happened around him. He had mastered the way to alter their course with a minimum of effort. And then, suddenly, in Bologna, César got insomnia. He wandered around like a bear with a sore head. He grew even thinner than he had been when I met him. For a week he did nothing but crack his knuckles and read and reread his *Lives of Napoleon*. Fournier's , Rusé's, Sloane's, Seeley's, all the lives of Napoleon that he had or could lay his hands on.

Elías came to visit us. He brought some of his belongings with him, and arranged to move in with us as soon as he had finished some 'business'. He took César back to Milan with him to reclaim our rings before we forgot. He also brought with him three tickets to Grenoble.

'Why Grenoble?' I asked him.

'I don't really know,' he said, 'I asked for Paris but since I wasn't paying, I thought it would be a bit much to complain.'

We agreed, and made ready to use the tickets. Otto had been given the use of the flat at San Salvatore for as long as he wanted it, and we decided to keep it as our base. It was a kind of Adriatic Oxford, more suited to our group than London or Milan. César returned cured of his sleeplessness. When we asked him how he had done it, he said, 'I've discovered the cinema.'

I was delighted. I had always liked the cinema but for some reason I had stopped going almost entirely since I met César. With Serge, in Paris, I had gone to a matinee every afternoon, and sometimes two. I didn't even mind if it was a bad film. I just liked sitting in the dark halls wedged between two seats, eating chocolates and watching the movements on the screen, however mindless they might be. Otto, on the other hand, insisted on a high standard of everything, acting, directing, script, the lot. But César's criterion became, in Bologna, films that would lull him to sleep.

Elías provided a sum of money every week for household essentials. He was the only one of us who still had a regular income, and it was this that subsidised Otto's sporadic extravagances of imported teas and eels' livers and the like and César's and my daily visits to the cinema. We couldn't afford the plush, air-conditioned ones, but we became connoisseurs of the flea-pits: the cinemas where the soldiers sat and threw gum at the screen, and where it never paid to look at what was going on in the back row, and where every time there was a kiss on the screen, the entire cinema would shout and whistle. The seedier the cinema, the more often it changed its films. We discovered two that altered their programmes every day, and we set aside our 150 lire each no matter how little was left with which to buy food. Most of the films were foreign and dubbed, so that well-known actors with deep masculine voices would twitter and prattle. Our two regular cinemas had 'seasons' of films. A 'season' usually lasted for a week, and consisted of seven different films on one theme, or starring one actor. Thus the Dracula season included Polanski, Laurie, Vincent Price and a medley of lesser-known Italian actors, while the Sordi season consisted exclusively of films by Alberto Sordi. Sometimes, the two cinemas would just swap their programmes, and then we would watch the Burton season and the 'Spaghetti Western' season twice. And on one deadly occasion, the two cinemas synchronised on Gina Lollobrigida, and we saw fourteen of her films in one week.

It didn't matter how small a part the star in question played in these films – he or she might have a role of a mere two minutes, or appear as a waiter in the first scene and then not come on again – if the actor appeared at all, the film qualified for a season. It was often more amusing to look out for these fleeting appearances than to pay attention to the plot. César slept religiously through most of the films excepting the war ones. He took these war films very much to heart, clenching his fists and muttering under his breath if a general took too long in deciding his course of action, and he would remonstrate with the characters when they made any false moves. He particularly hated any love scenes.

'Get on with it man,' he would shout out every time there was a last-minute kiss.

There was no air-conditioning in these cinemas, in fact there wasn't usually any air. But a very small war veteran in a stained uniform opened out a great shuttered vent in one wall which let in the hot sleepy air from the street, and also provided a free way into the cinema for anyone agile enough to climb over it. As a result of this, the veteran, who issued and collected the tickets, and opened and closed the grids outside the hall, and turned out the lights, and did everything except show the film, shuffled around from one row to the next shining a torch on to people's faces to see if they had paid. When we went to Grenoble even César hoped that we would be back before the Friday, when there would be a James Cagney double bill.

Otto accused us of growing old, he claimed that we had been postponing our trip to Grenoble like a couple of old maids with a Bible class. Elías had come to Bologna, stayed for a week and then gone on to Rome. Our rail tickets were now only valid for the day they were stamped, 6th September, and we set off on that day. We took with us one small leather bag between the three of us, and a crate of books that Otto insisted on dragging along. He was writing a study of Sartre, and he insisted that he needed them all for his research. Otto was in one of his manic moods from the moment we set off.

Chapter XIV

César was a great believer in destiny. If I were to believe in it too, I would say that our trip to Grenoble was doomed. We had six litres of wine and no food, and drank steadily from Milan to Vercelli. Once the train started moving out of Vercelli and on to Turin, César and Otto began to get maudlin. Torino they said, where Cesare Pavese committed suicide, Torino, the one-time capital of Italy. Otto brought down another bottle of wine. For some reason, we were drinking Tokay. I suppose there hadn't been any French wine in the shop where they bought it. Otto was a wine snob, or perhaps just an instinctive connoisseur. He used to claim that he could tell a bad bottle by the outside of a shop. We were often reduced to drinking very cheap wines, but even among these he would pick and choose and send a glass back if he didn't like it for what it was supposed to be. Once he was drunk, I think he would have happily downed eau-de-Cologne or meths, but reasonably sober, he was a principled drinker. Therefore we drank Tokay to boycott bad Italian wine.

We toasted Turin again and again, for its past and its present and its name. Otto threw a glass of wine out of the window, 'For the Vercelli book', and César began a long debate as to whether they ate vermicelli more in the north or south of Italy. It was only at the last minute and with the point still undecided that we remembered we had to change trains. We all jumped out in time, and salvaged our leather bag and the wine, but Otto's books were left behind. We stood on the platform and waved to them until the last of the train was out of sight. He looked so crestfallen that I forbore to tell him that there had been worse in the war. He looked as though he wouldn't have been sure about it.

We took the six forty-five to Grenoble, Otto drank his way through the wine in the same dedicated way he might take notes for an essay. When he drank, his cheeks flushed and gave him a boyish air. César slept for most of the way, but was woken up from time to time by Otto, who insisted that he drink occasional mouthfuls 'to stop him from getting hungover'.

Otto slipped into a different compartment just before the frontier, and returned once we were all safely through. As the night progressed, and we sliced our way nearer and nearer to Grenoble through the French Alps, Otto drank as though he were drinking the last wine in the world. The journey included a surprise change at St Jean and a switch to an even slower, more local train that paused to take breath at every village along its route.

We eventually reached Grenoble at about midnight. Otto was hopelessly drunk, and César and I weren't much better. We sat on the bench on the platform, and finished our last bottle of wine, then we passed through to the ticket hall and decided on a plan of campaign: more wine. César produced three collar stiffeners, and we drew to see who should go to buy it. I drew the short one. 'That's all right,' César said, 'you'd have had to go anyway, because Otto is too drunk, and your French is better than mine.' César never made any bones about his belief in dictatorship.

'Don't you believe in democracy then?'

'No,' he'd say, as though that were an end to the matter.

'Why not?' I'd demand, indignantly, and he'd say,

'Democracy doesn't exist.'

If I went on arguing after that, he would tell me to go and try 'the chaos of Venezuela for a few years' and then come back when I knew what I was talking about. And if I argued any more after that, he would whistle quietly and get bored. Otto once explained to me how Venezuela was the product of one man's dream. Simón Bolívar had moulded the whole country on the freedoms and democracy of England.

'The result is so different, it's like a bad joke,' he had said. 'César comes across like Genghis Khan, but there's a benevolence in his tyranny.'

I screwed up my courage, and set off for the wine. I could see there was no way out for me. César would just say, 'Dictadura es dictadura!' and that would be that.

I was afraid of the dark, and afraid of strange men jumping out of alleyways. With the money that César had proffered, mostly in lire and useless, I had less than two hundred francs.

It was a small thing to do, to walk into the night and bring back a bottle of wine. I thought anyone else might have thought nothing of it, but I was absurdly afraid. I walked out of the station precinct and across a main road, and to my immense relief there was a bar in sight; I went in, and a host of coarse bleary faces leered up at me. I ignored them and asked for a bottle of vin rouge. The bartender eyed me suspiciously. 'To drink here?' he asked.

I thought he was worried about my being under-age. 'Oh no,' I said, 'to take away.'

He didn't even bother to answer, but turned rudely back to his sink. It was as though I should have known something that I didn't. I reached the door, someone was talking to me, but I wouldn't stop.

After the glare of the bar, it seemed even darker outside. One of the men followed me. I hoped he wouldn't have a flick knife. My mother claimed that all foreigners carry flick knives, and even I had one back in Milan, and Otto had two.

When I was nine, the police had had to intervene when a strange man had followed me to school and waited outside the gates for me, until the lollipop lady reported him. And once a man had asked me to jump from a moving train with him, and I had been too embarrassed to pull the communication cord. 'I don't want to hurt you,' he had said, 'I love you.'

I was always being loved by strange men, the rank and file

131

of the sick and lonely mistook me for a kind of itinerant Red Cross.

I walked down the street in Grenoble, thinking about such things, and keeping my fingers crossed that I would not end up as a statistic in the Isère gutter press. Otto and the others had done the biggest bank robbery to date; their names would at least be remembered like that of Henri Charrière on the lips of the underworld. Future presidents might thank or penalise them for their work; they qualified for the Guinness Book of Records. (The Great Train Robbery wasn't a bank, Otto always reminded me.) And here was I, unable to complete this mission too insignificant for mention.

I tried bar after bar, cafés and restaurants, trailing my long checked dress through dirty sawdust, between crowded tables. In the workmen's café I was given the hardest ride, but everywhere I went, people pestered.

'Stay and have a drink,' they invited. Some of them seemed like the kind of people I would have liked to stay and drink with, but I was looking now, desperately, for one miserable bottle of vin rouge that no one would sell me. Most places didn't sell by the bottle, those that did had sold out, others quoted the law to me, 'to be drunk on the premises'. Others still turned me out for being under-age. César was right. The French were unspeakably mean. Now that I had braced myself to my mission, I needed to find the wine, I couldn't face the idea of failure. César wouldn't understand, he would look at me with his slow disbelief, and then he would look away. He had so few words anyway, no words to waste on a failure. He wouldn't understand why I hadn't just grabbed a bottle and run, or bribed a bartender, or broken a window. He didn't know what it was like to be seventeen and brought up in England. Age was never an excuse for César, he would have managed, no matter what his age.

The street seemed interminable, but finally petered out, and I tried the other side. Entering, as I had done before, every bar, systematically trying to buy the wretched wine. Halfway back to the station, I noticed a group of people ahead of me. After each bar, they were still there. There was one more bar in sight, and I tried it, but as I reached the door, someone barred my way. At the same time, I felt hands pulling at my dress.

I turned round slowly. I was being shaken, my hair had come down from its complicated mesh of pins, and someone was pulling it. Through the dark I saw my assailants were all women. I might have felt relieved but I didn't. My mother's experiences as headmistress of a girls' remand home had given me a lifelong dread of them. I could remember, instantly, the girl with the sixty stitches in her face from a mug of cocoa, and the girl who murdered her granny with a poker, and Mary Bell, who hid babies in a dust heap and slashed them with razor blades at the age of ten. And I had heard all about the razors in vaginas and the fights.

One of my arms was twisted behind me in an amateur half-nelson. I couldn't even see how many there were, six, ten, twenty, it was impossible to see in the dark. They were all talking at me, shouting, words accompanied by punches. The shock began to wear off, and I started thinking. First I ran over my mother's advice for dealing with violent adolescents. One, avoid eye-contact, two, always give a verbal response, and three, never smile.

A handbag struck the side of my face, and I began to hear what they were saying through the hum of my reddening ear. They were all prostitutes, and they were accusing me of soliciting on their beat. I was on their street. They said that they had seen me going into every bar, and they were going to teach me to get lost the hard way. I tried a direct verbal response, I told them that I was buying wine. They told me that they were the harem of Haile Selassie. When I told them that I was an English tourist, they bristled with rage; and then they moved back and prepared to close in.

As they drew back, I saw the glint of a blade in the streetlamp, and sharp costume-jewellery being adjusted. And I was faintly reassured to see that they were mostly middle-aged. I had no statistics on middle-aged female delinquency, and this in itself seemed to be an advantage. It occurred to me that I could probably out-run them. Only a good-looking girl and a couple of others looked game enough to catch me, and I was taller than them and therefore longer in the leg. I was standing up against a damp wall inside the half-circle of their taunts. It seemed that they couldn't make up their minds who was to get the first kick.

'You scab,' someone shouted at me in French.

'Go on, Lulu, get her.'

Lulu was squaring up, preparing a tremendous left-hander when a new, red-headed girl came forward and put her face almost into mine, spat and gave me a sharp kick on the shins as though to see if I was real. Then she said: 'Leave her to me.'

'I got her first,' Lulu told her.

'Shut your mouth!'

'Shut yours.'

'Up yours.'

There was a scuffle and a fight, and suddenly, I was forgotten. I broke through their ranks and ran, aiming myself in the direction of the station. I rarely run, believing, perhaps too readily, what I was brought up to believe, namely, that exercise is something that you give to dogs and horses. But under the circumstances, I picked up my voluminous skirt and was away before anyone realised what I was doing, sprinting out of the dark street to the lights of the main road. I could feel them in pursuit for the first few blocks, and I could hear them hurling every insult they could think of after me. Once again, I was grateful to my mother, who was educated in a French convent and for some reason had learnt every term of French abuse from the nuns. These she had taught me, and it was the one area of that language where I felt entirely at my ease. My assailants would have been gratified to know that none of their epithets was lost on me. They left me at the main road, and I straightened out my dress and found the station and César again.

César was angry. 'What took you so long?' he said. I could tell that he didn't want to know.

'Where's Otto?' he demanded.

'He's with you,' I said. I didn't even mind if César was cross, at least he was there, and I didn't have a cocoa mug buried in my face.

'Don't be silly,' he said.

Cesar didn't even ask about the wine, he didn't seem to want it any more. At any other time I would have been annoyed at having been sent out on a fool's errand, but the mere fact that César was no longer drunk, nor yet stretched out asleep somewhere, seemed to imply trouble.

'What's the matter?' I asked him.

He pointed to Otto's coat slung over our leather bag, and he said, 'He's gone.'

'Gone where?'

'I don't know, for Christ's sake, or I wouldn't be asking you,' he said.

I had never seen César worried like this before. I knew that in general they considered France less safe than Italy. I began to recap. We had just that evening crossed the frontier. Otto's documents could have been identified, his cover blown, they could have been waiting for him at Grenoble. Theoretically he could be arrested at any time by Interpol. There was an international warrant out for his arrest. Or worse still, he could just disappear. On false papers it would be easy for an authority to disclaim any knowledge of him. With a real passport he would at least have been entitled to consular rights – for all the good they ever did anyone, but they sounded vaguely reassuring. But if Otto just disappeared, he could turn up under the tarmac of a motorway, or in a car dump, or not at all.

César's face had gone pale with the pallor of the day of the pork when I had said that I would leave him, and the pallor of our talk before our marriage at the point when he spoke of his father's death. His face was set in an expression of grief. We didn't talk, he didn't want to, he wanted to find Otto. We searched the station, looking for him in the most improbable places. We checked the platforms and the waiting-room, we looked under the benches for any last-minute sign of him. 'If they'd have arrested him, he would have made a noise,' César said, convinced that there must be some scrap of evidence left by Otto and missed by his kidnappers that would lead us to him.

My moment of glory, my flight from the prostitutes, was lost in the past. Only Otto mattered as we scoured the lavatories and dustbins for him. We looked in the precinct outside, and on the tracks for two hundred yards each way. There was no sign of him. We checked the trains with the surly ticket man. There had been one to Chambéry, one to Valence, and our one.

'He wouldn't just take a train,' César said.

'But he doesn't turn up sometimes,' I reminded him.

'He doesn't come,' César said, 'but he doesn't go either.'

I reminded him about posting a letter to Berlin. 'He sort of hinted before he did it,' César said.

We decided to wait in the station for Otto, however long that might be. 'What if he doesn't come for a week?' I asked.

'Then we'll wait a week,' César said stubbornly.

'We can't stay here for a week,' I insisted, for the sake of saying something.

'If he doesn't come for a week, he'll most likely be dead.' César walked away from me to lean on a grubby window sill and stare at the night.

We waited at the station until a kind of unreal glow came through in patches, highlighting the litter on the floor. César had remained on his window ledge, and I had left him to his thoughts, and sat huddled on a bench with only our bag for warmth. I thought how much I would miss Otto if I didn't see him again, I had hardly noticed how he had grafted his way into my system. He had told me that César could graft anything on to anything. 'He can graft a tomato on to a potato and an apple on to a pear.' I didn't know if he was lying, but I knew that he had somehow grafted us together. Otto had become more than César's friend to me, he was a crucial part of my life. I forgot all his unpleasantness as I sat there. His faults shrank to insignificance. He wasn't touchy or rude or neurasthenic any more, he didn't nag or storm or insist on his own way. He assumed the status of the newly dead and all his peccadilloes receded to give way to his charm and charisma, his brilliance and his praise.

I imagined him floating down the Naviglio Grande, with his hand caught in the weeds, waving to me through the slime. I imagined his drooping moustache that gave him a sad Mexican air, wafting in the water as he was carried to the

Ticino. He became beautiful like Ophelia in the painting by Millais, drifting on the water. I became filled with the desire I had hitherto denied him. I repented of my coldness. He claimed that I tortured him. I imagined him tortured, but worst of all I imagined him dead.

César came and squeezed my shoulder on his way to the lavatory. He had aged again, like he had been when I first met him; it was partly his haggard unshaven look. He came back a few minutes later and stood by me.

'Come with me,' he said, dragging me to the men's lavatory. It was astonishingly dirty compared to the women's next door. He pushed me into a cubicle with a kind of furtive urgency. I thought, 'What a moment!' but he just said, 'Listen.'

I listened, and a strange rumbling sound came through the wall.

'Am I hearing things,' César said, 'or is that Otto?'

We stood on a slippery porcelain ledge and looked over the top of the partition. On the other side a strange heap was slumped over the mouth of the lavatory. It was Otto, doubled up with his feet on the seat, and his head in his knees. But for the snoring, I would have said he was dead.

'It's him,' I whispered.

'Is he hurt?' César asked.

'I don't know, he looks weird, but he could just be drunk.'

Otto had locked his door from inside, so we dropped things on him to bring him round.

He finally emerged in the most unspeakable rage.

We were both so relieved to see him that we didn't care. We didn't tell him how worried we'd been, and he never told us why he had curled up there and slept. If his feet had only shown on the floor we might have found him.

That was about all we did in Grenoble, get chased by prostitutes and search for Otto, because when we went to the one address we had, that of a cousin of Otto's, we were told that he had 'gone to Italy to visit a cousin'.

'I don't believe it,' César said, but there wasn't much else to do, so we went and sat on the edge of a low wall in one of the town's squares and looked up at the snowy peaks around us, and at the town hall. This last spurred César to reel off a list of the city's treasons; Otto argued for the resistance that had been particularly strong in Grenoble, César refused to concede, and said that we were probably sitting on the very wall against which the Maquis had been shot after being denounced by their neighbours.

We decided not to change our lire, and just make do with the francs we had, so we pooled them and bought some crêpes from a mobile crêperie. We bought one last one between the three of us, but I dropped it over the wall and into a sandpit, and it seemed such an excessive shovelling on of misfortune that I gave way and cried. Otto hugged me, and César said he would never speak to me again if I didn't stop immediately. So I did, and we went back to the station, and back to Chambéry and St Jean, to Susa, Turin, Vercelli, Novara, Milan and home to Bologna, eating nothing but the rock-hard rolls with the leather ham, and comparing our hangovers.

Chapter XV

Autumn came late in Bologna, in fact the summer seemed to hold out almost until the snow began. I realised that by waiting for some mass movement of leaves and climate, a gradual transition from season to season had slipped by without making much impression. The hills around the town retained their heat until well into October. We still took picnics to eat on the parched hills around the pilgrimage church of St Luke, and it was warm enough to fall asleep in the sun. I can't remember at exactly which point the dry grass and bracken gave way to scattered fallen leaves. The oak trees held their wigs of russet jigsaws right through the winter, and I suppose that it was the oaks particularly that I had been watching.

Our life in Bologna had an inalterable timetable of its own that lasted all through the tail-end of the summer, and the autumn that it merged into and the winter it became. It wasn't until the following spring that our lives were hectic again. We all returned tired from Grenoble, and happy to sink into the lull of Bologna and its quiet Renaissance charm. San Salvatore itself was like an island in the sun, with all the pros and cons of the tropics. It is often said that the English do nothing but talk about the weather, but I have never lived in a country where the vagaries of the climate were not discussed, daily, ritually and at length. In Bologna there were no vagaries, it was as hot as the sands of Africa, but the sheer extremity of the heat was commented on and tossed about.

'Che caldo!' the old ladies would say, sitting out on the landing with their panting spaniel, Chapolino, and fanning themselves with old magazines.

'Che caldo!' they would repeat every time they saw us. It was as though there was nothing else to say. Just 'How hot'. How hot could it get? How hot would it get? Sometimes there would be a hint of admiration in the 'Che caldo', as though every extra degree in the shade gave credit to their own endurance.

In London and Oxford and Milan, we had stayed in bed until well past midday, but in Bologna, bed was a kind of purgatory which made rising early seem like a reprieve. One thin cotton sheet was cooler than none, but the nights were wakeful and given over more to trying to forget the mosquitoes than to sleep. Despite its beauty, and the cauterised cleanliness of the terracotta façades and the rambling roofs of reds and oranges, there was something insanitary about Bologna that the mosquitoes seized upon. I would lie in my thin brass bed, with my sheet tucked in around me from head to foot like a shroud, listening to the measured frenzy of the mosquitoes on me. If I fell asleep, and moved, even an inch, they would find their way into my winding sheet and suck and bleed me until the itch created a strange limbo of its own.

They were single-minded, voracious, never ending, like the hungry millions of India. One meal of Red Cross blood was not enough, they needed more and more. I could hear them drone and whisper over my own thoughts, over the night, over the gentle breathing of the others. They wound their way into my head like the whispered prayers of my great-aunt Maud drifting through the panelled walls of her house: 'Lord have mercy upon our sins.' For hour after hour through the night I had heard her praying, kneeling against the wall where I lay on the other side, hearing her ghostly appeals to the God who had left her alone at the age of ninety-three with no other wish than to die, quickly, before things changed any further in the world where she was already lost, fossilised in her prayers, and fed by servants. Droning too close to my ear, 'Lord have mercy upon us, Christ have mercy upon us, hear your poor servant begging mercy.' Mostly, only half the words would drift through, on a line of esses, biting their way into my adolescence. 'Saviour . . . sanctify, we beseech, sickness and sense . . . s and seriousness . . . s and the residue in fear . . . or else grace.' My great-aunt Maud's prayers leapt from one subject to another, lingering on all the ess sounds, and the mosquitoes made a perfect replica of her prayer, closing in and withdrawing, then hovering on the same consonant, refusing to cease saying over and over again, 'Save thy servant, O Lord', determined to follow her husband the rector, who was forty years dead and had left her to cope with the servants, 'And forgive us sour trespasses as we forgive, And forgive Grace, O Lord, for breaking a saucer, for I cannot forgive her.'

For some reason, perhaps my mother's red hair, perhaps just my bad luck, the mosquitoes attacked me more than the others. They chewed and pestered and pursued me more, and nothing seemed to ease them. I kept a tally of all my new bites, and they averaged out at twenty-two a night. I divided this by two, and made a point of personally killing eleven of these delicate-legged, insanely annoying creatures each night before I went to sleep. As a result, the wall above César's and my bed was speckled with wings and blood and numerous strands of legs squashed into the whitewash. I was surprised to find how much I enjoyed swatting them, and even squeezing them between my fingers. I was unusually squeamish with other insects and animals, but I derived a very real, vindictive pleasure from hunting mosquitoes. It was no matter that the ones I caught had probably never bitten me, they were part and parcel of the same species, with the same tastes, and the same inane drone. There were mosquitoes everywhere, in the cinema, in the shops, on the stairs, but it was at night, in bed at San Salvatore, that they were worst.

Apart from the heat and the marauding insects, we had no other troubles during that first long summer. We had virtually no money, and when Elías was away, we had none at all, but we had grown used to that, and we managed. Once it became clear that bohemians no longer starved to death in garrets, the sense of impending doom that had dogged our actions in

Milan left us, and we were able to enjoy the more social side of Italy. We made friends with people in the town, and with some of our neighbours. It was Otto who made the first gestures. He had a way of tracking down friendly faces, and finding endless things in common with strangers.

Thus by the end of October we exchanged 'Buongiorno's and 'Fa caldo's with two of our neighbours, a cellist at the academy, an architect, an actress, two professors and a fishman from the market. We even had the unheard-of distinction of being invited back to some of their homes. Northern Italians, like the Japanese, have a friendliness that stops at their own front door. Since there were always three and sometimes four of us, we arrived like an invading army, and since we rarely ate a square meal at San Salvatore, we had to use all our restraint not to eat our hosts out of house and home. On the whole, we stayed in the flat during the day, reading and waiting for the sun to ease, and then went to the cinema, walked around the town, went to the cinema again, and then home, and talked as far into the night as the hordes of mosquitoes would allow.

Otto remained firm in his scorn of our flea-pit cinema, and Elías had a girlfriend who used to visit him when we were all out. We did our shopping at the local supermarkets. Except that it wasn't exactly shopping, more living off the land, since although we picked and chose what we wanted in the usual way, we always by-passed the cashier. I never managed to master the technique of this foraying, and César was so lazy that nothing would induce him to stir from his bed. But Otto and Elías made their lists and brought back the goods. Elías was the best at this. He just filled up a huge shopping bag and walked confidently out of the shop. So confidently that it never occurred to people that he shouldn't be doing what he was. Otto, however, went through agonies of surreptitious concealment. Hiding away his packets of Earl Grey tea, and his lapsang suchons while the sweat gathered on his face, and his hands trembled, and his face went green. Sometimes he would try to take something that didn't fit, and then have to take it back. At other times, the store detective would always seem to be behind them, and we would have to forgo one of our cinemas or go hungry.

There were few signs to mark César and his friends as any different from the other summer travellers in Bologna. Even when the winter came suddenly there, with frost on the Garisenda and the Asinelli, they could still have passed for any idle loiterers who chose to stay on in the city. All of them were so haphazard in their ways that the strains of exile and the constant sense of biding time were well concealed from outsiders. The old ladies who lived opposite us compared us to migratory swallows.

'When the spring comes, you'll go,' they said.

César said, 'No, we'll stay in Bologna', but the old ladies shook their heads and tightened their hold on their dog Chapolino's crumbling lead as though they knew better. Not for nothing had they lived for over sixty years in the same decaying building, fanning themselves against the heat, and sweeping up the dust that the woodworm left around them, and watching the comings and goings of the house.

'You're all young,' they said. 'Only old people stay here . . . San Salvatore,' she said, stressing the Salvatore, 'everyone here is waiting to die.'

César, particularly, became very fond of the two old ladies, and spent more and more time listening to their canary, and discussing the past with them. One day they talked about all the things they missed. Vienna, the waltzes, muffs in winter, holidays in Venice, and brown sugar in cubes like they had had during the war. César said, 'One day I'll send you some of that sugar.'

The old ladies shook their heads, they were sisters, one fat and one thin, but they moved in unison like a shaky cabaret.

'You can't get that kind of sugar any more,' they said, 'it was special for the war.'

César insisted that he would send them some all the same, and they smiled.

'And now,' they said, 'let the signor Cesare tell us what he misses most.'

Now it was César's turn to smile and shake his head, and he left them with their question unanswered, and was quiet and pensive for days.

'Why did you tell them you'd send them that sugar?' I asked him later in the evening.

'I like them,' he shrugged, and turned his face to the wall to sleep.

I looked to Otto for a more helpful answer, and he said, 'That's what César has on his land, sugar.'

I felt suddenly very stupid for not having asked him before what he had on his land. It had seemed enough just to own the land, it hadn't occurred to me that he would have something on it.

'Well, why hasn't he got any money?' I said, annoyed by my ignorance.

'Oh, he's got money,' Otto said, 'he's very rich.'

'Then why haven't we got enough to eat?' I snapped.

'Because he's not as wealthy as he's proud,' Otto said, and then, almost whispering, as he saw me go back to César, 'He's sad tonight, let him be.'

Over the next few days I quizzed César more about his lands, but he seemed reluctant to talk about them. All I gleaned was that he grew sugar-cane and avocado pears, and that he had an estate manager, and that all his workers had stayed on without wages while he, César, was in prison. It didn't seem to matter how many questions I asked, he had a genius for answering and telling me nothing at the same time. I grew curious for the first time about the size of his lands, how far they extended. However, each time I asked him, he said that he didn't know, they were just 'big'.

'How big?' Now that the thought had occurred to me, I wanted to know.

'Just big,' César would say.

'But how big?'

I could see that César was bored, but I couldn't stop, so he finally sighed, and said, 'There is a road that the dictator Pérez Jiménez built when my father was Governor. It runs through the hacienda. If you stand on one side and look as far as you can see to the skyline, that is the hacienda, and then climb over the hills and down and across the valley and up to the far crest, and that is the hacienda. It has never been measured.'

'And what's on the other side of the road?' I asked, trying to visualise the whole set-up.

'That is the hacienda too.'

My desire to see this hacienda in the Andes grew through the winter. I asked Otto more and more questions about it, and he sensed the turn of my thoughts.

'Even if César were pardoned,' he said, 'and even if he wanted to go back, they would never accept you there.'

'Why not?' I asked him, undeterred.

'Because you were not born into the family. César's family always marry within themselves, they have done for centuries, no one else is good enough for them. It is like a dynasty, and you are a commoner.'

César had seemed so eager to marry me on no acquaintance at all that this last piece of information seemed almost unreal. I retreated to the British Council Library, my one and only bolt-hole, to think it over. I purposely missed the afternoon cinema, as a mark of protest at my implied unworthiness.

It seemed preposterous. For sheer eccentricity my family could stand man to man against almost any other. Strangers knew and respected this. César's family should do so too. Even the Germans had, in the war when they occupied Jersey; it was Claremont, my mother's family home, they made into their H.Q., built in 1840 like a ship with portholes for windows and an upper deck for a roof. I sulked all afternoon until the library closed at five. When I got back to San Salvatore, César was so pleased to see me, and so worried as to where I had been, that I forgot my anger and even consented to join in one of Otto's ridiculous word games, forfeits and all. Claremont was a hotel I would never see, and the Andes were over four thousand miles away.

Chapter XVI

Our flat in San Salvatore was picturesque in the summer, but it proved hard to heat in the winter. We had eked out what little money we had for so long that it seemed inevitable it should last for ever. When it finally ended, we just assumed that it would start again, a trickle of lire would come from somewhere, not much, but enough for César's cigarettes, and bus fares, and the pittance for the cinema. We had been living for months on odd notes scrimped and squirrelled by me into my crocodile wallet in the lining of my Gladstone bag.

It was in mid-November that I went to the wallet in the lining, and found that it was bare. Even the lining itself, which had had loose notes in it, was empty. My pockets and César's aspirin bottles were empty. I rummaged for hours, looking in the places where I usually concealed notes. It didn't seem possible that I could have used up all my caches. There were so many of them: on top of the cistern, under the loose pamment in the kitchen floor, between the main beam and the plaster, in the hearth. I had always hidden notes. There had not been one day when I couldn't produce our 300 lire for a film and enough to buy ten cigarettes. I felt utterly cheated.

César was in bed, scarcely visible under a mound of rugs and blankets.

'Pass me a cigarette,' he said.

I pretended not to hear him. We didn't have any. We couldn't buy any. I had checked our pockets. Only Elías would have money on him, and Elías had left the night before for Milan.

'I want a cigarette,' he said.

'There aren't any,' I told him.

'Well, let's get some,' he said, pushing his ten blankets on to the floor with a thud. I didn't know whether to tell him or to let him find out for himself. He washed and dressed, adjusting his waistcoat with his usual care.

'Give me the money,' he said, putting on his overcoat.

'There isn't any.'

César smiled, he always smiled when he didn't believe things.

'Don't be silly, you always have some,'

It had seemed natural to César that I should have. He was never born to be poor. It was enough that in Europe he cleaned his own shoes and bought his own stamps, that he ran his own bath and made his own bed. Certain things he never mastered. Whenever he washed or shaved he left a trail of wet towels and flannels over the flat. In London, my mother used to get incensed by the heaps of wet towels trailing down the hall from bed to bathroom.

After about a week of grumbling at his nonchalance, she had asked him, 'Do you really expect someone to walk behind you and pick them all up?'

'Yes,' he had said.

'Well they won't here,' she had said firmly.

'Oh,' was César's bemused reply. It had obviously never occurred to him before. After that he made a token effort, gathering together his belongings in a deliberately martyred way that seemed to say, 'I've known worse times.'

So César refused to believe that our money had petered out. There had been so little that it hardly counted as money, it was just there to make ends meet. We were provided for, his cigarettes happened, he never questioned why. It was like the divine right of kings before the days of Cromwell. There had to be money for his cigarettes.

I could hear Otto getting up and dressed in his room. He came through and into the bathroom without saying a word. Then he made straight for the front door and left, making a cut-throat sign with his forefinger, and pointing towards César with a smile.

People never fully appreciate each other's vices. I didn't blame Otto for leaving us in our dilemma, I would have happily gone myself to the British Council Library or anywhere else until the storm blew over. But César was more than upset, he was shattered, propping his head up with one hand and grinding his teeth in slow desperation.

'I must have a cigarette,' he said, and waited.

It was as though he thought that the God in whom he no longer believed but whom he had once served so loyally would lift up the roof of San Salvatore and put a packet of Benson & Hedges down on the table. He opened his eyes and saw that nothing had happened. I could see him reasoning with himself. He didn't believe. Concentration and concentration alone could solve his problem. He closed his eyes and frowned ferociously. When he opened them again, and found the table still bare, the full horror of his situation seemed to hit him. His exile, his poverty, the waste and the failure, the uselessness of his life, the foreignness of Bologna. He didn't move an inch, but his nose began to bleed, violently. I passed him a towel, and he held it to his face.

César changed somehow behind that towel. I couldn't see his face, just a blur of blood seeping through the pile. He seemed to gain a new sense of purpose. It was as though he had shed a skin of inertia like a snake grown tired of basking in the sun and suddenly hungry.

'Come with me,' he said. And we set off in the direction of the town centre. We didn't stop until we reached the arcade of the Via Farini. César had walked so quickly I could hardly keep up with him, and I was out of breath when I arrived.

'Now what?' I panted.

'Now we are going to get a cigarette.'

'How?' I asked.

'That,' he said, pointing to a stone pillar ahead of us, 'is a bus stop. E vietato fumare on the buses. The smokers will have to throw down their cigarettes to get on the bus.' It was a good plan, but there were very few people queuing for the bus, and half of them were elderly ladies in black who would no more smoke than they would wear a bikini to Mass. One man alone was holding a cigarette.

'That's our man,' César said.

The bus didn't come and it was growing cold under the arcade. My shoes had worn thin on the soles and the chill from the pavements seemed to go straight up my shins. César watched his prey, he had lit up and was inhaling lightly, like one who hasn't smoked for long.

'Goddam him,' César said, 'he's not even enjoying it.'

The man was halfway down his cigarette and the bus still wasn't in sight. After ten minutes it was smoked. César began to stamp around angrily; he went and stood in the bus queue, slapping his sides to keep warm.

'Why doesn't that blasted bus come?' he said to no one in particular. He was frowning savagely.

One of the old ladies turned round to him, blind to his frown.

'Fa freddo,' she said. César smiled a kind of sickly strangler's grin. The man with the cigarette had finished, he was stubbing out the dog-end in a sort of lonely twist. The old lady turned back to her companion.

'Molto gentile,' she commented, referring to César.

'Did you see that?' César asked me, coming back to the wall. I had done; there was nothing left of the cigarette but a smudge of twisted tobacco on the pavement. 'The mean swine,' César said, and we walked on to the next bus stop, and then the next, discovering that trampling cigarette butts was a kind of national disease.

I could see that César, with his manic cleanliness, and his underlying misanthropy, couldn't bring himself to smoke just anyone's dog-end. At least at the bus queues he could see who had smoked them before him. But it didn't work. People dropped coins and handkerchiefs and even an aubergine in the Piazza Vittorio Emanuele, but not so much as a puff. We passed the cigarette machines, rattling their closed drawers as we went by. I couldn't help but see the irony of the man who robbed banks unable to bring himself to rob a slot machine.

As we combed the bus routes from one end of the city to the other, the seed of a thought took root in César's mind. He told me at least three times during the course of the morning, 'We've got to get out of here.'

After all the months of aimless drifting, it was finally this lack of tobacco that proved the last straw. He was trapped by his need.

'I must have a cigarette,' he repeated, to the street, to me, to the Torre Garisenda that refused to fall down, and to Standa, the supermarket that kept its cigarettes in the cash desk. We walked past the statue of Neptune with its fountain and trident, and the rows of plaques set into the wall to commemorate the glorious war dead.

'Glorious arseholes,' César said viciously as we passed them. 'I bet you they'd refuse me a cigarette if we were out in the desert now.'

This seemed unfair to me, and I said so.

'O.K.,' he said bitterly, 'so they would give me one if they were standing still, but they'd be too busy running away to stop and fuss around with packets.'

I let the matter drop, and we walked on.

'Whose side are you on anyway?' César asked, wheeling round on me, so that I nearly tripped over him.

'The war's over.'

'The war is never over,' he said, and then he waited, and he asked me, 'Will you go and get me a cigarette, Veta?'

'I would if I could, but how?'

'Just go up to someone and ask.'

'I can't.'

'You could try,' César said.

'Why don't you?' I asked him.

'I couldn't even try,' he said.

In the end, it was half-past three, and we were cold and ravenously hungry. We had been standing on the corner of the main square for two and a half hours, watching people come and go in an agony of smoke. We had decided to just stop and pick up any old dog-end that we saw. It wasn't easy, we were both too vain. We cased the street, waiting for total emptiness. It didn't happen. Someone was always coming. We couldn't decide who should be the one to kneel. We made a pact, and went down together and picked up one frayed, dirty cigarette butt, and made our way home in silence. César was too ashamed to speak until after dinner. But dinner was so scant that it needed all the conversation that the three of us could muster to fill the gap it left.

'How did it go?' Otto asked.

'Fine,' we both lied together.

Otto smiled knowingly, and I asked César what he had done for cigarettes when he was in prison.

'It's funny,' he said, 'but I never lacked a smoke in the cárcel. They'd send you out like a dummy, handcuffed into the line of fire, so that you'd get shot by your own guerrillas, but they'd always shove a cigarette in your mouth before you went. They'd take you out to the firing squad, and they'd give you a last smoke. You could sit in your own urine for a week, and they weren't at all keen on stitching up wounds or straightening out your ribs, but they'd always throw a cigarette through the grids. I've never really needed a cigarette until today.'

'It's like keeping elephants in a cage,' Otto said, 'we won't let them out, but we'll throw them buns, as though buns grew on trees by the Limpopo river.'

'When we go somewhere else,' César volunteered, 'I'm going to stop smoking.'

'Why then?' I asked.

'It's got to be in my own time,' César said.

Otto snorted, he was half-choked on some private joke.

'What's so bloody funny now?' César asked him. Nothing was going to make him laugh just then.

Otto put his hand in his pocket and brought out a packet of Gauloises, and slid them across the table like gambler's chips. César looked at him dispassionately.

'How long have you had them?' he demanded.

'Since our trip to Grenoble,' Otto told him.

César was speechless. You could see him hunting for something to say. His entire language was inadequate to express his thoughts.

'You're a mean, Frenchified bastard,' he said finally, through his teeth. 'You're an uncouth illiterate swine,' he said, seizing the packet and then finally, 'You're no good.'

Otto laughed, uneasily. 'I just thought it would do you good, César José, if you stepped down to the planet earth for a few moments,' he said.

'Well, next time you get one of those philanthropic urges, you unethical little pimp, take it to the viaduct, and get rid of it.'

César shouted at him, seizing the offending packet of Gauloises and crumpling it between his fists. 'And that's what I think of your lousy cigarettes,' he said, grinding them to a pulp inside their blue wrapper and tipping the bits of tobacco over the rug. 'And I can't even begin to tell you what I think of you!'

So saying he stormed out of the flat, and we heard him take refuge with the vecchiette in their flat across the landing. Otto was unrepentant.

'César thinks he's some kind of fairy tale,' he said, clearing the table in his usual meticulous way.

I awoke early the next morning to find César on his hands and knees collecting up the tobacco from the pulverised Gauloises.

'Sshh,' he said, holding up one finger and pointing to Otto's door. He had enough tobacco, eked into thin hand-rolled cigarettes, to last him for the next week. After that, he went out on his own and came back like a tramp with a little pouch of dog-ends. Sometimes I went with him to collect these, sometimes he went on his own.

There seemed to be no such solution to our missing the cinema. We just didn't have the entrance money. Sometimes we went and stood by the billboards, lingering to see what we were missing. After about ten days the doorman came up to us.

'Why don't you come any more?' he asked.

'We had our wallet stolen,' César told him, confidentially. 'There's been some delay with the reissue of our travellers' cheques.' The doorman eyed us, standing there, a good head and shoulders taller than him, and vastly fatter in our fur coats.

'You used to come every day,' he said wistfully. 'You were my best customers.'

'Yes,' César continued, 'we have to see a lot of films, you see we are in films ourselves.'

'Really?' the doorman said. 'Well, of course,' he paused, 'I'd rather suspected something like that.'

César turned as though to go away. 'Good-bye,' he said to the doorman, who was still labouring with our last admission.

'Don't go,' he said, 'I mean, come whenever you like. I mean, while you're waiting for the bank.'

'Thank you,' César said, 'if we get the time, we might just do that.'

The slate of César's faults was wiped clean for me from that moment. His long silences, his refusal to take an interest in things, his almost constant hibernation, his addiction to the television, were all forgotten as my own addiction to the big screen was catered for.

Elías returned. He was having an affair with a girl called Clara Lanzini, a cellist from the academy. It didn't seem to matter much, that we had gone from having virtually no money to no money at all. We had the flat, and Elías had done something to our electricity supply so that it ran, magically, from the flat below, and as many books as we wanted, thanks to the unwitting local bookshops, whose stock was constantly thinned while our own shelves bulged and grew, as the piles of books heaped up beyond all proportion. Even the brand-new books that were displayed in the window and kept in a case behind the store detective found their way on to our shelves: the silver-grey cover of *Zelda, A Biography*, and the new editions of the classics.

Elías had abandoned his last Mercedes somewhere. He seemed to know instinctively when to sell a car and when to just walk away from it. So we were once more on foot, and, without the money to pay for buses, we were obliged to join ranks with the gypsies. The zingaros who were thrown off buses and out of shops and who were not allowed within the Red precincts of the town. We also took great pains not to collect dog-ends anywhere near our cinema, since it would have ruined our new image as movie tycoons. César liked walking around the area of the two leaning towers best of all.

'Don't you find it worrying,' I asked him, 'the way they

seem to be coming at you?'

'No,' he said, 'it's all the other buildings coming at me that I don't like. The towers are real.'

He was also very fond of the sette chiese, a conglomeration of seven churches all joined into one. We would spend hours and hours sitting on the cold pews of one or other of these churches, and César, who was usually so silent, would insist on talking in a stage whisper through Mass. He seemed to enjoy disrupting the service.

'Why don't you just let them get on with it?' I asked him. 'No one is asking you to join in.' But he wouldn't.

'They have betrayed themselves,' he would say, 'someone must stand out against them.'

'Yes,' I'd say, blushing with embarrassment as a host of disapproving faces stared at us from under their weeds, 'but why does it have to be you?'

'Why did it have to be Loyola, Columbus, Napoleon?' he would say, and then continue to point out to me the different architectural points from the reredos to the door. I was determined not to assist him in his one-man crusade. Savonarola had done it alone, I thought, so let César subvert the matins or the vespers on his own.

Chapter XVII

We spent all of that winter of 1970 in Bologna. Tito wrote to us for Christmas, and invited us back to Milan for a week. We were glad of someone else's company, because, however hard we tried, Christmas wasn't happy for us. It was forced and hilarious, tiring and besotted, but always full of thoughts about the past. I began to miss London, I missed the lights and the carol singing, Harrods and Jackson's and the Norwegian tree in Trafalgar Square, and it seemed like too long a time to have not seen my family. Over a year without seeing my mother or my sisters Lalage, Resi and Gale, and all the ramifications, the step-families, the friends, my Siamese cat, Bosie; who hated Otto and had scratched his face to the bone.

We didn't stay in Milan for the full week, César was prostrate with his hangover, and Otto was liverish from all the grappa and maraschino. He got liverish on everything except aquavit. But most of all, we just wanted to be quiet for the New Year. The New Year seemed instinctively more important than Christmas then, the one was a celebration of things past, the other a hope for things to come. None of us had the heart to celebrate a wasted 1970, but we all entered optimistically into 1971.

Elías came and went through January and February, as he always did, arriving unannounced, and leaving with a casual 'Ciao' and no fuss. He had been seeing more and more of Clara

Lanzini, the cellist, and often, after he had gone away on one of his lightning trips, she would turn up at San Salvatore. She told us how bored she was with her life and her studies at the academy. She said that she wanted to be like us.

'Elía' has told me all about you.'

César, who was in his permanent winter position, propped up in bed under a patchwork of history books, sat bolt upright in alarm.

'Yes,' Clara continued, 'Elía' has told me, about il Dottore', here she nodded to Otto, 'and himself and il signor César; how you were all expelled from the university, and how you all continue your studies here, on your own. I want to do that too!' she said, dreamily. 'I have my own ideas about music, I don't want to go to that academy any more. All my life under the same professor. I want to travel with you.'

After she left, César said, 'I wonder where Clara got that story from. It's the first I've heard of it, but it's an odd thing to invent.'

Clara began to come every day, skipping classes to be with us. Elías would make a point of not being in when she came.

'Please,' he would say, holding his hands together in an attitude of prayer, 'deal with her. Tell her I'm dead, perverted, backward, all three.'

We did our combined best to dissuade Clara from her infatuation with Elías. But, as is usually the case, the more we maligned him, the more she adored and defended him.

'You don't understand him,' was her answer to everything.

'Clara, Elías will be leaving soon, you've got to realise that,' Otto told her, once, twice, any number of times a day. But she was undeterred, the less she saw of her idol, the more she loved him.

'He'll take me with him,' she said stubbornly.

'He won't, you know he can't.'

She refused to believe this, and none of us had the heart to tell her the simple truth, that Elías didn't love her.

Elías himself became the villain of San Salvatore. We felt that he had behaved badly towards Clara, but since we had all behaved badly in one way or another about walking out on people, about moving on to the next place, we didn't really feel that we had the right to say so. One evening, as we sat huddled over the table, by the one electric fire we possessed, drinking tea, Elías said:

'You look at me as though I was poisoning the old ladies from next door. What are you so damned mealy-mouthed about?'

We didn't answer, and Elías broke the embarrassed silence himself.

'I know it's about Clara,' he said bitterly, 'the trampled damsel and the horny deserter. I never told her that I loved her. Never!'

'She had some cock-and-bull story about us being expelled from the university,' Otto said, 'she must have got that from you, she seems so sure, that's all, and she's a pain in the neck, Elías.'

'Yes, well she went through my trouser pockets one day, and found some papers, nothing much, but it seemed best to make us all protesting students, a cause that is dear to her heart, rather than have her discussing my papers with her friends.'

'But why dodge her?' César asked. 'Can't you just tell her straight out?'

'I've told her,' Elías said. 'It doesn't make any difference. I've told her that I don't want to see her again, that I don't love her. I've told her that I don't even like her, which is a lie, because I do. But she doesn't believe me. She thinks I'm a model of self-sacrifice. She's convinced that I secretly love her and that is that.'

'Well, that's different,' César said, 'it was probably her first time or something.'

'Her first time?' Elías said incredulously. 'She practically raped me. I think she does it to annoy her mother. She says that her mother checks her underpants every day when she comes back from school to see if there are any tell-tale stains, so Clara makes a point of "fraternising" with her fellow students class by class, and then changes her pants and goes home to her mother's scrutiny.'

'Does her mother know about you?' Otto asked.

'No, that's the problem, as you know; the signora Lanzini is rather taken with me herself. She'll have a fit if she finds out. I swore Clara to secrecy, but God knows how long it'll last, every time she has an argument with her mother she rings the alarm bell in her block, so that all the neighbours can come down and hear. It won't be long before she lets the cat out of the bag.'

Clara continued to turn up at San Salvatore, she even came in the evening, hoping to catch Elías unawares. She pretended that she was still seeing him, she even brought a ring to show us.

'It's our engagement ring,' she said.

Her fantasies grew more and more extravagant.

Elías saw her for one last time, instructing us all to hide in the boxroom and listen to what happened.

'Why?' we asked.

'Because she's mad,' he said, 'and I'm afraid you'll all have to deal with her after I go.'

The boxroom was long and narrow, and crammed full of dismantled brass beds and irons, and broken chairs that would never be safe again but that we couldn't bear to throw away, and all the electric fires that had packed up on past inhabitants but had been kept in case they came in useful some day. Some day when everything got so bad that even relics would have a revival. It was extremely cold and uncomfortable crouching under the sloping ceiling. There wasn't one point in the room where any of us could stand up.

The interview that was supposed to take a 'few minutes' dragged on amidst tears and accusations. Elías was very quiet, but Clara refused to listen to him as flatly as she had refused to listen to us.

'I'm leaving tonight, Clara, for good.'

'Non è vero.'

'I won't be coming back again.'

'I don't believe you.'

'Good-bye Clara.'

'You love me.'

'No.'

'You do.'

'No.'

The conversation went on and on and on. César's legs were bothering him.

'I'm going out,' he said.

'You can't now,' Otto told him, and held on to his jacket to make sure he didn't. Clara heard the scuffle and asked what the noise was.

'Rats!' Elías said, emphatically.

It was more than three hours before Elías finally got her away.

César was livid and blue with cold.

'I'll sue him for damages,' he said, when he had crawled out of the room and into his bed. 'I'm not only crippled, I've missed the cinema.'

'You've been watching "scenes from real life", what do you want with the cinema?' Otto said.

'Because real life is tedious, as you well know, or do you think you're some kind of Che Guevara like Clara Lanzini does?'

'Maybe,' Otto said, 'but ask Lisaveta who looks more glamorous, me or you, masquerading as a granny with those shawls round your head. All you need is a pair of knitting needles, and you'd get the part for Little Red Riding Hood.'

There was rarely any arguing, apart from Otto and me, but once a quarrel got going, an immense amount of dirt was dredged up from the past, and scores of minute grievances were aired and ripped apart. By keeping entirely out of the fray, and keeping my ears open, I could learn more about the three of them and their respective pasts in these brief harangues than I could in a whole year of my own questions. But the quarrels would always reach a certain pitch, and then pause like a note held on crescendo, and then stop abruptly, and one or other of them would put on some music.

After a misunderstanding, quarrel or calamity of any kind, it was always Carl Orff's *Carmina Burana*, with César conducting the gramophone record with an imaginary baton for the first few bars. 'O fortuna, velut luna.' Always the same music over and over again. It was the Brandenburg Concertos for Otto to work to, whenever he stayed at home alone, while for César it was Tchaikovsky's First Piano Concerto, which he knew by heart and never tired of. He once told me that his ambition in life had been to be a pianist, but that his mother had forbidden it and sold their piano, because she believed that 'pianists are homosexuals'. Whenever we were drinking at home, after a certain point was reached, it would become time to listen to Tonia la Negra, a black singer with a deep syrupy voice that was instantly recognisable. Even after one word of a song, it could be her and no other, and her voice would be met with enthusiastic praise. But strangely, whenever I tried to play her tapes by day, or sober, I'd be met by a chorus of:

'Turn it off!'

It was mysteriously only suitable for the night, and even then it was ritualistically saved for certain moods.

Elías went to Milan. He had embraced a new interest in aviation design, which had taken over from hydraulic engineering, which had taken over from photography in all its forms. Elías didn't actually lose interest in his past hobbies, he just filed them, cataloguing them in his mind and feeding them from time to time. But he leapt into his new ones with such enthusiasm that his voracity blinkered him to the world, and he had eyes for only one subject at a time. During the time these crazes lasted, he would acquire phenomenal stocks of information, and then, once he had mastered a thing, it would cease to hold him spellbound, and he would take up something else. If a subject took longer than he usually allowed for, he would juggle with it, tagging it along through other bursts of interests, and then give it a second run. He had a way of being very good at whatever he turned his hand to, whether it was flying or topography, mechanics or photography, forgery or guns. He was never discouraged by failures. 'Failure is the beginning of success,' he would say, and try again.

Elías also had a knack of never being short of a car or enough money to run it. However, during our months at San Salvatore, even Elías had been hard up. His banking arrangements had entirely fallen through, not once, a contingency that he always allowed for, or even twice, but three times. There was money sitting in his name in two banks. But he had twice been forced to change his name, and the money was in his discarded identity.

'It's an occupational hazard,' he joked, but poverty didn't sit easily on his shoulders. Perhaps it was just because he refused to fall into any category, but he wasn't a natural poor man.

César tended to ignore his lack of funds, but Otto and Elías railed against theirs. Elías, particularly, because he wanted to fly again, and the fees were exorbitant. He wrote from Milan to say that if some money didn't turn up soon, he was going to go to Scandinavia and work. Otto half-agreed with him, but César said: 'Never!'

Clara still came to us, inventing letters from Elías, and insisting that he would shortly return for her. She was skipping more and more classes at the academy, and in danger of failing her next exams. She came only to talk to us, not with us, she didn't want advice and she didn't want the truth, she just wanted the chance to unburden herself and romanticise. After Elías returned to Milan, our weekly invitations to dine with Clara and her parents began to tail off, until one evening at the end of February when we arrived at the Lanzini flat only to be told that the signora had changed her mind about us. It was old Signor Annibale, Clara's father, who spoke to us.

'I'm very sorry,' he said, 'she doesn't want you to come any more.' He seemed to want to say more, but was too embarrassed, however his wife came out to the hall, red-faced with anger, and said it for him.

'Annibale is pussyfooting,' she shouted, 'but I'm not. I'm not blind. Clara is falling for César and you're all encouraging her. I don't want you to see my daughter again.'

We were sorry to miss our meal, our one good meal of the week, with three courses and wine, and as much as we wanted. We were sorry even to miss Signor Annibale, with his tin banjo and his small stock of jokes that he told over and over again. And we were sorry not to hear Clara play any more, because she always ended our evenings there by playing her cello for half an hour or so. But we were delighted at the thought of her no longer coming round to San Salvatore and

plaguing us with her infatuation, and her increasingly hyster-
ical scenes.

However, in practice, the new prohibition only applied to
the meals. We never went to the Lanzinis' home again, but
Clara kept coming and pestering us. She even came with new
vigour, staying for longer and longer, and, short of barring
the door, there seemed to be no way of getting rid of her. We
began to lie low when she called. But she would sit on the
landing for hours, waiting until one or other of us emerged,
and then either barge in or follow us out. She was as blind to
our growing reluctance to see her, as she had been to Elías's
lack of love.

Otto was growing restless again, and Clara's invasions
weren't helping him.

'I have enough problems babysitting myself,' he said, 'I
refuse to cope with her,' and he upped stakes, to join Elías in
Milan. He urged us to follow him, but César didn't want to
go.

'What are we going to do in Milan?' he asked.

'What are we doing here?' Otto answered him.

'I like Bologna,' César said.

'But we have to stay together,' Otto argued.

'We'll join you for the slow train,' César promised, 'next
time you get tickets for France.'

Otto agreed reluctantly. He didn't like us splitting up, even
for a few months. Elías always came and went, but that was
different. We three had to stay together, in a kind of supersti-
tious clan, as though we were safe only in numbers.

After Otto left, Clara's visits increased, as though she were
afraid that we too would leave overnight, and she would turn
up one day at an empty San Salvatore, and have no one to talk
to. The winter grew daily harsher, and as the temperature
dropped César became less and less willing to venture into the
street. He stayed in bed for most of the day, swathed in all his
and Otto's blankets, hardly able to move for the weight of
them, nursing his arthritis. Our one electric fire was on day
and night, but even so, it was inadequate for anything more
than taking the chill off a small half-circle around it. The rest of

the flat was unimaginably damp and draughty. Also, when César didn't go out, we had nothing to eat, since we depended entirely on his scavenging for our food.

As the month of February progressed we ate less and less, depending more and more on tea bags, sugar, and bruised vegetables from the market. I was brought up on hot chocolate, and this was the one thing I couldn't bear to forgo. After Otto left, however, we ceased to have milk, since he alone knew how to provide it, so I made do with plain cocoa (of which we had many tins) with water and sugar, and drank it black rather than not at all.

Sometimes Chapolino would come snuffling at our door, and the old ladies from across the landing would knock and bring in a little dish of crème caramel, or one profiterole, 'E per la bambina' they always said, much to César's annoyance. Both the old ladies insisted on calling me 'la bambina'. I think this was because when we first arrived, they had met Otto, Elías and César on the stairs on three separate occasions, and each time they had asked, 'Chi è la bambina?' referring to me, and each time they had been told that I was their wife. That is, Otto said I was his wife, Elías said I was his wife, and César said I was his wife. It was only after we had been at San Salvatore for months, and I had been commiserated over and cross-examined endlessly by the old ladies, that we realised what had happened. They were determined that I wasn't a day over twelve, and they even told me off for going out on my own. I think that they were so bored that they were glad to have anyone to talk to. But rather than accept what they must have seen as our gross immorality, they stuck to calling me 'the child' and occasionally, 'la poverina'. This last, especially, after Otto and Elías had left, I suppose because they thought that I had been abandoned by two of my husbands.

Some days, their little offerings of food were all we had to eat in the day. They would come round with a wing of grilled chicken or a toffee apple. and tap on the door, saying, 'We've only brought a very little, because you probably won't want it. Just a bite for la bambina.'

Although they rarely came past our first bare hall, the vecchiette would always catch hold of something, a book or rug, lamp or tin, and pouncing on it they would ask, 'Where did you find it? What did it cost?'

And we found that the only way in which we could repay their kindnesses was to invent places and prices for them, so that everything we had and wore could enter their mental catalogue.

It was in the second week of March that the winter seemed to reach its coldest point. The snow wasn't thicker, or the ice any harder, but the effects of not eating were wearing us down. We still went out every other day to collect cigarette ends for César, and we would return with our fingers stiffened and blue with cold, and our feet in a blaze of chilblains. We had just returned from one such expedition, and I was taking what was left of my shoes off, to warm my feet, when the electric fire literally exploded. There was a great thud on the floor from the people below. Every time there was any noise, the people below banged on the ceiling; one of them was crippled, and she used her crutch as a weapon of protest. A rush of flame was travelling along the wire, from the back of the fire itself, up the wall and along an ancient worm-eaten beam. Before either of us could move, the flat was on fire. After a moment of paralysis I turned the electricity off at the mains, and then we both stood helplessly watching the curls of flame and black smoke swallowing up one whole side of the room.

'I'll call the fire brigade,' I said.

'You can't,' César told me, 'the flat is illegally wired to the one below.'

'What shall we do then?' I asked, feeling suddenly useless. The entire building was made of wood. I envisaged four centuries going up in flames.

'Help me with these,' César gasped, shifting his pile of blankets into the fire. Between us we managed to put it out, but the walls were burnt, the room was full of fumes, and smoke was beginning to find its way through the chinks in the shutters. We could hear the neighbours gathering outside our door. It didn't take them long to start banging at it.

'Go away,' César said sharply.

'There's a fire,' they called.

'It's my wife,' César called angrily, 'she burnt the food again. She can't cook, she's useless. I'll kill her,' he shouted, spluttering with the fumes, and heaping curses on me. Then he turned to me and said: 'I've warned you Lisaveta about burning any more meals. You're going to get it now.'

Although the fire had lasted scarcely two minutes, the flat was thick with fumes. I looked at him in amazement. He was signalling to me with his hands, but I couldn't make out what he wanted through the smoke. 'Shall we call the fire brigade?' the neighbours clamoured eagerly from behind the door.

'No, no,' César choked, and then to me, 'Shut up crying. When we have fish, you burn the fish, when we have chops, you burn the chops.' He said all this in Italian, and with his mouth virtually up against the front door. I joined him there, and we proceeded to enact a fight entirely for the benefit of the neighbours, slapping the walls and screaming, while I sobbed and he cursed me. After some ten minutes, they dispersed, grunting approvingly. Nothing goes down better in an Italian tenement than a really good family row. For a heady week after our fire, we became the most popular couple in the block, but our fame was short-lived because someone threw his wife bodily through their first-floor window on the following Saturday and we had to surrender our limelight to them.

Chapter XVIII

César and I stayed on at San Salvatore after our fire, more out of stubbornness than anything else. It was bitterly cold, the two gas rings in the kitchen were our only form of heating, and these finally guttered to an end after four days of constant use, and we were left with nothing but an empty cylinder and the charred remains of our blankets. Some of these blankets had holes burnt in them, and some of them had just melted into glue-hard wedges in odd places. We tried to light a fire in our one open fireplace, but the smoke curled back on itself and into the room, adding to the sooty streaks that blackened every wall and shutter. It wasn't enough to see that the fire didn't draw, or to choke on the smoke; it wasn't until I had squeezed myself up the chimney shaft and poked around it with a brass pole, and found that it had been cemented over, that I was content to leave it alone.

It seemed hard to believe that the same San Salvatore that had been such a godsend in the summer should have become our undoing. I had heard Otto say often enough that you had no allies when you were down, and I began to see that this applied to places as well as people. I couldn't bring myself to tell my family the truth, or even any part of the truth about our plight. They knew that I was in Italy, they accepted that my honeymoon should last for years. I could imagine my mother defending me to outsiders, 'Why not, if she wants it?'

I had 'postponed' my academic plans to become a full-time

member of the idle rich. I never told her that César was penniless in Europe. It would have been too long a story, men who dressed and acted like César just weren't penniless, and I was too proud to tell her about my split with Serge. I refused to go back to London while I still needed help. Having spurned all their suggestions for my future, I had to make my own way work, and if it didn't, I would bear its failure on my own.

I knew that César was following the same policy, and that his family had no idea of his want. I wondered how long he would wait before he admitted that he needed money. Otto had told me, 'César will never ask his family for help. It's his money and his land sitting there, but he'll die rather than admit that he can't manage.'

During our last week in Bologna we went out less and less, just not bothering to bring back food, it wasn't worth getting cold for, there was no way of cooking it and no way of warming ourselves after coming in from the street. Clara still came, but most days we left her hammering on the far side of the door until the neighbours told her to go away. She was undeterred by this treatment, and returned time and again, regailing us with her woes from the landing.

'I'll break the door down,' she shouted, throwing herself against it in floods of tears. 'I know you're in there. César, Lisaveta, let me in.'

But we didn't care any more. It was cold, and the room was growing still. There was no glass in the windows, only shutters, and it was dark all day and all night, so we couldn't read. We lay in bed, under the stiff patchwork of burnt rags, and for the first few days, we talked. As the cold got worse, and the lavatory cistern froze, and the tap and the sink as well, we just lay under our barricade of blankets, and slept fitfully and listened to the muffled sounds of the building, and our own numb thoughts.

Once in a while, one of us would say, 'Are you still there?' and there would be a need to answer, despite being wedged together in the same bed.

Everything I thought or said began with 'If only'. If only the three hundred and forty thousand dollars had not been stopped at the bank in London, then we could have been warm, and able to read, and have chocolate cake, and all the gateaux from the cake shop on the corner, and even the full-length fox-fur coat I had seen in Paris. If only Clara would stop banging on the door, if only the gas stove worked, if only we weren't so lazy we could go to the cinema, if only the dog-ends didn't smell so foul. César would listen to so much and no more of my regrets and then come out with, 'If only you'd be quiet, I could get some sleep.' César always talked about 'getting some sleep', as though he hadn't had any for weeks.

I believed that we didn't go back to Milan and join the others, who were bound to be having more fun than we were, because of not wishing to admit defeat. Since we had insisted on staying on in Bologna, I thought that we were honour bound to do so, even if it entailed freezing to death. It was like staying in Italy instead of packing up and going home to London: once we sank below a certain level, we had to surface under our own steam. So I lay, swaddled by the converging draughts, and waited. But César's apathy was sheer obstinacy. His reactions to changes in his fate were so slow as to be imperceptible. He had a love of history almost unequalled by anything else, and he resisted any change that threatened to destroy the past. It was always the future that needed change for him, the past was untouchable, good or bad, it had a place in history. But the future needed remoulding to be made worthy for the place it would sometime take beside such heroes as Napoleon and Alexander the Great. So every move meant slow machinations churning relentlessly in his mind. Usually, whatever problem needed attention was already solved by the time César had finished thinking about it, sorted out its future historical implications, weighed it with all the weight of a crucial strategy. When this happened, when problems just went away or lapsed, César would shrug and say, 'Well, they weren't really problems then, were they.' He was never one for snap decisions in a crisis.

One morning, I woke up, my legs rigid with cold, and every joint in my feet and hands stiff and cramped, and I whispered,

'Are you there?' to César, and was horrified to find that he wasn't. I extricated my fur coat from the blankets and put it on, noticing that César's was gone. I had fallen asleep convinced that I was rigid from malnutrition, but having found myself alone, I staggered out of bed and was on my feet in no time. I had hardly the time to consider how angry I was at this desertion when César appeared, laden with everything from hot food to letters from home, and even a minute cylinder of Calor gas.

I was so hungry that I couldn't face the pizzas César had brought, so I left them to him, and ate my way steadily through a whole box of cakes and pastries and a litre of pear juice. When I was about halfway through, I asked him how he had acquired such wonders, but he wouldn't tell me.

'We're going to Milan today,' he announced.

I was glad. San Salvatore had become embarrassing, it indulged all my fantasies of death by wasting. I was glad that Otto hadn't seen me over the last few days, he would have said that I was on vocational training. He claimed I was determined to be a martyr.

'You're like the Last of the Just,' he said, 'suffering for the sins of others.'

We packed a few books and clothes, and locked up the flat, and took our leave of the vecchiette. César had brought them a potted cyclamen.

'E bella, guarda che bella,' they said in chorus as they so often did, and then they paused. I knew that they were waiting to ask their questions. It was always the same, as though they wanted to label the whole world.

And then it came, 'Where did you buy it? What did it cost?'

'We'll see you soon,' César said, ignoring their curiosity.

They shook their heads sadly and one of them said, 'You don't have to pretend. We have seen you all come and go, the one with the beard and the one with the limp, the one with the child and the one with the rings. They never come back again, and nor will you.'

I hoped they were wrong about this, since I had left half my belongings in the flat, and I had every intention of returning once the weather turned.

When we reached the station I said to César, 'I've forgotten my rings.'

'No you haven't,' he said, 'we ate them this morning', and he handed me the pawnbroker's ticket.

'Why didn't you pawn yours,' I said, noticing that he was still wearing them.

'I don't know if we'll be coming back,' he said calmly.

'I like that!'

'You've still got your icon,' César said. 'You know that's what you really care about.'

'You can't even begin to know what I care about,' I lied, but he was right. He had a way of being infuriatingly right, it was my icon that mattered most. I still thought it incumbent upon me to make a gesture about this possible loss of my rings, so I said, 'Give me my ticket, I don't want to sit with you in the train.'

'We haven't got any tickets,' César said.

'Why not?'

'We haven't got any money, remember.'

'Well, I'm not hitch-hiking,' I told him. I had a horror of hitch-hiking, not that I had ever done it, but it seemed like the Hanratty murder in slow motion to me.

'I wouldn't dream of hitch-hiking,' César said, 'we'll just jump off the train before it gets to the station.'

'I'm not jumping off any train,' I said, appalled at the mere thought of it.

César shrugged, and boarded a second-class wagon.

'Suit yourself,' he said, finding a seat.

The whistle blew, and the doors were slamming all along the line, and I jumped into César's compartment and sat down opposite him, feeling a kind of hatred.

By Modena, I had calmed down, and was reflecting that this was the second time I had thought that I hated him. By Reggio Emilia I had weighed up his infuriating calm against his many assets, and decided that there were worse faults than immutability. By Parma I had decided that I did love César best of the three. And all the way to Piacenza, across the River Taro and on through Lombardy, I wondered when exactly I had come to love any of them, and I thought that it must have happened at some time in Bologna. At Piacenza, I couldn't resist smiling at César, who looked immensely relieved and wanted to talk, but I wanted to watch the fields race past us and to feel the full force of the journey. It was the very first journey that I had made to be with someone and not just for the ride. Before we reached Lodi, César handed me my cameo ring with the silver Florentine setting.

'I kept this one back for you,' he said, 'I know Andrew brought it back from the war.'

He was human again for me, but it didn't last long.

'We'll have to jump off soon,' he said. 'It's quite easy.' He could see my reluctance, it was the face he didn't like, the ferried donkey. 'You don't have to,' he said, 'but they'll arrest you in Milan for defrauding the railways.'

We didn't actually have to jump, as such, it was just a long step down on to the tracks, when the train slowed to a standstill outside the signal boxes at Milan.

'How did you know the train would stop here?' I asked him, hitching my skirts up as we ran across the tracks.

'It always does,' he said.

No matter how awful Milan looked when we left it, there was always a brightness under the grime when we returned. The same thing applied to Paris, and Bologna, and all the other places where we stopped and stayed. No matter where, during our last days there, the very place would eat into us. The streets would become blanks, the shop windows full of forebodings, the people predatory. We would come to believe that everyone was following us, the police were always reaching for their guns, other cars aimed at us, even the food would become tasteless and the wine sour. And we would leave, glad already, because we were getting away. And then the new place would begin to pall, and we would return, and see all the things we'd missed from the time before. So Milan became the prima donna once again.

We rediscovered Il Duomo, feeling its slabs of white marble as though for the first time, and we found the model of it inside, scaled down to the size of a royal toy, complete with all its pinnacles. And we fed the pigeons at the foot of the monument in the Piazza del Duomo, and Otto climbed on to the horse of Victor Emmanuel II and declared himself Otto I, one night when he was drunk, and César told him that he would have to be Otto II, and Otto had pretended to cry, so loud that the carabinieri came, and we had to run, pursued by them down the cobbled backstreets, and it took us till dawn to meet up again.

Elías had found us a new place to stay in Milan. It was in the old quarter, near the Via Dante, and the trams rattled right past the windows. It was part of the mezzanine floor of a converted palace, and the panelled walls and floor-length shutters had an elegance that we were unused to. There was virtually no furniture, just beds and canvases and a pair of easels, and a makeshift kitchen, and nothing else.

'We can stay here until June,' Elías told us. He obviously wasn't volunteering any more information, and he didn't like being asked, so we never knew whose flat it was.

The weeks went by very quickly in Milan, sightseeing again, and visiting Tito, who was planning some new raid, and constantly offering to recruit us, and Athos, who was still managing to make ends meet, with cloths wrapped around his hands to ease his arthritis, and his rationed wine, and his sculptured glue. It was Elías who financed us during this period, with a seemingly endless trickle of ready cash from one of his many mysterious bank accounts. And it was Elías who was determined to leave Italy once the worst of the winter was over, and go to work in Sweden. Like Tito, he spent a good part of his time trying to recruit us. But César was adamant. He would rather fall into the hands of the Nazis than be the slave of some obscure Scandinavian brewery. In vain did Elías explain the advantages of spending the summer somewhere new. 'You don't have to work,' he said, 'you can just come along for the ride.'

'And live like some pimp off your earnings,' César said, 'not likely.'

'But we share our money here,' Elías argued.

'Yes, but we all pull our weight here. I don't mind work-ing,' César said, 'but it's got to be my way. I will not be anyone's porter.'

'Not much,' Otto mocked him, 'you'll pick up dog-ends on your hands and knees, but you won't take a job.'

'No!' César said, and his arms were crossed, and that was final.

Elías had grown so brash about 'shopping' in Standa that he used it as though he had an expense account there. He even asked the shop assistants to pass him things that were behind counters or out of his reach. He would ask for delicacies: did they have eels' livers, or Tiptree jams? He moved in and out unchallenged, carrying away our every necessity and my every whim.

'All you need is confidence,' he'd say. 'If you take my advice, don't ever shoplift,' he told me, 'you blush too much, and you just haven't got that natural flair. You might do for something big, but it often takes more sang-froid to go into little things. You see you have to go in like a big-timer, like the Aussie gang, and then nobody dares to stop you.'

Judging by his own success, I thought he must be right. There was nothing that Elías couldn't steal, however awk-ward or however large. If it took two people to take out a television set from a department store, then he would ask someone to help him, and wheel it out, so that César shouldn't be 'deprived'. If it was raining, he would dash into Standa, and reappear with four umbrellas, one for each of us. Elías flaunted danger for the fun of it, and we'd come to think he would never get caught. And then, one day in the middle of April, he was trapped in Standa.

He had been with Tito, and it was he who brought us the news.

'Couldn't he have run?' César asked.

'No,' Tito said, 'it was a trap from the start. He went down the escalator to the food store in the basement, but they were waiting for him. I had to buy a new plug, and I went upstairs to get it. The noise brought me back. It sounded as though the whole shop was screaming. Elías was downstairs, they'd stopped the escalator and cordoned off the food hall, there was a crowd of customers herded into one end, and Elías, with his clothes all torn, fighting like a madman. He had policemen on the floor, whole racks of food knocked down, and six men tackling him. I don't know who was the worse off physically, but they got him in the end.'

Nobody wanted to say anything, but we all had the same thought. All evening we kept a vigil, hardly daring to break the silence. We kept the lights off, and sat on the floor under the window, listening to the rumbling of the trams and hoping that Elías would somehow escape, knowing that he would most likely die. Prisoners had a way of falling to their deaths in Italy, it had happened already that year to a friend of Tito's. As the night progressed, I felt again like an outsider, the neighbour attending Elías's wake. We were all there, only the corpse was missing. I thought that we would probably never see his body again, his copper-coloured perfect body like a red-stone statue of Atahualpa the King.

Chapter XIX

We ran the risk of being arrested by sitting through the night in our flat, which was Elías's flat, and they must have known it, but they didn't seem to care. Tito was the first to move. He had wept, with his back against the shutters, and I had envied him his tears. I was too stunned even to cry. Theoretically, I had known that this could happen at any time. There had been occasional reminders; once, outside Oepli, the bookshop, a car had backfired like a gun, and thrown out a stone from the gutter which hit Otto in the leg, and I knew that when he moved, he did so believing that he was shot. And the greyness of César's face, reflected in the shop glass, was resigned grief. They were always ready for the one beside them to fall down dead, and ready for their own arrest. But they put it out of their minds, concentrating on their success. Every day was a success, for Elías, it was one more day of avoiding the warrant out for his death.

Tito rose to leave.

'It's just possible,' he said, 'that his cover will hold. If anyone is lucky, it's Elías.'

He squeezed César and Otto by the shoulder, picking his way over their legs as he went.

'I have friends with friends,' he said, 'I'll find out what I can.' The room was dark, and he turned the light on, by the door, and then thought better of it, and turned it off.

'You shouldn't be here, Otto,' he said. 'They were waiting

for him in Standa, they could be waiting outside this door.'

'No,' Otto said, 'they haven't found this yet. I think it would feel stranger than it does.'

'This is no time for voodoo,' César butted in. 'Tito's right. Why don't you go with him and see what you can find out.'

Otto didn't answer but he stood up and left the room. He returned with his shoulder bag and a box of papers. He seemed glad to be on the move. He turned the light on and pointed to the papers.

'Burn these,' he told me. I nodded but didn't move. 'Now!' he said, 'and then scatter the ashes. Then stay here with César. If you're gone when I return, I shall assume that you are arrested.' He kicked a socket in the skirting-board lightly, 'If anything happens put that switch down with your foot.' He was talking to me. César was lost in his thoughts, stone-faced on the floor. 'I'll be right back,' Otto added as a parting shot.

I began to rummage through the box of papers and then for something to burn them in. I wondered how long Otto would be. His 'right back' was no guide. They always said it, and I knew it bore no relation to time. I supposed that Tito would tell us if anything happened to him. He was more likely to be arrested than us. I wished that we had all gone together. It was always fatal to split up. It was what happened in horror films. Ghosts only came to you when you were alone. But César was immovable in a calamity. It took time for him to react. Once he decided on a course of action, he was a strategic genius, but while he decided, he was cataleptic. As I picked over our papers, I wondered if he could even see me.

I burnt all that we had except for clothes and books. I burnt Elías's photographs, especially those that contained people. Even unknown figures who happened to be standing in front of the Duomo had to burn. Those photographs that were of César and me, with no one else, not in Ticinese, not at Tito's, just César and me and famous places, were allowed to stay. I burnt the driving licences and permits, bank receipts and security cards. There were two passports. It seemed wrong to burn them, so I asked César. I had to shake him he was so dead to the world.

'What shall I do with these?'

'I don't know,' he said.

'But Otto told me to burn them.'

'Then burn them,' he said, 'why are you asking me?'

There was no one else to ask. The stuff didn't burn easily. Especially the photographs and the passports with their stiff covers. I used a flowerpot as an incinerator, but after each blaze there were still tell-tale bits left over. The remains of my pyre looked more incriminating than the originals, and I lost track of the time, mixing a black paste with pestle and mortar, and burning my own letters as fuel to the reluctant box of documents and papers.

Otto returned alone, he looked at my blackened hands and the heap of charred evidence with indulgent approval.

'Good,' he nodded and then left me to talk to César.

I was surprised to see how alert César had become, I had thought that he was sleeping.

'What news?' he asked, and then before Otto could say a word, 'Tell me first, is it good or bad?'

'I don't know yet but it might be good,' Otto told him, and then turning to me he said, 'You can listen if you want to,' which I was, and then to César again. 'They took him down to a local station and they beat the hell out of him and then a chap from the Immigrazione was called in. Elías was carrying his Peruvian papers today. He's been moved to a central interrogation block.'

'How do you know?' César asked.

'Tito's friend knows someone in reception.'

'Did they see him?' César asked.

'Yes. They said he looked like one man going in and another coming out, they've beaten the shape out of his face.'

'Thank God,' César said.

'What do you mean?' I asked him.

'There's a chance they won't recognise him.'

'But what about finger-prints?' I asked. Even his passports had finger-prints on them, they all did.

'Elías has never been taken before,' Otto told me, 'they can only identify him from photographs and if he talks.'

'What do you think?' César asked Otto.

'I hardly like to believe it,' Otto said, 'but he could just get done for shoplifting and the brawl at Standa. He could just get out.'

César took out a cigarette and lit it.

'Will Tito come back?' he asked.

'If he thinks it's safe, if not we're to meet him at the corner of the street where the tram stops, every two hours on the hour.'

'Has he got a friend in the new block?'

'Sort of, there's a cousin of that chap Marcello's. Tito says he's never been very forthcoming but he's O.K.' Here Otto turned to me and asked if I had finished burning the papers.

'Not really,' I said, and I knew I had said the wrong thing. He glared at me, there was only ever yes or no. I went back to the flowerpot, which was cracked.

'Use a saucepan,' Otto snapped.

When I came back from the mini-kitchen he and César were discussing something under their breath. As I drew near them, Otto stuffed two bundles hurriedly into his bag. I recognised them by their shape and bulk.

'Why the guns?'

'We might leave suddenly,' César said.

'Well, why hide the guns from me?' I asked indignantly.

'Are you good with one?' Otto demanded.

'No, but . . . '

'Then get on with what you are good at, and don't ask questions.'

I cleaned up all the pieces of ash and flushed them down the lavatory in three successive lots. A film of grease collected around the bowl and I set to cleaning it. Otto came in and stroked my hair.

'I know you don't really ask questions,' he said. His talking to me made me want to cry, so I stayed stooped over the lavatory bowl. 'Tito says they won't kill Elías here in Milan, unless he falls through a window. He's a foreigner, they don't need to account for his body, so they'll probably take him away. Tito's men are watching all the entrances to the interrogation block, they might try and snatch him.'

'It would be suicide,' I said.

'They'll want to do it. I never knew till tonight how popular

Elías is here. They want to try.'

'Thank you,' I said.

'Now do something for me,' Otto said, 'get out of those long clothes for once in your life. If you're coming with us, look like us at least.'

I cleaned the lavatory bowl, and then went and changed, borrowing clothes from all three of them, until I was dressed to my satisfaction. But we didn't go anywhere, we sat and waited in the empty flat. Otto came and went twice more during the night, but he brought no news with him of any kind. César slept, leaning against the wall, and then moved to his mattress.

'Elías knows how much I love him,' he said, 'but I can't stay awake any longer.' He covered himself and curled up. 'Call me if you need me.'

Tito arrived at seven in the morning, haggard and un-shaven. He brought a bag of fresh rolls with him.

'I have to go to work,' he said. He had an office job as a civil servant. 'I'll keep in touch with the boys and with you. I'm afraid there's still no news though.'

'None?' Otto said, looking hard at Tito's hands. Tito was fiddling with a scrap of paper from the bread bag.

'Well . . . a man from Interpol went in this morning, and . . . "the Apostle" was seen to go in.'

Even I had heard of this 'Apostle'. He was the scourge of Milan, the most ruthless interrogator since the S.S. left the city.

'There's just a chance he's been called in to someone else,' Tito added. 'We don't know it was for Elías.'

The others weren't listening any more. Tito could see that. He picked up his hat and scarf, and said good-bye.

'I have to go to work now.' He was reluctant to go though, he had something else to say. 'I . . . I could move the things from Ticinese,' he said quietly.

'It's all right,' Otto said, 'Elías won't talk.'

Tito looked relieved. 'I know myself,' he explained, 'with "the Apostle", I might talk; I'm sorry.'

'No,' Otto said again, 'Elías won't talk, but "the Apostle"

is an animal, if Elías doesn't pretend to talk, he might kill him for fun.'

'Elías isn't stupid,' César said. 'He'll say something; he knows.'

Tito returned at lunchtime.

'He is with "the Apostle",' he confirmed. 'But Marcello's cousin says they don't know who he is yet.'

After he left, I asked Otto how long it would take before they discovered that Elías's passport was false.

'But it isn't false,' he said.

'That's not his name though.'

'No, but it is somebody's name, someone who has never had a passport, and who has agreed to lie low for a year or two. It has Elías's photo and Elías's fingerprints, and all the right seals and signatures.'

I hadn't realised before that a false passport could be real.

'Do you mean that if Elías doesn't talk, and they don't recognise him, they really can't trace him?'

'That's right,' Otto said, without much hope, 'if that bastard leaves him alive, they could just call in the Peruvian Consul, and deport him.'

'What if the Consul recognises his accent?' I asked, doubtfully.

'Do you know, the man who shot Trotsky spoke a host of languages, and Elías is like that, he is just South American, from anywhere in the continent, always a stranger, always a native. He's been roaming since he was fourteen, and he has a brain like a computer.'

Tito returned in the evening with the news that 'the Apostle' had been seen to leave the building.

'They've contacted the Peruvian Embassy,' he said, 'the Vice-Consul will see him tomorrow. If he doesn't recognise him, and I don't think anyone could, the state his face must be in, they'll deport him.'

Tito took back his guns, wrapped in the same cloths they had been in the night before. 'You won't need these now,' he said, 'they're more of a liability than a help at the moment.'

We spent the evening together with some of Tito's 'men'. We didn't know most of them, but the events of the past twenty-four hours had drawn us suddenly close, with Elías as a common cause. As Elías's chance of escape grew, the air of reverence with which we had treated him in his absence slackened off. Everyone was struck by the absurdity of the situation. Here were the Milanese police holding an internationally wanted criminal, whom they were interrogating for information about far less significant people wanted for far smaller crimes, and they didn't know. The very police had punched his face to an unrecognisable pulp. If only they could see under the bruises, they would see the man whose poster was in every police file in Europe, whose photograph would be in the hands of every casual hit-man whom Interpol had ever hired: Elías who said, 'I'm not a gangster, I'm a soldier.' Elías who had turned a pogrom into a civil war. I had seen a C.I.A. photograph in Paris of Elías in action with a target dot on his chest in the angle between his arm and his machine gun. I found it impossible to believe that the police could really be so stupid as to catch him, question him, and still let him slip through their net.

Elías was finally taken from the central interrogation block on the following morning. We were kept closely informed by Marcello's cousin, who was kept informed by converging gossip and chance sightings of Elías himself. On one occasion he saw Elías being carried down a corridor. He was unconscious. Tito spared us the details, but we heard them later from Marcello's cousin, who described the scene with a wealth of gory Latin zest.

'He looked like a monster,' he said, 'a monster with no skin on his face.'

Elías was deported. He had a police escort to the Italian frontier. Ironically, they took the slow train to Simplon, the same that we had travelled on so many times together.

Our informant told us of the time of departure, and Tito drove us to the station. Elías was handcuffed to two uniformed guards. That was how we recognised him, and by the way he walked, because his face was swollen into a horrifying purple mess. They led him like a blind man, his eyes were so nearly closed.

'How will he manage when he arrives?' I asked.

'He'll manage,' Otto said.,

I was the only 'legal' person of the group, the only one who had nothing to lose by being seen with Elías.

'Follow them on to the train, and then say good-bye,' Otto told me, 'let him know that we know he's all right.'

As I stood in front of Elías, facing him and his armed escort on the train, I suddenly didn't know what to say. I might never see him again, he might still die, and I had never told him how much I loved him, missed him, wanted him to stay. I needed one perfect phrase to sum up all the worry and goodwill. The whistle blew, and the train was about to leave. The police guards pushed past me, pulling Elías by the wrists. It was now or never, and no single sentence would do.

'Good-bye,' I said to him. He could just see me through his one half-open eye.

'Geronimo!' he croaked, and followed the guard.

I bit my lip and jumped off the train. The others were waiting for me.

'What did he say?' they all asked together.

I told them, and they laughed, but I felt miserable and depressed.

'Say something then,' Otto nudged to cheer me up.

But I didn't have the heart to.

'I bet you're upset because you couldn't think of what to say on the train,' Otto whispered to me in the car.

I nodded, and we let the matter drop. It was the second time in a year that I had been lost for words. In Venice, leaning over one of the minor bridges, I had seen an old man walking towards me in a haze of white hair. He was bowed and seemed more ancient than is usually possible. Something about him forced me to stare, and I recognised him. As he drew nearer, I told César, 'That's Ezra Pound.'

'Speak to him,' César said, 'you'll never have the chance again.' I stepped into the via, and all my language left me, looking at an old man with a wind-tanned wrinkled skin, enjoying his walk.

'Speak to him,' César urged, 'now or never.'

But nothing I could say could mean as much to him as to say nothing and let him pass and enjoy his ninety-year-old walk through Venice undisturbed. Again, cramped in the back of Tito's ravaged Fiat Cinquecento, I felt cheated by the eloquence of silence.

Chapter XX

Otto always used to say that bad news came in threes, and he was often right. Although if you start living by numbers, it is easy enough to adjust things to fit them. Elías's arrest could be seen as good or bad luck. Bad luck to have been arrested, put on file, beaten up, deported, but good luck above all to have got away. Our trouble with the Lanzinis, on the other hand, though on a much smaller scale, was just bad luck and bad news and there was nothing good about it.

We left Milan, after Elías was gone. It didn't seem the same without him. Milan in a strange way had always been more his city. It was where he studied, and worked, and where his daughter lived, albeit briefly, since she returned to Germany with her mother, and we never saw her again. All the streets seemed to ring with his last word, 'Geronimo!', his battle cry copied from the Indian warriors in cowboy films, as he rattled over the cobbles, scattering pedestrians and showing off his skill behind a wheel.

Elías had a horror of keeping things. In that, he was the opposite to César and myself. We were both hoarders, keeping everything from bits of wood to bus tickets. But Elías liked to live surrounded by expensive things, and then just leave them, move on, and start again. Perhaps it was a built-in defence that enabled him to cut his strings and go with such apparent ease.

So after he left, we had all his belongings to deal with. His stereo equipment, and his camera, his books and his clothes. Otto picked out a pair of suede shoes, and a combat jacket, and two volumes of Liddell Hart.

'He'll want to keep these,' he said, 'he would have taken them with him, and maybe a couple of cameras.'

'What about the rest?' César asked, adding a pair of German binoculars to the pile.

'We may as well sell them,' Otto said.

'Does that seem right?' César asked rather uncomfortably.

'Well, under the circumstances, it seems more right than putting them on a raft and pushing them out in a blaze of flames into the Adriatic,' Otto told him. 'He isn't dead you know,' he said primly, 'I'm not a turkey vulture.'

'I suppose so,' César agreed reluctantly. But he kept back a few of Elías's things to satisfy his own sense of ritual.

It was a fair assumption that everything Elías had was illegally gained, so we didn't risk pawning it, or even selling it on the open market. Instead we took refuge in one of the many disreputable dealers who were only too happy to lay their hands on a stack of high-quality equipment. We didn't get even a quarter of what the goods were worth, but after our transaction, we had enough money to go to a trattoria, and to buy tickets for Florence that allowed us to loop back to Bologna.

'Why Florence?' I wondered.

'You can't come to Italy and not see Florence,' Otto said. 'And it'll take a couple of days to sort out the wiring at San Salvatore. I've found someone who will put us back on mains electricity again.'

Our train stopped at Bologna before going on to Florence, and César said that he was tempted just to get out and go home to San Salvatore. Otto and I wanted to go on.

'I'll get seasick if I go,' César warned us.

'But it's inland.'

'I don't care, I tell you I'll get seasick if I go.'

We arrived in Florence through a haze of ill-will. I had a list of places I wanted to visit, and which I insisted on seeing, despite César's miserable mood. I knew that he wanted to get back to Bologna before the end of the year. It was 27th April, and one end of the year for César was always his own birthday, which was 29th April. He pretended not to notice his birthdays, but secretly, he set himself targets to be completed before them, arbitrary goals, like the crossing of paving lines in a given time. And now he had some ritual need not to be sightseeing at the beginning of his thirty-seventh year.

Each year ended several times within its usual span for César: there was the New Year itself, his birthday, the 18th of August, the day of his father's death fourteen years before, and the day that his uncle was buried and the funeral that he was forced to miss. On all these days, and on the ones leading up to them, César would be unapproachably gloomy. And so he was in Florence, although he refused to admit the cause of this gloom, which came to him like an annual miscarriage of his ambition.

We visited as many palaces as we had time for, before César insisted on our return. It was late and dark, and it seemed absurd not to stay in Florence for a couple of days. But César's need to leave was stronger than our curiosity, and we gave way. It was too dark to see anything from the train, only the names of stations as we came to them and left them behind, Firenze, Prato, Pistoia. I slept through the lull of the wheels, with my head resting on Otto's shoulder, since César always liked to sit alone.

We could hardly open the door of San Salvatore, there were so many letters slipped underneath it. We lit a candle and went to bed, sharing for warmth.

'Who do you think all those letters are from?' I asked Otto before we went to sleep.

'It looks like our fan club,' he said.

'Who are they?'

'There's only one,' he said, 'Clara Lanzini.'

'How do you know it's her?' I asked.

'She's got the worst handwriting this side of the Alps,' he said, 'I'd know it anywhere.'

'If you don't let me get some sleep . . . ' César threatened.

Next morning, César was already awake when I woke, and

sorting through the pile of mail with Otto. There were twenty-two messages from Clara herself, written in spidery grey ink, and two long manilla envelopes as well. These last were from the Lanzinis' solicitor, and they constituted a preliminary summons to César and myself for what they called the 'corruption of minors'. Otto was, among other things, a lawyer himself.

'Just ignore them,' he said, 'they're off their heads if they think they can prosecute either of you. Elías is one thing; but Lisaveta is a minor herself.'

At that hour, before breakfast, with the window shutters wide open to the morning frost to let in light, the whole business seemed like a lot of nonsense, and we put all the letters in a Saratoga trunk full of miscellaneous junk, and made ready to repair the damage to the flat. By the 1st of May we were armed with paraffin heaters, oil lamps and candles, and a good supply of basic food which I insisted on buying, despite the protests of both the others who dismissed my forethought as 'boring'. Once the flat was warmer, instead of staying in and enjoying our newly acquired comfort, we spent more and more time on the street. We watched the May Day marches from the steps of the Cathedral, and we watched an itinerant puppeteer perform to a handful of frozen children who heckled him to a standstill and then went away, and Otto persuaded him to do the show again, to the three of us, alone in a cobbled courtyard with hailstones settling in our hair. And after a young student threw herself from the Torre Garisenda, we were there, with the crowd, cordoned off from the covered blanket that looked too flat to have a real person underneath it. We were with all the fat old ladies who were shaking their heads over the suicide. 'What a pity, what a pity,' coming from all sides. But only a few had any pity for the dead girl. The Bolognese were braver than some of their compatriots; harder, they didn't sympathise with 'the easy way out'. And it was easy to fall from the leaning towers, in fact, it was difficult not to. And they had no belief in the frailer sex, they had had women teachers since the fourteenth century. But they mourned the fate of the towers themselves.

Pisa's was one of the seven wonders of the world, while

their two were forgotten and ignored. Remembered only by themselves, and celebrated only on these rare occasions, when someone honoured the city by flinging themselves down. And then they all joined in that chorus of 'what a pity'. What a pity that the world didn't recognise their leaning towers, the learning and the beauty of their city.

Clara Lanzini came, inevitably, but Otto ordered her out of the house.

After she had gone, he said, 'It's for the best if she just doesn't come again.'

'How can you stop her?' César asked.

'You just have to be firm,' Otto said, 'like me. She won't bother us any more now.'

To César's and my astonishment, she really didn't come the next day, but on the day after, she arrived, suitcase in hand.

'We're drifting apart,' she announced, 'I've left home, and I'm staying here. It's the only way,' she said.

Otto was furious, César was speechless, I don't know whether with anger or surprise.

'Look here,' Otto told her, steering her bodily in the direction of the door. 'We can't use any groupies . . .' He used the word groupies in English.

'Any what?' Clara asked.

'Any groupies,' Otto repeated, more hesitantly, and obviously wondering if he had got it right.

'What do you mean?' Clara asked, quite thrown off balance by this new word.

'You are lowering the standard of life,' Otto explained. 'We would have liked you, we all do like you, in theory, but I am up to here,' he shouted, drawing his finger across his forehead abruptly. 'We are not Elías, and Elías is not God,' he said, holding the door open for her.

Otto was never at his best before breakfast, never at his best when he was hungover, and he had a horror of being manipulated. He was, that morning, unusually hard on Clara, but I am bound to say that no other form of treatment had managed to relieve us of what amounted to her persecution. On the other hand, Clara had a way of giving in to hysteria: sometimes, she positively encouraged it. At her home, I had seen here more than once kicking on the floor in fits of screaming. So it didn't really come as a surprise when she greeted Otto's outburst by a series of piercingly sharp yelps. Once in her stride, she quickened these into measured screams that came in a perfect staccato that made the entire building vibrate.

The two old ladies from across the landing were the first to arrive on the scene, dragging a reluctant and barking Chapolino behind them. They looked at us, as we stood helplessly in our hall, and at Clara, standing on the landing with her hands on her hips, increasing the volume of her protest as the audience around her grew. I had no idea that we had so many neighbours. They seemed to come out of the woodwork. San Salvatore was a lonely building, with never more than an undertow of gossip, and only the rarest of visitors to the upper floors, and yet, there they were, crowding the stairs as they piled on to our landing.

'Che cosa? Che c'è? Che cosa?'

Everyone wanted to know what was happening, and even more, they wanted to know what had happened. Clara was unstoppable. I could see Otto toying with the idea of just closing the door, but there were more feet over the threshold than he could really deal with, so he waited with the others to hear Clara's story. She ceased screaming as abruptly as she had started. She refused to answer the clamour of questions, dealing with none specifically. But she picked up her music case, and pushed her way downstairs, saying only: 'They have done this to me. They have kept me apart from the man I love, and they are breaking my heart.'

A loud wave of commiserating 'ah's followed her downstairs, and Clara slammed the door to the street with the final bang of the prima donna.

'Poverina,' the neighbours murmured, even the vecchiette joined in. I looked at them reprovingly, I was the poverina. They caught my eÿe, and I detected a glimmer of loyalty, but the others were set against us. I thought Otto was going to make a speech. He was a powerful orator when he chose, and I had heard that he could sway a hostile crowd of thousands. But he just looked at the faces glaring up at us and turned to

César and said: 'Have you noticed, there's a kind of law of gravity about people? And we three are definitely going down.' He shook his day-old *Corriere della Sera*, and I could see that he was smiling behind it. It was a grim, mirthless smile, such as I had sometimes noticed during moments of stress or disbelief.

'Deal with them, Veta,' he told me.

I was determined to have nothing to do with the gang of irate ladies in front of me, but Otto said, 'Be an angel, Lisa, I think I am allergic to the whole lot of them.' He smiled, bowing a little towards the crowd, who were puzzled by his Spanish, and had stopped talking for a moment. I stepped out on to the landing, and Otto, like a good friend, slammed the door behind me, leaving me in the midst of the mob. I succumbed to my natural reaction and burst into tears.

It was the two vecchiette who helped me out, putting words and reasons into my mouth.

'She's only a child herself,' they explained to the others. 'I think that hussy has been tampering with her husband.'

'Which one is her husband?' the others demanded. Here, I broke into vociferous wails, thinking that if it had worked for Clara why shouldn't it work for me, and at the same time, saving the two loyal old ladies from the embarrassment of saying that they still didn't know which one was my husband.

'What was all that about?' César asked, when it was all over.

'It's summer in the air,' Otto said. 'I haven't got the strength to see Clara through her neurosis,' he added, 'I think we should all make tracks. We could go to Sweden and make some money, and get away from all this hysteria.'

But César didn't want to go, he couldn't bear to leave the route that stretched approximately from London to Milan, and I didn't want to return to London in our present state, and César said that he would rather die than live in Paris, and Milan was full of the lack of Elías, so we couldn't agree.

Finally, Otto went on his own, tearful at the last moment, torn between the two halves of our group. Elías sent daily cables from Strasbourg, urging us to join him on a venture into Scandinavia. But in some things, César was unerringly firm, and this was one of them. He seemed to need Italy, with all its upheavals, he seemed to need to keep to one route, to move only along one line with Milan at its core. Otto asked the vecchiette to look after us.

It was summer again, but early enough to enjoy the heat, and soon enough after the winter to remember the cold.

The two old ladies were very sweet to us, and they interpreted looking after us as keeping us amused. This they did by bringing daily piles of old court magazines, which they left outside our door. Each evening they came to collect them, and we would spend an hour or so, discussing the exploits of Princess Alexandra, or Queen Sofia and her black sheep brother-in-law, Jaime, and a scandal in the Spanish court about a certain Don César, whom they always mentioned as 'Cesare-like-you'. And they approved of certain matches, and compared one wedding to another, recording the appropriateness of the choice of flowers, or lack of sufficient pages. They knew about every scandal that had ever been recorded from every royal court in Europe. They had an endless stock of magazines that covered two decades, and ended abruptly in 1966. I never had the courage to ask why they ended then, but I gathered that their third sister had died in that year.

They kept all their magazines in a series of metal trunks on the landing, under the crook of the attic stairs. And they used to sit in a half-circle around these trunks, with always an empty chair for their dead sister, and one for the son of one of them who never came, and they would read through the magazines, up one pile and down the next, recycling them, year after year, until the pages became frayed and the print faded in their lower corners.

Through May and June and July, César and I took a crash course in court etiquette, learning of every royal birth, death and murmur that occurred between 1949 and 1966. We even found ourselves discussing these affairs on our own. Why did the crown prince of Greece marry as he did, and not one of the other royal princesses. Why had one married a commoner, while another had refused to. Why did the Grand Duchess deny any knowledge of her niece. We even spent hours wondering in what order the different royal families would stand if they were all to be gathered together.

I don't know if the summer of 1972 was really any cooler than its predecessor, or whether we had just grown more able to withstand the heat, but we managed to get through the hottest months with far more elegance and ease than we had the year before. We still slept through most of the days, although sometimes we joined the vecchiette in their silent vigil in the half-light of the landing, filling the two empty chairs that they dragged out each morning, and put away each night. And we still slept shrouded by our sheets while hordes of mosquitoes ravaged our skins, chewing and biting with the same ravenous frenzy. But we had learnt to expect less in the way of food, money and post, and the flat seemed to run itself with a kind of monastic order that maintained itself and carried us along with it. We no longer even tried to fight the heat, but accepted that it was inevitable, and when we exchanged 'Fa caldo's with our neighbours it was without our former mutiny. Just as the wind sweeps over the county of Norfolk, unstopped from the Urals, and no one tries to change it or complain, the hot air blew directly from the Sahara to Bologna, and no one tried to deny its force.

Chapter XXI

The ritual of our second summer in Bologna grew until it was second only to the ritual of the two old ladies who lived across the landing of San Salvatore. And their patterns were so set, that when one of them fell on the stairs, twisted in Chapolino's lead, and sprained her ankle, the other did not change her routine and take her sister's turn on the rota of daily walks. And Chapolino was left to pine on alternate days with his sad spaniel eyes. Chapolino's walks consisted of being escorted downstairs, and being allowed out on his own in the desultory street for just enough time to relieve himself. This was followed by a run, which was always the same run, climbing back to the top floor where he lived.

The two elderly sisters were firm in their views of what a dog needed and what a dog didn't, and they were convinced that Chapolino was content to climb the stairs and scarcely ever see fresh air. He merely shared their own cloistered lives. Their shopping was brought to them, and their laundry was left in the lobby, and their only friends were those who came to see them on their landing. At various times over our stay, César had offered to take Chapolino for a proper walk. But the two sisters regarded this as an improper suggestion. Chapolino was as shielded from life as they were themselves, and they deemed no one else reliable enough to chaperone him appropriately through the town, which they regarded as some kind of pit of depravity. I suspected that their last foray into its streets could have been in March 1966, the date of their most recent court circular.

César had asked them if they would like a regular order for one or other of these magazines, but they had said 'No,' in shocked tones, 'someone might read them.' As though they were intended for their eyes only, and for the eyes of an initiated few. When César offered to bring them some more recent news of the crown princes, they declined.

'O no, we don't have the influence we used to,' they explained, 'it's a long time since we retired.'

I hadn't the heart to ask them from what, I knew that they believed that they were the bastion of the city, and that one day, when the whole town had worn itself out, they would remain, like the survivors of some nuclear holocaust, untouched on their landing, where life itself was unreal. They treated themselves like a museum in formation. Every item in their flat had a place that was sacred to it, and things were never shifted except in certain prearranged lanes, and only the chairs were really ever moved, with their tooled leather, taken in and out, religiously, and two extra ones for the two missing persons. Everything in their flat was labelled, like the rooms of Queen Victoria, and the luggage tags with their perfect italics hung from thin string everywhere. There was grandmamma's sewing box from Vienna, 'pantry stool', 'carving knife', 'Jenny Lind's cage', and so on. Jenny Lind was their canary who lived under a cloth in the kitchen, and who seemed to like the light as little as her mistresses.

The more of their magazines that we read, the closer we became to them. They invited us in to see their life's work of cataloguing. Everything they had ever had was listed and labelled, and there was an overwhelming smell of mothballs from every corner. César and I were rivalling their former status as advisers to the royal courts of Europe. Sitting on the airless landing, we discussed the comings and goings of the different palaces with more and more fluency. We were finally speaking their language. Before, we had exchanged words, but apart from César offering them some sugar, we were in a modern world that bore no relation to theirs. Now, we were drifting back into their past, and they ushered us into it with a friendliness hitherto unknown.

One evening in June, after we had weighed the merits of the younger English princes' schooling, the two sisters produced a bunch of keys, and asked us rather shyly if we would like to see what they kept in their loft. It had never occurred to us to think about the loft, but we said we would love to, envisaging that yet more court circulars would appear, piled high, from the turn of the century to the war. However, the worm-eaten ladder and the plain battened trap-door held back a long low room packed full of treasures of every kind.

'They are all mamma's things,' the elder of the sisters said proudly.

There were rolls of Persian carpets, immaculate in their asymmetry, with their flaws woven in, because only Allah is perfect, and there were carved and gilded overmantels stacked one on top of the other. There were pier tables and candlesticks, chandeliers and rows of boxed decanters. And around the low walls, behind the legs of the chairs and tables, and a dismembered harpsichord, there were framed and unframed paintings, portraits and landscapes with the occasional streak where the sun had faded a stripe into their canvas. Everything in this loft went under the one label of 'mamma's things'. Who 'mamma' had been, and how, why and where she had owned such wealth, we never asked. It was enough merely to sleep under such a treasure trove, and to see the pleasure on the two sisters' faces when they asked us, as they did, daily from then on: 'Come vi pare? What do you think of it?' and for César to go into raptures of appreciation.

One day I asked him if he or any of the others would ever steal the old ladies' things.

'Of course not,' he said, deeply shocked.

I was relieved but puzzled. Why should Alexander Borgia's tomb be fair game and the vecchiette's attic not?

'Why not?' I asked out of sheer curiosity.

'Because they mean something to those two old ladies,' César told me. He was silent for a while, and then he said, 'And if you so much as touch any of those things, Lisaveta, it'll be the last thing you do.'

He was pale with anticipated rage. I didn't point out the

ludicrousness of what he had said, I was just reassured that for once he had voiced my own puritanical qualms.

'I'm going round to them,' he said, and hurried to their door, as though fleeing from my unclean thoughts. He stopped in front of the vecchiette and produced a brand-new leather lead. 'I am going to take Chapolino for a walk,' he announced.

'E bello,' one of the sisters remarked, 'where did you buy it?'

'What did it cost?' her sister echoed.

'I said I'm taking Chapolino out,' César repeated.

'Where did you buy it?' one said dreamily.

'What did it cost?' the other added.

'Where did you buy it, what did it cost?' they repeated, spellbound like magpies about to dive. One of them tugged at its brass clasp, 'Dove l'hai incontrato, quanto ti costò?' They were implacable. César ignored them, pushing through to Chapolino on the floor at their feet. He clicked the lead over his collar and pulled him downstairs. For some reason, he had them in his power, he took their dog away, and they didn't even protest, they just insisted, 'Where did you find it?' trailing down the dry stairs after him.

Despite the heat, I followed him, intrigued by the feeling he evoked in others. I kept my distance some ten paces behind him, and listened. He was talking to Chapolino, bobbing his head as they went along. He was moving steadily with the built-in stagger of a train. He had acquired a sing-song railway rhythm in his voice as he spoke to the dog. 'Where-did-you-find-it, what-did-it-cost. Do-ve-l'hai-incontrato, quanto-ti cos-tò?' He was gathering speed, hurrying along a delighted Chapolino, through street after street of unprecedented freedom. Widows asleep in their doorways awoke to stare at him, but he was unawares, repeating the incessant questions of the two old ladies, the words that Chapolino knew best. He passed under a balcony, and a tall sunburnt woman leant over to watch him. A few moments later she appeared on the street, and followed César and the dog, and we made a slow procession led by César hammering out his tune, and Chapolino the cocker spaniel, whose lead he had dropped, but who followed him all the same, and the sunburnt woman who followed his every move, fascinated, and myself trailing behind like a surplus wagon unable to unhitch itself.

It was so hot that the heat throbbed through my temples like a drumbeat. César's voice carried along the empty arcades, bursting through the five dead hours of the siesta like a proclamation. All the shops were barred and the blinds drawn, the city was mourning the midday sun, while César marched through its deserted streets, mustering the city's strays as he went. Where did you find it? What did it cost? In the Piazza Vittorio Emanuele, we were joined by a gypsy boy and his dog, and a thin tired man took his place behind him outside the Palazzo della Podestà.

César's voice had grown louder now, and was reaching me clearly at my position in the rear, it was grinding through the terracotta, gathering children and beggars on its way. He paused momentarily beside the plaques commemorating the war dead, and took his breath. And then he seemed to remember where he was, and a faint hint of what he had been doing dawned on him, and he turned and blushed. There was quite a crowd waiting behind him. He looked at them in icy embarrassment, and then catching sight of me, he called, 'Veta, take this dog', as though Chapolino had caused his aberration, and as though Chapolino were a stranger to him. I took the offending creature, and we waited, César whistling slightly, and me looking at the war plaques, as though nothing had happened, for the crowd to disperse.

Eventually no one was left but the sunburnt lady who had come down from her balcony.

'I've always wanted to do that,' she said, introducing herself simply as Bianca, 'but I never dare let off steam in the city. I'm glad I'm not the only one here to be sick of business.' César was too embarrassed to say anything, and I could see he was wondering exactly what he had done, and how he had let off this steam that Bianca mentioned.

'I have a little place in the country,' she continued, 'you must both come and stay with me there.' So saying she thrust a card into César's limp hand, turned and was gone.

Chapolino was returned, the incident was never mentioned again, but two weeks later we visited Bianca, and accepted her offer to stay at her place in the country. It turned out to be near Ravenna, and in the end, Bianca didn't come with us, but entrusted us to a tall good-looking man of about fifty, whom she introduced as her husband, Gianni.

'Gianni will look after you,' she said, 'don't worry.'

César climbed into the car reluctantly, I could see him trying to decide whether to make a run for it, or just let it happen.

'If it's a kidnap,' he whispered, when our host and driver was out of earshot packing the boot, 'they'll kill us.'

'Why?' I asked.

'Because my mother would rather cut off her own hand with a breadknife than pay money to strangers.'

I failed to see the logic of these thoughts, and sat back, determined to enjoy the countryside, even if César did insist on composing his last moments in this gloomy way.

On the road to Ravenna, I began to miss Elías with an urgency hitherto unfelt. Elías was in love with speed, but this Gianni was a maniac behind the wheel. Like many Italians, he took his driving very personally. Any car that dared to overtake us was 'taught a lesson' that threw us from door to door like shuttlecocks in the back seat. Everywhere we passed through was obscured by a furry haze of sheer speed. Even César was shaken out of his reverie, and realised that our most immediate predicament was far more likely to end tragically than any kidnapping. But he still found time to say ominously, 'We're heading for the Abruzzi.'

The Abruzzi were the bogey-men of the south. Tito, Otto, Elías and César all believed the most astonishing things about them. And indeed they had a reputation for being wild, unruly, illiterate and bestial. But César and the others heaped the whole nation's blame on the heads of these unwitting herdsmen. Thus when Elías was arrested, it was because of the 'vindictive brawling' of the Abruzzi, and he escaped, thanks to their 'inherent stupidity'. Taxi-drivers who overcharged more than was decent were automatically 'Abruzzi' and all the cut-throats and gangsters, drunkards and brigands were, 'obviously Abruzzi'. Only d'Annunzio, the poet-orator, was redeemed from among his lost race, and that was only because, as Otto said, 'No one is perfect, so why should the Abruzzi distinguish themselves by being entirely bad.'

We bowled along at one hundred and eighty kilometres an hour screeching our brakes and taking even minor bends in the road on two wheels, while César watched us approaching the Abruzzi territory with increasing gloom. We were surprised, therefore, when long before we reached Ravenna, we turned off the main road, and terrorised a couple of small villages, and stopped, abruptly, outside a pair of wrought-iron gates with a pair of griffins bearing shields glowering down at us from the high gateposts. Gianni pressed a button and the gates opened electronically, and then he forced the car into one last spurt which ended on the front terrace of a massive Palladian mansion.

'I can't stay,' he announced, 'but I'll get you settled, and then leave you to it. But first, come and meet my father.'

A bowed old man had come to the door, and I was about to give him my hand, when César pulled me back.

'Wait,' he said.

The man came up to the car, said good morning and began to unpack the luggage. When he reached our battered Gladstone bag, Gianni said, 'Take the signori's luggage up to the barn.'

César gave me a significant nod, but I refused to be drawn into his paranoia. None the less, the sealing of the gates behind us had made me a little uneasy.

The entrance hall was cool, with a coolness that we hadn't felt all summer. It stretched back some fifty feet and was virtually empty. But the walls were hung with pictures in elaborately gilded frames and the ceilings had a painted frieze of rather hectic cherubim, and the floor was a beautiful pastel-coloured mosaic.

Another man, rather less ghostly and less bowed than the first, greeted us in the entrance hall, and showed us into a long dimly lit room to our left. This room also seemed empty at first, but as my eyes grew accustomed to the dark, I made out the figure of someone, sitting bolt upright in an enormous whicker wheelchair. Gianni stepped forward and, half-kneeling before this chair, he asked, 'Benedizione, padre.'

The old man in the chair neither moved nor spoke. He was wearing the dress uniform of the Italian army, and by the clusters of insignia, I judged that his rank had once been very high, but he himself was so worn and thin that he was swallowed by the uniform, the collar of which framed his old head unnaturally. Gianni introduced us to his father, and César put out his hand. 'He's blind,' Gianni told him.

César withdrew his hand and clicked his heels, uttering a few formal words of greeting. 'He's deaf,' Gianni told him.

The old man hadn't moved since we came into the room, and I wondered if he was dead as well. But I kept this to myself, and we took our leave from the silent figure, and backed into the main hall again.

'I thought you would feel more at your ease in the barn,' Gianni told us, 'I'll show you where it is.'

Even the barn seemed preferable to the ghostly household we had just left, so we followed Gianni up a winding path, and were amazed, once more, to be brought to the door of an eighteenth-century mansion.

'This is the barn,' Gianni said, waving his hand in the general direction of the house, with its terraced lawns, and its live peacocks, and its stone urns.

'Who lives in the pigsty?' César joked.

Gianni laughed. 'My great-great-grandfather was a stubborn man. He was paralysed, but he refused to die. His eldest son waited in vain to inherit the estates, but nothing happened, and still at fifty his father forced him to sleep in his suite of nurseries like a child and forbade him to marry until his own death. One day the son told his father, "Either you give me a house or I shall emigrate." But his father said, "Son, you are still a child, it is your place to play. You cannot have a house but you can have the barn to play in." And the son took the barn, and designed this house around it, which his father never saw since he could not move from his bed. His father lived for another eighteen years, and for all that time, his son perfected this house, and it has never been known as anything but "the barn".'

Gianni showed us around, and he led us to a fist of rooms that fanned off a back hallway, and introduced us to a stout lady called La Romana.

'La Romana will look after you,' he said, both to us and to her, and then left us admiring his wondrous barn to the screech of his car's brakes as he backfired away and out of earshot. The structure of the barn was still there, like a kernel inside the house. On the ground floor, it was a long flagged kitchen opening out into a rambling conservatory, while on the first floor, it was a library that ran for some eighty feet on one side, with a dining-room on the other. Higher up, there was a succession of bedrooms and sitting-rooms, with so many attics above that I lost track of them.

We learnt from La Romana that we were on the Azienda Santa Maria, a vast estate of vineyards and olive groves. César spent his first two weeks there saying, 'Pinch me, and tell me if it's real.'

And it was hard to believe that we had been let loose in this garden of Eden, with the added delights of eighteenth-century architecture, and all mod cons as well. After the infernal heat of San Salvatore in July, César said that the course of events was almost enough to make him believe in God.

Our hosts made two fleeting appearances during the first week, and were gone again, without our getting a proper chance to know or thank them. Every morning at exactly nine o'clock, La Romana came to our room, drew the curtains and told us that our breakfast was served. She always came, pen in hand, and asked us what we wanted to eat that day. César asked for nothing but pork, pork and more pork.

'But La Donna says you are to have whatever you ask for,' La Romana would complain.

'Then I want pork again,' César would insist.

La Romana couldn't understand him. 'Such a fine gentle-man,' she once confided to me about César, 'and wanting to eat peasant's food.'

I added to her lists more adventurous flourishes, taking

advantage of this opportunity to eat all the things I had craved and missed over the past year. I ordered chocolate and chocolates, asparagus (which she managed to find out of season) and artichokes, salmon and mushrooms, prawns and steak and every kind of fruit imaginable. La Romana would pretend to write these down, but I soon discovered that she couldn't write, and brought her paper entirely for show, remembering all we asked for in her head.

There was a round swimming-pool in the garden, with blue-tiled mosaics on the inside that always made the water blue, and around the edge, there were wedges of marble cut into the lawn. La Romana brought up half a crate of wine every day, a Sangiovese made on the Azienda, and half a bottle of olive oil, also home-pressed. César spent long hours in the swimming-pool, with bottles of wine in strategic positions around the edge, and he would swim from one side to the other, filling his glass from one bottle and then another, and occasionally taking a swig from the bottle of olive oil as well. This last he claimed was the best of all, but I couldn't bring myself to try it.

Although we explored the Azienda, taking occasional walks through its groves and orchards, we spent most of our time basking in the garden of the barn, or sitting in the long library. The whole house was like an antiques warehouse in the Portobello Road, with so much furniture that racks of table tops, games boards and stray pedestals were stacked and piled in every room and the tapestries and rugs were, in places, three-deep. The house had the air of a film set that was either coming or going – a crystallised elegance that was gathering dust.

On one of her brief visits Bianca told me that the house had been underfurnished when she married, and that she had 'picked up' a lot of the things in Paris just after the war. She didn't talk much, but she was very intense, and her eyes were eloquent for her. 'Some of the things we picked up were too battered,' she went on, 'but I still keep them in the attics, because I haven't the heart to throw them away. I've got a favourite tapestry like that, it's beautiful, but it's too ruined to use. Some one like you could probably fix it,' she said, 'but I haven't the patience.'

I felt a sudden urge to show my gratitude in some way, so I asked Bianca to have the tapestry brought down for me to repair, and we went together to Bologna to buy threads for the venture.

I regretted my offer almost as soon as I saw the piece; it was ten foot by eight and centuries of moth had played havoc with it.

'I'll just start it,' I said, rather ashamed, 'it would take years to finish.'

'It would take me years to begin it,' Bianca said.

Before she left that night she called me out into the garden and we walked around in silence for some twenty minutes. Then she cleared her throat and said, 'Has anyone ever warned you not to get too absorbed in César?' She pronounced it Cesare as all Italians do.

'Sometimes,' I told her defensively.

'Well, just let me say it again then, just not to leave it unsaid.'

We went back in and Bianca left for Bologna. Years later, I learned that she was a writer. At the time, it never occurred to me to ask who she was. I thought I knew; she was a woman who came down from her balcony, and followed César through the streets. And then she was the woman who gave us a month of happiness in her barn, and who said the same thing that Serge had said, warning me away from César as though he were some kind of virus disease.

So, for the last three weeks, I sat by the edge of the pool, or in the old bentwood rocker in the conservatory, or on one of the crumbling chaises-longues in the library, lugging around the heavy tapestry that I had begun to re-embroider. Working at it until the thick needles made my fingers bleed, working longer and longer hours, as though to prove to our half-known benefactress that I was still capable of patience, still able to turn her tattered cloth into a cloth of gold, even though I was 'absorbed' with César.

By halfway through our stay César accepted that it was real, and changed his tune to 'Otto will never believe this' every time he felt like saying something. As the month of August wore on, and neared its end, we began to feel embarrassed by the length of our stay. Neither Bianca nor her husband, nor the old man at the mansion whom we never saw again, nor any of the servants, made any mention of our leaving, but César decided that we should leave on the first of September, so as not to outstay our welcome. We had passed the anniversary of his father's death there, and he had taken me to a hill above the olive groves and he had sat there with me beside him all day, saying merely, 'My father would have liked to see that.'

I knew that his father had pioneered the planting of avocados in Venezuela, and I realised that the olive groves must have looked rather similar to his own estate in the Andes. His father had died of his sixth heart attack on 18th August 1958. After this fifteenth anniversary of his death, César changed his form of speech, and instead of saying, 'If we ever go to Venezuela', he said, 'When we go to Venezuela', and he began to take an interest in life again, in a way that he had not done before.

Chapter XXII

After over a month of blissful existence on the Azienda Santa Maria, we returned to Bologna full of good resolutions. I had even picked up the very slackened threads of my education, where I had left them, just before my illness in Milan. And both César and I spent several hours a day practising our various newly acquired languages. English was never among these for César. It had become part of his 'destiny' that he should not learn it. The most that he would concede would be to say 'later'.

The two old ladies and Chapolino were overjoyed at our return. They had saved up all the magazines we would have read had we remained, and they commented on the coronation of 1953, and on that whole summer season, as though we had just missed it. As we were about to leave them for the evening, the elder, who often spoke for them both, called after us, 'I didn't tell them anything.' César wheeled round, and returned to them as though tugged on Chapolino's lead.

'Who didn't you tell?' he asked, fiercely.

'The carabinieri,' she said, 'the police. They have been here, looking for you.'

César had moved into slow motion. He even spoke slowly, with a long pause before his next words.

'When did they come?'

'They came up during the coronation,' her sister reminded her.

'Yes,' she mused, 'October . . . that would be two weeks ago, hmm, about the middle of August.' Their dates were often vague, calculated by whatever magazine they were on, and then slotted into reality.

'What did they say?' César asked.

'They wanted to know where you were. It was easy enough not to tell them, we didn't know. And they just wanted to see you.'

'When you say "they", how many of them were there?'

'Lots,' the other sister threw in.

I had visions of an entire brigade goose-stepping up the crumbling stairway, shaking the woodworm dust out all around them.

'There was a man, and two carabinieri, and the signora Lanzini and two more.'

'How do you know it was the signora Lanzini?'

The two sisters blushed, and coughed half-heartedly.

'We just happened to see her when she came here to visit you.'

There wasn't much that your neighbours didn't 'just happen' to see about your life in Italy. They probably knew our meagre guest list inside out. They probably knew where we had been before we even learnt the name ourselves. These two sisters were seasoned watchers.

'Well, that's all right,' César reassured them.

'Are you sure?' they asked doubtfully.

We thought we were and smiled.

As it turned out, we were wrong. The campaign that the signora Lanzini led against us made Interpol's exertions look like a parish fête. Clara Lanzini herself seemed to have forgotten us as passionately as she had picked us up the summer before. And, infuriatingly, she took as little interest in her mother's wishes as she always did. So it was of no matter to her that her mother was persecuting us with positive relish, hounding us down with a vindictiveness of which I couldn't have believed her capable. She was determined to get us arrested, tried and convicted of 'corrupting minors'.

Despite what Otto had said on the subject, we were

informed by Bianca's lawyer that under Italian law it was quite possible to reach such a conviction, and that the maximum penalty was nineteen years. César received all these facts, and took them in, but refused to move. He sat all day in the window of San Salvatore, looking down in the small courtyard below, where an old man was carding wool, and from above, he looked as though he were sitting in a white fluffy cloud.

'I don't want to go either, César,' I told him, 'but I think we should.'

'No,' César insisted.

He wouldn't run away.

'When we leave Italy,' he said, 'it'll be because we want to, or because we have to. But the reason must be good.' I didn't like the thought of having to leave the place we had chosen to settle in solely on account of the signora Lanzini's farcical accusations. Clara and I were actually the same age, and far from wishing to pervert her ideas, we had long since wished for nothing but that she should leave us alone.

The signora Lanzini came with and without her lawyer. She collected statements from everyone in the building, which built up a damning picture of Clara's trials there. Only the two loyal vecchiette had a good word to say for us. The other neighbours all agreed that César and I were an unnatural couple, that we had had only one fight (the fire), which was evidence enough of our being perverted, that we boycotted the radio, that I wore long dresses, and then the story of Clara's hysteria on the stairs, repeated and inflated and distorted in fifteen different versions.

'If it's any consolation,' Bianca had said, 'if it came to court, I think Lisaveta would be acquitted.'

After that, whenever I urged César to leave, before things came to a head, he would say, 'You don't need to worry, Bianca said you'd go free.'

I hated watching César through that August; I didn't hate him, just his helplessness.

'What's the matter with you?' I'd taunt him. 'Do you want to go back to the cárcel?'

'I'm tired of running away,' he said, 'I'm tired of hiding, of strange noises on the stair, of people saying "boo" in the dark.' He didn't really want to talk about it, he never did, every word had to be probed out of him.

'If something is going to happen, let's see what it is. This way of living can turn a man into a coward. Why should I fear the Lanzinis? I don't fear death,' he said. 'Why should I fear them?'

'It isn't them,' I told him, for the umpteenth time, 'it's what they can do.'

'Don't be so childish, Veta,' he would say, 'think about it. What can they do?'

The sight of César sitting like a trapped fly between his chairback and the open window made me more uneasy than anything he had done before. It looked as though he was just watching the old man carding below, but he could also see the stairs, turning in front of him, and so he was watching for the return of the men who claimed they could arrest him when they wanted.

'There are times,' César said, 'when you just have to face the enemy.'

'Yes,' I would say angrily, 'but why bother when all the evidence is banked up against you like this. Clara's mother wants blood, she doesn't want justice, and in a strange country, you haven't a chance.'

'Maybe,' César would say, 'but a man has to live with himself, and I couldn't if I ran away from la signora Lanzini.'

'For goodness' sake,' I told him, 'can't you see the difference between being brave and being just plain stupid?'

'Is there a difference?'

One day, on my way to the poste restante, I met old Signor Annibale Lanzini in the street. He was going to walk past me without a flicker of recognition. But I spoke to him as he lowered his head and hurried his step.

'Buongiorno, Signor Annibale.'

'I'm sorry,' he said, waving his hands in a half-circle of eloquent gloom. 'I'm sorry. I don't want this,' he stretched his arms even higher, as though to indicate the falling in of the sky, 'but Luciana wants it. When she wants something, she gets it. She wants a new car, we get a new car,' he said shrugging helplessly, 'she wants a new flat, we get a new flat, she wants more money, I work my fingers to the bone. She gets everything she wants,' he said, smiling sadly, 'but she wants me to be young again, and I am an old man, so she is always so angry. I don't want it, I like you, César è un bravo ragazzo.' He was silent, tapping his polished shoe on the pavement. He obviously felt that he had said all he could, done all he could. Then he flushed, suddenly irritated by his guilt. 'Porca Madonna,' he said, 'it's not my fault.'

I smiled and we parted, but he wouldn't shake hands.

'Luciana has spied on me all her life. If I am seen talking to you, I can say that I was giving you a piece of my mind. But if I am seen shaking hands,' he raised his shoulders and rolled his eyes in horror, 'you understand,' he said apologetically and walked away.

The Lanzinis' lawyer was the kind of man that my mother would have described as not to be trusted with small children and furry animals. We had sought legal advice through Bianca and her husband, and we had been informed of our rights, and told that we were under no obligation to let this man into our house. However, he came frequently and stood on the stairs, staring into the window where César's statue sat staring out at him. Each time he came, he brought a file with him that was growing daily thicker. This, he informed us, was the file of accusations against us. It was all the evidence that he had unearthed. The whole process hung in suspension while he and the signora Lanzini insisted on knowing the whereabouts of Elías.

'Dov'è Elía'?' rang through the building.

The carabinieri returned. They had no record of 'this man Elía''. Every foreigner with a visa was recorded in the inspectorate.

'Who is Elía'?' they had demanded.

'I don't really know,' César answered, slowly.

'He lived here,' a caribinieri snapped, lowering his rifle threateningly near to César's arm.

César pushed the butt away.

'No,' he said, 'we live here, my wife and I.'

All their questions were stopped at the same source, Elías wasn't a person, it was a name, and it wasn't a proper name at that. There was no surname, no nothing. Clara had come up with one of his aliases, but it just confused matters more. In the end, they were bound to record that two men, the alias and one who called himself Elías, had disappeared. So the signora adjusted her statement, and let the entire brunt of the accusations fall on César and myself. But, now, principally on César, who was accused, among other things, of rape.

'It's more serious than you think,' Bianca told us, 'all they have to do is examine Clara, and if she's not a virgin, and she has been known to visit you, you are the guilty party.'

César still refused to stir.

'Let them come, if they dare,' he said.

But it was Tito who came, one night towards the end of September.

'We're moving,' he said, excitedly.

'Where to?' I asked.

César and Tito each gave me a long hard look. I had said the wrong thing again.

'When?' César asked. He had said the right thing, because Tito began to explain what he meant in a kind of conspiratorial whisper.

'I won't give you the details,' he said, rather grandly, 'but my group is moving into action in two days.'

Neither César nor I said anything, since we were a little unsure of what was expected of us. Tito waited, and then said, 'You both look very serious, what's the matter?'

'Nothing,' César lied, 'it's been a long summer.'

'We've got a bit of a programme worked out,' Tito said, gaining his second wind. 'We'll start off with a bank, and I hope you won't criticise my methods as much as you do some of my compatriots.' César protested. 'And then,' Tito continued, waving him aside, 'we're going down to Naples, then back to Rome and then we'll take cover for a few years.'

'What about your job?' César asked.

'I'm on compassionate leave,' Tito said, 'in America, Piscataway to be precise, with my aunt.'

'Why three banks?' César asked doubtfully.

'Because we can't handle one really big one,' Tito explained. 'If you three hadn't retired,' he said wistfully, 'we might have managed the whole thing better. But it's our first time here, so we're taking three. If it works,' he added, 'we'll have enough to finance ourselves and really *do* something.'

'Like another President Tito?' César asked.

'I wouldn't wish the presidency of Italy on my worst enemy,' Tito laughed, 'but we could get pretty near him.'

I made some tea, and we moved back to the window, and reopened it. It was very quiet with only the hum of the mosquitoes in the air, and the faint smell of raw lanolin wafting up from the well where the heap of uncarded wool was waiting. There was also a stronger smell of oil of citronella, which my mother had sent me to ward off the mosquitoes. It had a peculiar smothering effect. Oil of citronella is most commonly used as a cat repellent, to keep off unwelcome toms. Tito drank his tea and sniffed.

'What a strange smell,' he said.

'Yes, it's Lisaveta,' César said, 'it keeps off the insects.'

'I bet it does,' Tito agreed, 'it'd keep off a Panzer Division. With a smell like that, you could take over Europe.'

I was so used to the smell that I scarcely noticed it. I treated Tito's comments as grossly exaggerated, doused myself with another liberal sheen of the oil in question, and wondered why Tito had really come, and what he had really come to say.

The evening seemed to pass very slowly. Tito asked the odd question and César answered him, but Tito wanted to say something that he couldn't quite formulate, and he was uneasy about it, and that made us uneasy too.

'How's Elías?' he asked.

'He's fine,' César told him, 'he went to Strasbourg, and now he's in Scandinavia.'

'Scandinavia,' Tito said in surprise, but we knew he already knew, we'd told him ourselves before going into the country.

'Yes, he's working in Sweden with Otto, in a beer factory. Otto arrived at the beginning of August and he's still on the one hangover.'

'Beer's heavy going,' Tito nodded.

There was another long silence. The whole evening had been composed of long silences, and repeating news that we all knew about already, and commenting on the oil of citronella.

Tito lapsed from his native Italian into Spanish, which he spoke fluently with a Cuban accent.

'I'm not kidding you,' he said, 'I know, but what I really want to say is that we're all so fed up with doing nothing that we'd rather do something even if we bungle it.'

César nodded his head encouragingly. Tito was only a few years his junior, but he held César in a position of reverence.

'If we do get caught, someone might talk, or the police might trace things, put things together, find out about the equipment, find out that you lived there . . . '

Tito was talking very quickly, working up to a crescendo of reasons. But César interrupted him.

'We've got twenty-four hours to get out of this flat, right?'

Tito heaved a sigh of relief.

'Yes,' he said.

I didn't understand it, so I asked: 'Why?'

'Because Tito used to live here, briefly, and if he gets caught, the police will trace him to this address, and find us, and assume that we are connected with whatever our friend has done.'

'Don't you mind?' Tito asked guiltily.

'Of course we don't. We were thinking of going anyway, weren't we, Veta?' César accompanied his 'weren't we' with a tremendous kick on my shin. I winced, and he glared.

'Yes,' I said.

'You'd better be getting back,' César suggested, 'to your sick aunt in Piscataway.'

'Yes,' Tito said, 'I'll be back in Milan in three weeks if all goes well. I'll get in touch with you at the poste restante, here and through the usual code. If you don't hear from me, then don't bother, just go away. Meanwhile, lie low for three weeks, or whatever.'

'Don't worry,' César said. 'I know just where we'll go.'

Tito rose to leave. We wished him good luck and saw him to the door.

'Good luck with the play,' César said again.

'Look out for the reviews in the papers,' Tito said.

Instead of going straight down the stairs, Tito turned back and kissed us both. I kissed him an extra time, for having saved us from the wrath of the Lanzinis.

After he had left, César seemed quite jolly.

'What about all our things?' I said.

'We could take them, or leave them, or store them.' I had grown very fond of some of the things at San Salvatore, mostly books and bric-à-brac, but all full of memories and hard to leave.

'Let's sleep on it,' César suggested.

There were five metal trunks at San Salvatore, two of them covered in khaki canvas, and three not. These we filled with books, with one-half of one for our clothes and odds and ends. We arranged with the vecchiette to leave two of the trunks in their flat, and for three to remain on the landing, against the wall, and out of the way.

'Where are we going?' I asked César.

'We're not really,' he said, 'we've no money, and nowhere to go. We'll send a cable to Otto, and wait in Bologna till he replies.'

'How will you pay for the cable?'

'With your savings,' he said.

'And where will we sleep?'

'In the open air.'

It isn't easy to sleep in the open air in a city as well kept as Bologna. There was a diligence about its planning that was reflected in everything we did. No matter where you went the town council was watching you. We cabled to Otto, at his beer factory, and hoped that he would be sober enough to appreciate our need.

'What if he doesn't answer?' I asked.

'He will.'

'But what if he doesn't?'

'Then I'll write to my estate manager and have him cable some money.'

I was astonished, this was a measure to which César had never showed any signs of resorting, even in moments of dire need.

'Just like that?' I asked, snapping my fingers.

'Yes,' he said, 'so don't worry.'

But for four days Otto didn't reply, and we didn't cable the estate manager either. We just lived from hand to mouth, seeing the underbelly of the city. I thought that we should go back to Bianca and her husband, or stay with the vecchiette, or return to Milan. But César said, 'If things turn nasty, we don't want to involve any of them. All they've ever done is be kind to us. The least we can do is stay away from them all.'

To begin with, we pooled our ideas, sorting out the different places where we might be able to sleep. There were many to choose from; there were the churches, the station, the waiting-room there, the park, Neptune Square, leaning against the fountain, better in summer than in winter, but still possible. There was the cinema, and observer benches in the museums. We tried them all by a process of elimination, but we were moved on from each one. It was far more important to César to sleep than to eat or do anything else, while I would have happily stayed awake for all four nights, if only there had been the chance of a hot drink, and some food.

Trouble sits visibly on people's shoulders, like dandruff, and it announces itself like a leper's bell. The doorman at the cinema took one look at us and scuttled into his inner room, closing the heavy doors behind him. There was something down-trodden about us that he picked up on, and I could see that not only was he not going to let us in for free any more, but that he was making a mental note of all the times we had been in without paying, and he held a grudge for our debts. At the station, a vigilante checked tickets every ninety minutes.

'We're waiting for a train,' César said.

'Oh yes,' the vigilante nodded. 'Which train?'

César looked up at the board of announcements, he had very good eye-sight, and read, 'Bari.'

'You can't wait in the waiting-room,' the vigilante said, 'you'll have to sit out.'

There was an element of a crusade in the diligence with which the city officials made sure that everything ran smoothly. We were turned out of the station, and we took refuge in one of the gardens. But everywhere the act of sleeping was persecuted, like some kind of crime. Every time César's head lolled on to my shoulder, someone in uniform would come up and remonstrate, as though they had caught us chalking up graffiti on one of the immaculate burnt-red walls. The churches were mostly closed except for Mass, so we traipsed around the town until night fell and then took refuge on the Cathedral steps, swathed in our coats and propped against the stone pillars. We had sat there so many times before that there were some people we knew during the early evening, discussing politics and the price of bread, but it was no longer summer, and they drifted away.

At midnight, the clocks around the city began to toll. An old beggar gathered up his belongings, knotting them into a threadbare tablecloth.

'You can't stay here,' he said to us, as he stumbled down the steps.

'Why not,' César asked as pleasantly as he could after having been abruptly awoken.

'They won't let you,' the old man said ominously.

'Who are they?'

But the beggar was tired of us, and he just pursed his lips and shook his head and went away.

'We'll be lucky if we don't catch his fleas,' César said, rolling over and nuzzling back to sleep.

At one o'clock, a van drew up and a great hose was unreeled. We were alone on the steps, since the last of our companions, a boy with bad lungs, had looked up at the Cathedral clock and hurried away some ten minutes before. A team of men in helmets jumped down from the van.

'Uno, due, tre,' they shouted in chorus, and the great hose began to thrash over the steps, drenching every ledge and corner until there was no dry place to sit or hide.

At two o'clock the sick boy and the beggar and a couple of gypsies returned.

'I told you you couldn't stay there,' the beggar said triumphantly.

'You rotten swine,' César muttered under his breath. We were still squeezing out the water from our clothes.

'They come every night,' the sick boy said, 'this is the only place in the city where you can sit all night, so they come at one, and again at four, and hose down the vagrants.'

Despite the damp, and the discomfort, these steps did prove to be the only place to stay and we took up residence there, beside the sick boy's pitch. He said his name was Umberto Nobile.

'My mother called me after a famous general, she thought it would bring me luck. I'm glad she's dead,' he said, 'she wouldn't like to see me here, not with this cough.'

When you need to rest, it's surprising how few places there are where you can sit down for more than a few minutes without being disturbed. Even in the ladies' lavatory at the station, following Otto's example from Grenoble and sleeping on the lavatory seat, the fat attendant would come and bang on the door after ten minutes with a bad-tempered 'Time's up'.

'Why don't they leave us alone,' I grumbled to César.

'Because you're panicking,' he said kindly. 'Relax, and they will.' But I couldn't relax. Then a cheque came from Otto, cabled to the poste restante, and we took it to a bank and they said, 'That'll take three days to clear', and I began to enjoy the novelty of living on the street, and to see the advantages of our nothing-to-lose situation. Things could only get better. Even a prison cell would have four walls and a roof. But César told me, 'You're a fool. We'll all wind up some day dead or in the cárcel; why wish it on yourself? You're the only one of us who isn't trapped, can't you see that.'

I could see that there was no price on my head, and my name wasn't down on the blacklists that sit on the immigration desks of every airport. But the day had passed when I dared make César another ultimatum. I knew that I needed César, and the others. I needed all three of them just to get by. Whether it was really love, or how much went to each, or whether it was just force of habit, I didn't even want to know.

'We'll lie low,' César said, 'till the cheque is cleared, and then we'll go to Venice, and then Paris.'

'Why Venice?' I asked.

'You can't live in Italy, and not see Venice,' César explained.

'But I saw Venice last year,' I reminded him.

'This isn't a coach tour,' he said testily, 'most people would think Venice was worth seeing twice.'

Chapter XXIII

We went to Venice, armed with a guidebook and César's Gladstone bag fitted out with a week's supply of chocolate, clean socks, reading matter and such oddments as I could squeeze in between. For some reason César insisted on avoiding the Lido, and the main square, and gradually, everywhere else I suggested that we might begin our tour. We ended up drinking beer in a waterfront café by the harbour. After a couple of cans, César was sleepy, and he found himself a bench on that windy edge of the Adriatic with its skyline of factories on the far side. With his bag as a pillow, he prepared himself for a winter siesta.

'You have a sleep, too,' he suggested. But I preferred to find my way back to San Marco, and some of the other churches, and to walk through the narrow streets on my own. It rained, and it was cold, and it took me all afternoon to work my way back to César and the café and bench where I had left him. He seemed unusually glad to see me and apologised for having fallen asleep so soon.

'We'll have a fine time tomorrow,' he promised. But I had no time for tomorrows. I had felt all day like a new girl at school, a freak in the grey mist. The stares of the great city had hurt me as I explored it, like a crab on two legs, and I had no desire now to heal my raw underbelly. Venice had brought home to me my loneliness. Its bells had spelt my name, the corroded angels with their crumbling eyes and noses had

mirrored my face. Even the canals, with their passengers of
lovers who spoke to each other for whole minutes on end and
held hands, had brought a bitterness to the toll of my eighteen
years. I felt that I had wasted my life – Rimbaud was nineteen
when he finished – I was the wicked stepmother in *Snow
White*, with nothing left but to dance with rage and run away.
It was raining and it was cold, and I was in no mood for
dancing, so I would run away, take the first train to Paris and
not return.

I told César that I wanted to go, and he shrugged, and told
me kindly not to worry.

'What's one bad day?' he said. 'You have all of your life in
front of you.'

But for me, he was wrong, I had all of my life behind, with
the last remnants of it flapping on the tracks. I had heard many
a woman meet her middle age with the consoling thought that
'life begins at forty' but no one had ever warned me of the
bitterness with which old age begins at eighteen.

We went to Paris. And we looked every day for news of
Tito and his gang. There were seven robberies in the two
weeks following his visit, and two shootings in Rome, and a
host of kidnappings, hold-ups of security vans, failed attempts
at jewel thefts, and no details that could answer any of the
questions burning in our minds. At the end of two weeks, Tito
didn't contact us, so we could only assume that all was not
well. But his name didn't appear in the headlines, and there
wasn't even so much as a mention of him on the back pages of
the local press. So we followed his instructions and 'stayed
away'.

We stayed in Paris as long, as César said, as was humanly
possible. Otto had arranged to meet us there, but it came as no
surprise when day after day he didn't come.

'It's like making an evening appointment with a prostitute,'
César said, 'he'll always turn you over for a better offer.'

We stayed once again with Melina and Vitaliano in their
voodoo flat by the Bastille. Vitaliano's father had died, and he
was going home, to Venezuela. Melina, however, was
obliged to stay on. They had been on the point of divorce for

months, but now, on the eve of their separation, they had come together again, and buried their grievances. Vitaliano was waiting only for his ticket to arrive, and he talked about Venezuela all the time. It made César doubly restless, and he took out his spleen on the most despised of all his targets: the Parisians. There were few places that we could visit without running into trouble. At the Louvre he was nearly arrested for causing a disturbance. He had paid his three francs entry, and made a beeline for the Department of Greek Antiquities and stationed himself, arms akimbo, in front of the Venus de Milo, staying there, motionless, for three and a half hours. I came and went, through the rambling halls, and was finally driven back to him by the sheer quantity of things to see which was blinding my appreciation.

'Don't you want to see any of the paintings?' I asked.

'I can't come in a morning and see 200,000 of them,' he said, 'but I can see one. So if you don't mind, I'm seeing this Venus.' Little batteries of guided tours came and jostled him every half-hour or so, but he didn't move, ignoring the different languages as they drummed out the same lines over and over again. Then, quite suddenly, he dropped his arms and gasped, 'I can't breathe, they're all French in here, quickly,' and he dragged me out of the museum. Ten minutes later, he went back 'to finish the Venus' and was told that he would have to pay again. We didn't get back in, but I think the doorman will think twice before bothering to insult someone of César's size again.

'Why didn't you keep your ticket?' I asked him afterwards.

'I don't know.'

'What did you do with it?'

'I ate it.'

'Why?' I insisted.

'Since when did you join the Inquisition,' he said, leaving me to catch up with him or get lost, as he strode, silently angry, back to the flat at the Bastille.

We received two cables from Otto, one from Stockholm saying 'Arriving Orly 2nd October', and another, stamped Jönköping, with a cryptic 'Forgive me, mon général' and dated 10th October. My birthday had come and gone on 2nd

October, unnoticed by César who claimed that birthdays were meaningless, unless they were his own. And I had received a substantial cheque as a present from my mother. It had come, to avoid the currency embargoes, via Che Chouen in Morocco where one of my brothers-in-law was running a Red Cross clinic, and it was the first money I had received in my own right since my estrangement from Serge.

César immediately purloined a part of this money and cabled back to Otto at the poste restante in Jonköping, 'And I'm not God, you subservient swine'. There then followed a whole correspondence of telegrams which ate into my birthday money, and which traversed Europe in a twine of *non sequiturs*. We received his telegrams but I don't think he got any of ours. The last word we heard from him was a night cable from Göteborg with a single cryptic 'Avanti!' which César interpreted as meaning that we would meet up again in London.

'How do you know that London is forwards and not backwards?' I asked him.

'Because it is nearer to Southampton,' he said.

I failed to see any logic in this remark. 'What has Southampton to do with Otto?'

'Not Otto,' he said, 'us, we're going to Venezuela.'

This was the first time I had heard of any concrete plan, and I felt cheated and left out. I wondered how long they had known this. There must have been a series of letters of which I knew nothing. The letter from Caracas itself, clearing César to return, the inevitable discussions. I knew that the others were thinking of going to Chile, and I remembered one evening, some weeks before, when César had asked me, 'Where would you rather go, Veta, Chile or Venezuela?', I had chosen Chile, and now we were going to the other place, leaving the others.

We walked home in silence from the poste restante. Home was still beside the Bastille. César put his arm around my shoulder and squeezed me. I was so surprised that I forgot my grief, it was the first time that he had ever touched me in the street. He remembered himself a few seconds later, and let me go.

'Let's go tonight,' he said, and then confidentially, as

though telling me something I couldn't ever have guessed, 'I don't like Paris.'

The journey from Paris to Dunkirk was unusually quiet that night. Far quieter even than the empty benches of the Luxembourg had been on the rainy days when we had sat there, and watched the leaves fall and the puddles spread. Inside the train, the worn chequered plush of the seats merged into the extension of my own tartan dress faded by the last damp days spent in Bologna, and worn threadbare on the Cathedral steps. César's grey tweeds were also worn through, but he didn't care. 'You can wear rags so long as you wear them well,' he would say.

Our compartment was empty, and César seemed even more distant than usual, girdled by reading matter, laid out like a seat-belt. He had two lives of the 'Great Emperor', as he called Napoleon, on one side of him and the diaries of Columbus the admiral on the other, and in front of him lay a thin book in Italian, called *Lavorare Stanca*. César often carried this last as a kind of placard since the title was especially apt for a man of his idleness. In his more talkative moods, he would quiz me on all these books.

'Who betrayed the British in Morocco?'

'Pétain?'

'Who sailed with Columbus on his third voyage?'

'Briceño, the Bishop.'

'And where are the Briceños now?' he would ask.

And I would shrug, knowing that he wanted me to say 'all dead'.

I knew that there weren't many left, and that César himself was actually one of them, but in his fervour he would deny this kinship. 'I am a de Labastida,' he would say, as though that lineage excluded any other. César was often the first to tire of his quizzes, and he would doze, and then continue darting his questions like a nineteenth-century dominie.

'Who had a bath before every battle?'

'Napoleon.'

It was more reassurance than pleasure that César derived from these sessions, as though he was just checking to make sure that I had my facts and priorities aligned. I think the priorities came first, and I humoured him a little sometimes. However, in our dull compartment, I didn't want his guessing game, and I let him be, lulled by the engine and the movement of the wheels into alternate bursts of reading and sleeping. I looked across at him with a mixture of surprise and relief; after two years he was still the enigma who had put his foot in the door and sat down in the kitchen.

There were draughts coming through all the cracks in the windows and irregular blasts of hot air from the ventilators behind my feet. I would have liked to have read or slept like César, but I seemed to be caught in the cross-current of hot and cold air in a state of hyper-alertness, and the train was like a wake for the years that I was leaving behind me. After two years of drifting, someone had pulled the communication cord on our life, we would have to stop and start again. There was a canopy of sumptuousness in my grief, and I conspired to help everything make me sad. So the dust in the corner of the seats made me sad and the black grease on the grid. And the smeared looking-glass over my head, and the frayed mesh of the luggage rack and the broken blind on the door. And even the half-hearted graffiti pencilled over the blinds acquired sudden weight and menace.

This journey to Dunkirk seemed like my last journey, and I wanted it to be especially significant, like a last outing before an operation. César had dimmed our light and was sleeping now like a propped corpse in his corner, breathing heavily through his mouth as he did when he slept, on account, he claimed, of a malformed cartilage in his nose.

The train itself divided into vertebrae, linked shapes like planed coffins flick-tailing along the tracks, and the old lump in my throat had come to tell me that I would never return to this slow train. It was a familiar lump bringing a familiar bitter twist to my thoughts. It fed on whatever sad memories it could scrape together, it was the shrine of the martyr. It was splattered with the blood of my pet rat axed by our neighbours in Wimbledon in a fit of well-meant frenzy, and it was old Dr Tausig, refugee, fleeing the Germans and coming to land in the barren land of south London, feeding the five thousand with anti-depressants, until death eased the black bruises from under his eyes. And it was Veronica in Leningrad, with her hand-painted box that she gave to me because she had no heirs or family. She told me that after the cats and the dogs and the rats and the shoes had been eaten, they had all starved anyway in the siege, and only she was left with the Paliak box that should go to her daughter. And it was the newt that I had paid threepence for at school to take home and look after, and that had died in its glass jar outside my window, and sat on the ledge in the growing slime, dead for three months, unwitting lord of my guilt and fascination. The compartment was like a thin crate, and the crate was strapped over a mule, head-heavy at one end like a coffin, see-sawing in the wind, it was being dragged up a winding track up the low brush slopes of the Andes. Inside this makeshift coffin, tacked down with old gramophone needles instead of the usual nails, were César's words, and his *Lives of Napoleon*, and a pillow, and my five trunks of books and my long dresses, my letters from Serge, and then there was my Russian box, the dead aster from the statue of Tolstoy and as much as I could remember of my family, wrapped up in Elías's anorak and wedged between his two volumes of Liddell Hart. The mule lost his footing and the coffin began to slide, it clattered over the rocks, tore open and broke, falling to a halt. And then a voice screamed, 'Dunquerque!', and the train jolted back on the rebound of its brakes and then stopped and a slow slamming of doors came towards us, as the guard cleared all the carriages, and herded us on to the quay. César was half-asleep. He looked unspeakably haggard in the dawn light, ill and unshaven.

'You look awful,' he said.

We queued to get near the sea. Our luggage, the five metal trunks from San Salvatore, was travelling separately, and we had only a case and a Gladstone bag to carry. There weren't a lot of people waiting to board the ferry, but that didn't seem to make any difference to the waiting time. There were statutory delays. Both César and Otto were intrigued by queues.

'The world divides itself into those who queue and those

who clamour,' one of them had said.

'Are you going to sleep on the ferry?' César asked me.

'No, I think I'll drink lemon tea,' I said.

Amid the cardboard rolls and the cotton-wool bread, and the ham that literally dripped water from its swollen cells, and the polythene chips and the toasted-flannel fish, and the varying standards of both the French and British fare on the ships, the lemon tea was always good. And by elbowing relentlessly through the crowds to the outer restaurant, it was possible to secure a table for two, or more, with a clean starched cloth, for as much of the crossing as required. There was no view of the sea, and no blasts of cold wind, but a faintly barnacled smell drifted down, even to the lower decks, and it was the best way out of the scrummage.

We went on deck an hour before Dover, and stared down into the waves, leaning over the railings while the sea lolloped against the side of the ship and the spray and the savage north-easterly kept us gasping for breath. Then there was the usual excitement as the ferry drew near to the famous white cliffs. If Elías had been with us, he would have said, 'What is it that makes a pond so fascinating in a field, and land so amazing from the sea?'

It was his 'coming into Dover comment'; it was expected of him. Just as César would always say, 'Dunquerque!' with a sigh of admiration as we stepped on to the platform there. Once I had asked Elías, 'Why do you say the same thing over and over again?'

'It is a survey,' he said, 'like the Kinsey Report on sex; I want to see how long I can get away with it.'

'And how long can you?'

'Apparently, for ever, but I can only really calculate the time when I die,' he had smiled apologetically, and shrugged, 'Science is science.'

'Like Geronimo?' I continued, determined to get things straight.

'Yes, that's right.'

'What does it mean?'

'Geronimo? It doesn't really mean anything; it's just a battle cry. It could as easily be "shampoo" or "Pepsi Cola". I just prefer Geronimo.'

It was easy to miss Elías.

It took five days to settle back into the English language, and even longer to get used to the general change. For César, though, the switch was instantaneous. He had no sooner set foot on English soil than he adopted a new code of chivalry, more exacting and elegant than any he had held in Italy. He was again the perfect gentleman. He was the classic anglophile blind to all of England's misdemeanours and the passing of time.

We spent five days at my mother's flat, mostly eating and bathing in a very hot solution of coloured bath oils that made the water turn to the consistency of thin marmalade. Otto arrived noisily on the fifth day, laden with presents, and too drunk to find the door knocker. He banged and called at three in the morning until he was let in.

'Elías is coming,' he announced, and promptly fell asleep in an armchair in the sitting-room. We waited expectantly until half-past four, and then went back to bed ourselves.

Otto didn't come to until the following afternoon. He looked far from well, and his skin was quite alarmingly jaundiced. Unlike César, this time, he wasn't going to pretend that we hadn't been apart. He didn't want us to go.

'We've been together here for nearly three years now,' he reasoned, 'what difference can another year make to you?'

But César was adamant. 'I'd rather die,' was all he would say.

'But nobody is asking you to die, César, just to stay.' He paused. 'We've got money now,' he coaxed, 'we're going to Chile soon. South America. Isn't that where you want to go?'

'No,' César said flatly, 'I want to go home.'

'But we can't do that,' Otto said, 'and we could all stay together.'

'I don't ever want to leave you, Otto, you know that, but . . .'

'But but but,' Otto mocked and then stormed out of the room.

Elías arrived in his own time, and then we took a flat in a hotel in Evelyn Gardens in Chelsea, and continued our argument there for a full week. Otto and Elías wanted us to stay together, César wanted to go, and I wanted to stay with César and the others and not split up, and secretly, I still wanted to go to Chile too. César remained immovable. The others worked on me together and individually, trying to win me to their side, but before I could tackle César on their behalf, he volunteered another compromise.

'If you really don't want to go,' he said one night, 'we'll stay.'

I knew by now how much it meant to him, and his offer broke down all my opposition, I found my whole campaign collapsing into a simple, 'I'd really like to go', and I went to sleep feeling like a complete turncoat and the idiot that Otto always accused me of being, and I felt as though once again I had chosen the broken collar-stiffener as at Grenoble, and once again that I would have been given it anyway. Once I had thrown in my lot with César's, Otto and Elías gave in with a good grace and the arguing stopped. There would always be a moment in the day or night when Otto would contrive to be alone with me, and he would always try and warn me against the place I had chosen to go.

'It'll destroy you,' he said, 'I know where you're going, and believe me, it's all right for César, he is part of it, but it's feudal and it's evil, and they will never accept you.'

I told him that I would manage, and he would say sadly, 'You don't understand.'

Perhaps I didn't, but I began to look at this remote estate in the Andes with new eyes; in the life of cloistered isolation to which I had imagined I was being taken, I discovered an intriguing undertow of violence. It wasn't just a place where sugar grew, it was a place where people were hounded to their deaths, a place where César with his sleepy charm was said to be a tyrant, a feudal overlord, it was a place of insidious evil. All Otto succeeded in doing with his well-meant advice was to show me the relative boredom of going to Chile and having a house there by the sea. I began to feel that I was now going not just to the estates that already fascinated me in themselves, but to a generally interesting and sinister place, somewhere with a challenge.

Chapter XXIV

Elías and Otto went on what they called a business trip to Lyon, and we saw them on to the boat train at Charing Cross. Then César and I moved back into my mother's flat in Clapham to spend some time with her now that our journey was sure. César was once again waiting for a letter. This time it would contain our sea passage to La Guaira in Venezuela. We waited and waited, and nothing came. The phone would often ring at two or three in the morning, and César would stagger down the long hall to answer it, and talk for anything up to half an hour in the most emphatic monosyllables. On the morning after each of these protracted trans-Atlantic calls, César would announce, 'The tickets will be here any day now.'

For a fortnight I waited for that 'any day now' and savoured my every movement as a last before sailing to this strange new place in Venezuela. But gradually, it dawned on me that these tickets could be as mythical as César's other letters, they might never arrive.

The others had returned with yet another Mercedes, even more brilliantly silver-grey than the last that Elías had so proudly driven home from Sweden. On his return he gave this earlier model to César and me, tossing us the keys with a nonchalant, 'Here', and then, 'Don't get stopped, though, I didn't exactly buy it from a showroom.' With the coming of this new car to Clapham, César finally reached those heights in my mother's mind from where he could do no wrong. Elías had often driven her in it to the remand home where she worked, and she had enjoyed reverting back into something of her old style as the guarded gates opened to let her through. And she had, occasionally, hinted to César how wonderful it would be to have such a car always. Now she took the arrival of Elías's 'old' Mercedes as yet another sign of César's chivalry. We didn't, of course, tell her that it was stolen, and even if we had, I don't think that she would have believed it.

We battled along with the car for five dreadful days. César had never driven in England before, and had, therefore, never had to deal with a left-hand drive. He knew none of the road signs and his knowledge of the streets of London was negligible. I already knew from the way Elías drove that cutting across roundabouts and driving on pavements and doing U-turns wherever you pleased were probably second-nature to the average Venezuelan. I think that César might still have managed if he hadn't insisted on having me as his co-pilot. He refused to believe that I really didn't know my way around London, and that I didn't understand the highway code. For the first three days he was constantly saying, 'What do I do now?' or, 'What does that mean?'

Perhaps it didn't actually happen more times than I can count on the fingers of one hand, but my memory of that car is of driving against streams of hostile traffic in the wrong direction up one-way streets, the worst time being when we found ourselves driving the wrong way up the A40 on our way to collect a beagle puppy that César wanted.

'Why a beagle?'

'Because my grandfather kept beagles,' César said. 'He brought the first one back from New York in 1904 – it was called Reddy.'

The breeding kennels were just outside Oxford. The journey was a disaster and César arrived speechless with rage. We chose a puppy, Ross, and took it home with us, managing to be stopped not once but twice on the way: once for failing to observe a one-way sign, and once for parking on a double yellow line while Ross, the new puppy, was violently sick. Each time the police constable in question let us go with a cautionary word and even a word of advice about how to deal with the puppy's nausea.

Everywhere we went, the police were there, flagging us down, even if only to tell us about a traffic diversion; and we lived in dread of being asked to show its papers. My mother was the only person to enjoy that car, but even she seemed to join in the conspiracy against it, and would press down her window and summon stray policemen to direct us when we were lost. In this she was incorrigible. César would sit rigid at the wheel with beads of icy sweat forming on his upper lip, and I with my heart in my mouth while my mother passed the time of day and discussed the paint shade and the electric windows with every representative of the law she could lay her hands on.

After we had collected the puppy, and safely parked the offending automobile in front of the flats, César said, 'I don't like that car.'

We tried to give it back to Elías, but Otto said that he had gone to Hastings. 'Do you want it then?' César asked him.

'Not likely, that thing is a hot biscuit. If you don't want it, dump it.'

César was hurt by Otto's lack of sympathy.

It seemed a terrible thing to do to a virtually brand-new Mercedes.

'What's wrong with it, anyway?' Otto asked.

'I don't like it,' César told him.

We decided to drive it to a quiet road somewhere around Regent's Park and just leave it. But the next day, we found that the petrol had been siphoned out of the tank. César went on his own to the garage on the corner of Abbeville Road. I watched him from the gateway, and I saw a man step out and accost him beside the murderer's house on the corner of the road, and I saw César freeze. They talked for some minutes and then César walked on. He returned some ten minutes later. He set down the petrol can and said, 'I'm in trouble, Veta.'

'Was it that man?' I asked him.

'Yes,' he said. 'The funny thing is I thought it was about the car.'

The shock had made him strangely voluble.

'I was sure it was about the car. But he says he's a C.I.A. agent.'

'Well, at least he's not from Venezuela or Interpol,' I said.

César ran his fingers through his hair with short despairing tugs. 'Surely you can see that it's worse,' he said eventually.

But I couldn't, and I asked, 'Why?'

'Just think of the word "oil",' he said, and then he waited. 'We have a puppet president in Caracas, and most of our oil is in U.S. hands. If he really is from the C.I.A., they're boss. Anyway, we've been under surveillance. He told me my every move in Italy last summer.'

'All two of them?' I interrupted.

César wheeled round on me, flashing his eyes. 'It's not funny, Veta. He followed us to the kennels to buy Ross, he follows us to the remand home, he knows our café, the Embankment Gardens.'

'And?' I asked.

'And why me?'

'Do you think they'll shoot you?' I asked, out of the blue. I thought he'd say, 'Don't be silly' or something, but he didn't. He said, 'Maybe. Maybe we won't get to Venezuela, after all.'

I could see that he was thinking very quickly.

'It's funny he didn't mention the car,' he said.

'What about the others?'

'He mentioned my "friends" twice; he didn't name any names. He wants me to meet him at the Cumberland Hotel tomorrow at three.'

'You won't go?' I said, shocked.

'I will,' César said, 'I want to know what he wants.'

'What about the others?' I repeated.

'We should warn them,' he said.

'I could get out through the back garden and be there and back in two hours,' I suggested, without the slightest hope that César would approve or adopt the plan, my suggestions for tactical manoeuvres usually struck him as ridiculous. But for once he said, 'Good', and then, 'Tell them what has happened, and that I don't know what's happening.'

I climbed over the high fence of our communal back garden into an equally drab stretch of grass on the other side which was another communal back garden and then I made my way past the dustbins of a private alleyway until I reached the street on the far side of our block. I had often seen trespassing children rampage through our garden and over the fence on what was for them a short cut to the local primary school.

Otto and Elías were playing chess at their service flat in Evelyn Gardens, and, to my disappointment, they showed no signs of immediate surprise when I told them of the new turn of events, but they insisted that I stayed for some tea, and then we drank a bottle of wine between us and then Otto said, 'You'd better get back or César will worry, and we'll have to pack and go.'

They called a taxi for me, arranging for me to wait for it at the corner of the road.

'Thank you for coming,' Otto said, adding, as I left, 'If anything happens to César, come to us.' And then yet again, 'Do you know how to get in touch with us, not here?'

I knew. There was a system of codes designed to operate in all emergencies, and it was the one thing I memorised in each city we went to.

It was dark outside, and I couldn't tell if I was being followed. I hadn't been followed on my way to them, and that seemed to be what mattered most. Back in Clapham once again, I entered the flats by the back gardens but I couldn't face the outside dustbin-lift with its creaking ropes to our second-floor flat again, so I just went in quickly in the dark and hoped for the best. There was nobody on the stairs, and when I let myself in, I found César asleep in an armchair in front of the television, wrapped in a tartan rug that my mother had covered him with.

Next day, I insisted on going to Hyde Park with César, and then on waiting for him at a little distance across the road from the Cumberland Hotel while he went for his meeting with the C.I.A. man who had called himself Mr Green. He took the most meticulous care in his dress that day, discarding even more shirts than he usually did, and winding and unwinding his silk cravat an unnecessary number of times. His preparations made me impatient.

'Why bother?' I complained.

'Why not?' he said, mysteriously.

'If you took Ross,' he added, 'you could take him for a run in the park while you waited.'

César told me that if he hadn't come out in three-quarters of an hour I should go home.

'What about you?' I asked him.

He shrugged. 'You won't help me by being there.'

'But if anything happens to you, there must be something I can do.'

'No,' César said, emphatically.

'Then there's no point in my coming,' I said angrily.

'Exactly,' he smiled, 'that is why I told you to stay here.'

We took the Underground to Marble Arch and César read while I tried to keep Ross from chewing the cuffs and sleeves of our fellow passengers. And then we walked in the November park for twenty minutes to kill time. Inevitably, I wanted to know about the C.I.A. man whom César was to meet.

'Who is he?' I asked.

César shrugged.

'What does he want?' I insisted.

César shrugged again.

'Where did he come from?'

César stopped. 'I haven't seen him yet, remember,' he said, 'I only know that they have followed us from Italy. I don't know for how long, I don't know why, I don't know who he is and I don't know who the hell he thinks I am either.'

It was time to go. I took up my post on the little island in the traffic in what was, I soon realised, the most dramatically obvious place in the neighbourhood, while César made his way to the Cumberland Hotel with a parting, 'I won't be long.'

Ross didn't like waiting and he was determined to get away from the place I had chosen to stand. When I held him, he struggled frantically to the ground, and when I put him down, he strained and twisted himself under the low fence into the road. It was all I could do to keep him from diving under the wheels of the oncoming traffic and he whined and squealed like a stuck pig. Cars that were caught on a red light rolled their windows down, and outraged drivers shouted, 'What are you doing to that dog?' and 'Leave that dog alone.'

Pieces of fur were flying out and catching on the wire fence, not from Ross but from my own fur coat that his thwarted paws were ripping bald. I became unnaturally afraid of these passing comments. They seemed like so many ill omens come to say that César was gone for ever inside the carpeted lobby of the Cumberland Hotel, and in his place, as a token of his having been, there was Ross, imprisoned in my arms with no alternative but death under the lanes of car wheels, and choosing death. And César's continued absence seemed like proof to my paranoia.

'Don't you hurt that dog!' a taxi-driver told me.

But Ross was hurting me, clawing at my hands and chest, terrified by now by the shouts from the traffic. I didn't pause to reflect that almost any dog, whether mongrel or hound or toy, could rally the support of total strangers in England, regardless of the rights or wrongs of the case. The canine presence has merely to be there, and the invisible third lid on the eye of the English is drawn back and the sympathy that we deny to each other is poured publicly over these chosen animals until it cloys. And it flowed then, shouted and shaken through the Bayswater lane of the road; and in my fear for César I believed that I held his unwilling substitute. Strangers shielded and defended César, too, they cosseted and restored him. Everywhere he went he was treated like a listed building. No one could resist his indifference.

Half an hour passed, and he didn't come. Three-quarters of an hour passed and he still didn't come. And then the time had spilled over into the time he said he wouldn't stay there for. I imagined him bundled into a laundry crate and carried out through the back door. I imagined him being thrown down the rubbish chute, or strapped to a chair in one of the countless bedrooms of the Cumberland with their drab modern furniture and their intercoms. And I wondered how many days it would take to find him if he was hidden in a dressing-room, like Coliseo in Rome. Would the room service finally discover the source of the smell?

An hour had passed since I took up my post, it was raining a thin drizzle and Ross was eating his own sick. I crossed the road and sat down on the edge of the grass. I had looped Ross's lead round a post some yards from me, in the hope that this would dissociate me from his renewed burst of yelps. César had told me to go home and stay there if anything went wrong. But now that he had been gone so long, I felt too numb to move. Ross was still rallying his supporters.

'Poor thing,' I could hear them say, and, 'Poor little blighter.'

I nursed my hand where Ross had scratched me. It was swollen and grazed, and I was feeling sick.

'Is that your dog?' a fierce-looking woman demanded, looking down at me.

'I'm looking after it,' I said lamely.

'Well, you shouldn't treat it like that,' she said. 'Can't you see it's unhappy? No, a young girl like you should be up taking him for a run.'

I staggered to my feet and untied the protesting Ross, and walked a few steps with him.

'Why don't you let him off the lead?' this woman insisted, following my slow heels with the sharp point of her brolly.

'Because he'd get run over,' I said shortly.

This last of Ross's champions continued to follow me along the road. I thought, 'I am being hounded', and smiled.

'It's not funny,' she said, prodding my boots with her umbrella. 'Poor little wretch', and then, from the corner of my eye I saw César crossing the network of roads to me.

'Good-bye,' I said, pushing past her as I ran to meet him, then I remembered that he might never forgive me if I hugged him in the street, so I slowed down and met him more formally.

I didn't ask him what had kept him for nearly two hours. I knew I had to wait for the information to flow. He picked up Ross and swung him around and then cuddled him.

'Have you been nice to him?' he asked me.

I didn't answer. It was I who had fed and brushed and washed and groomed and wormed and walked that dog, and now, out of the blue, not five minutes out of the Cumberland and the jaws of death, he had joined sides with all the dust raisers of my paranoia. I repeated Otto's frequent words to myself: 'O to be a dog in England!' Ross had won the day.

I had to wait until the evening to hear the details, and when they came, they were reassuringly simple. There was the man César had spoken to, flown in from Washington D.C., and there was the surveillance, but there was no mention of Otto or Elías as such, under any of their guises but the ones they had assumed on their return from Sweden, and even then they were just two of a list of friends.

'They just want me,' César smiled bashfully.

'What do you mean?'

'They want me to work for them.'

There was silence in the room for a few seconds, and then Elías said, 'How much?'

'Twenty thousand a year to begin with.'

I whistled despite myself and Otto pinched me in the ribs.

'What for?' Elías asked.

'For keeping an eye open when I get back to Venezuela.'

'Pounds?' Otto asked.

'Dollars,' César said.

We had all gone to the 'safe house' that we had arranged to meet in. It was an empty house in Chiswick to which we all had keys, but had never used before. Otto and Elías had moved their belongings into it, but César and I planned to return to Clapham later that same night. However, we drank so much aquavit with powdered bird pepper that César and I stayed over there with the others until late the next morning. César's encounter and would-be recruitment were treated as a joke, but underneath the joke, we could all feel a cold grid of reality.

'How do you know that was what he wanted?'

César didn't. Not for sure.

'And how did they find you?'

He said, 'My name came up in Bologna, on the "Lanzini

case" and somebody noticed it so they put a couple of men on to Veta and me there, in Paris, here.'

'What did he do when you refused?'

'He kept trying, and then he said that he didn't blame me; and then he got quite friendly.'

'What did you talk about?' I asked, bitterly, remembering my two hours in the rain.

'Well, we talked about James Bond and cars and things for a few minutes, and then he said that he knew from my file that I grew fruit trees, and we talked about oranges versus avocados for his plot in San Diego, and the risk of phytoptera sinamoma.'

'Of what?' I asked.

'It's a root fungus,' César said.

'And who won?' Elías asked.

'I think he'll be getting himself some avocados,' César beamed, 'and I recommended he join the Avocado Society.'

'Well,' Otto said, 'if you ever get to California, perhaps you'll see him there.'

César shrugged.

That night, when we were all in bed, César in the only real bed 'for his rheumatism', and me on a sofa, and Otto and Elías with eiderdowns and duvets on the floor, Elías whispered in the dark, 'Did he really tell you to phone up the U.S. Embassy in Caracas and ask for George Washington if you ever changed your mind?'

'Hmm,' César said.

'I don't know,' Elías proclaimed to the room in general, 'it's one thing if the most efficient intelligence agency in the world fails to spot two fools like us from under their very noses, and if a stolen Swedish Mercedes means nothing to them, yes,' he mused, 'even if they're dumb enough to think they could recruit César, but that their code-word should be George Washington! I ask you,' he said, sitting up. But Otto was asleep, or passed out from the aquavit, and César was breathing heavily, through his mouth, because of the misshaped cartilage in his nose, and Elías was left to mutter, 'George Washington, indeed!' until he too fell asleep.

Chapter XXV

Christmas came and went, and then January, and it snowed but still no tickets came. A sum of money even came, cabled from Caracas. But, when I said, 'Shall we buy the tickets now?'

César said: 'No, the tickets will come any day.'

And we spent the money buying presents and what César called 'the indispensable' for our voyage and for the time when we arrived at the other end of it. The indispensable included two dozen pairs of knee-length socks that we went to Edinburgh for so that César could personally supervise the choosing of them from among the stocks of the shop that he revered as part of his father's memory. And it included another beagle puppy. Enough sharpening strops to last a lifetime, an antique-gold fob watch, two thousand aspirin, and a collection of eighteenth- and nineteenth-century door knockers.

By the end of January our money was gone and the others were ready to sail to Chile. They booked themselves two tickets for the end of June, sailing from Genova.

By mid-February I had made my farewells to all my friends and relations, our trunks were packed and catalogued and padlocked, and César didn't seem to mind, or even notice, the waiting. However, I was growing daily more restless, I wanted either to set sail or to return to Milan. But César was positive, the tickets would arrive any day now.

'But when?' I would ask, and he would always reply,

'Mañana', and cross his arms in the elaborate way he had, and have nothing more to say on the matter, and I would never know what to reply after that. I remembered, particularly, a dinner that my stepfather had attended in Dublin where an advertising executive from Connemara had made friends with one of the South American delegates, and they were discussing and translating for each other the various intricacies of their languages, and the South American had asked, 'How would you say "Mañana" in English?'

And the man from Connemara had said, 'We have a lot of words to convey time in English, but nothing with that specific urgency of "mañana".'

And now I lacked that specific urgency to retaliate. I was drifting like Lopez de Aguirre down waters unknown to me in an empty dream of grandeur.

I made a few half-hearted attempts at weighing anchor. I suggested that we borrow the money. But César said no. I had suggested that we sell the Mercedes, but César had again said no, and we ditched it in Hanover Terrace two days after meeting the man from the C.I.A.

'What about Otto?' I said. 'He could get us the fares.' But César wouldn't hear of it.

'They don't want us to go, I cannot let them pay for us, we have to get there under our own steam.'

So I kept paddling around, not in steam, but in the tepid water of that London winter, moving between Evelyn Gardens and Clapham South like a stray shuttlecock caught in the wind, dividing my time between reading and sitting by the statue to the Camel Corps in the Embankment Gardens on a cold bench that made a poor substitute for a train.

It was sitting there that I had the idea of getting our tickets myself. My father had a friend who had a shipping line and it suddenly dawned on me that I too had a way of producing tickets. César wanted our passage to fall out of the sky, his return to the hacienda had to be devoid of all sordid transactions.

All right, I would arrange it.

It took me one day to locate my unwitting patron and

another to break through the barrier of secretaries, assistants and couriers that stood between me and the great man himself. And then I failed to get an appointment or even so much as a word with him. His lordship was unobtainable. It was on the third day, through the help of yet another friend of the family, this time an ambassador with access to the inner hive, that I asked for two berths to La Guaira. On the following morning a special courier arrived at my mother's flat with a paid booking for the suite of honour on the *Montserrat*, sailing on 11th April from Southampton.

That morning I made my daily visit to the South London Hospital for Women with all the gloom and boredom of the last month gone from me. The kidney trouble and the haemorrhage of Porta Ticinese had returned and I was now in my third month of antibiotics. I made my way past the steamy corridors by the kitchens to the laboratories in the basement, where I handed over my usual phial of pink urine.

'You look very pleased with yourself today,' one of the analysts commented.

'I'm going to Venezuela,' I told her.

'You can't,' she said, 'you're ill.'

'I'm ill because I can't go,' I said. 'I'll be fine when I get there.'

She took my phial doubtfully and said, 'I shall have a word with Dr Wilcox about that.'

César was waiting for me outside. He never went into hospitals if he could avoid it, and we went together to tell the others of our good fortune. He even asked me how I was, a rare thing with him, since he assumed that everyone who could get to their feet was well, and that everyone had a moral duty to get to their feet. Notwithstanding, he inquired: 'And how is your kidney today?'

'Fine,' I said.

And everything did feel fine. Gone were the days when Dr Wilcox could put the fear of God in me, not even the South London Hospital itself could haul up the memories of the months I had spent there in a bleak sideroom off the children's ward with a drip and a catheter and a tube. Each time they had operated, they had reopened a previous scar, but we were going to sail to Venezuela, we had become suddenly invulnerable and no one had the power to reopen wounds any more, not even the South London, not even the sight of Stewart Ward with its windows hung with grime on the top floor as we crossed the road to the station.

Nothing much happened between then and the beginning of April. César and I took the dogs for a walk every day on Clapham Common, passing over the hump-backed bunkers that remained from the last war, and the points littered all over the grass like the marks on an anatomical drawing charted for acupuncture where all the different murders had taken place, and the plague pond where the bodies had been dumped in the twelfth century, turned now into a duck pond with a willow island and a muffled halo of inveterate optimists casting their lines into the burial mud in the hope of a fish. Every afternoon was spent with Otto and Elías, avoiding any mention of our future voyages as one might avoid any mention of death to a friend with terminal cancer. There were occasional visits to the Royal Festival Hall, and frequent visits to the cinema. Elías was the most restless of us all, and he seemed to survive the time of our waiting to sail by inventing a constant relay of things to do and different places to stay. But mostly, he was bored with a contagious boredom interspersed with manic bouts of organised entertainment. Our departure had become inevitable, and we were all anxious for it to happen as soon as possible to relieve the strain.

Only two weeks before we were due to set sail, our ship was damaged by fire.

'You see,' Otto said triumphantly, 'now you can't go,' and he threw a newspaper with news of the fire on to the breakfast table.

'It is destiny,' Otto added, delighted, 'now you'll have to stay with us. The *Montserrat* is dockbound for repairs. It says here that . . . '

Otto turned to César and so did we, and we were all struck by a kind of stillness that had taken over his face; behind the pallor there was a sort of shifting-sands expression, as though he had been sinking but now he had sunk.

'It says here that it'll be ready again soon,' Otto concluded.

'Anyone would think you hated each other,' Elías said. 'No nonsense about the greater love, but I am sick of the bickering, and you know I don't like being sick so let's go somewhere tonight', and the mixture of enthusiasm and menace in his voice made us forget that we went somewhere every night, and Otto stopped his banter, and César stared morosely out of the streaked windows into the bleak concrete spring of central London.

'A party,' Elías added, 'there is a party tonight with some Venezuelans in Chelsea, we never see our compatriots, so we'll make an exception and go tonight.'

On a normal day, it would have been the last thing any of us would have done. Unlike the English who seem to gather like migrating martins when abroad, César and Otto and Elías shunned their countrymen whenever possible. Even when it might have been politically 'safe' we avoided Venezuelans like a virus disease. I had asked Elías why this should be and he had said, 'The decent ones stay at home, on the whole it's only the dregs of the Maracuchos, the people of Maracaibo, who come with their big mouths and more dollars in their pockets than they can even count and they all have names like General Electric Ramírez, and J. Edgar Hoover Márquez. Names are a tricky business,' he said, 'if your parents had called you Trans World Airlines instead of Lisaveta, it might have changed your attitude to life, and if you then discovered that life was wholly a matter of buying and selling in which your role was only to buy, you too might have become brash. I don't really blame them,' he said, 'I just can't stand the sight of them.'

It was a tense day, with César pacing our rooms like a dose of flu in search of a victim, and it was a relief to look ahead to the evening, when we would be able to share the silent burden of his ill-humour with a crowd.

When we arrived at the house in Chelsea where the party was to be held, I asked Elías, 'Are these Maracuchos?'

Elias was shocked.

'Of course not. They're Andinos,' he said, and released my arm with some displeasure.

Since my first visit to Vitaliano's flat in Paris, I had never again been confronted with more than one or two Vene-zuelans.at a time, so the sight of a roomful of unknown faces was too much for me, and I retired to a far table in one corner of the room, and the company of a boy whom I took to be of about my own age, but who turned out to be only thirteen.

We had arrived one step removed from gate-crashers, not unwelcome but uninvited, and of the three brothers in the room, it was Lenin, the youngest, who held my attention all evening, with his boarding-school talk.

Before we arrived, Elías had briefly filled us in on the Ramírez family. The father was a journalist and a Communist who had left Venezuela years before to escape political persecution and to spend the fruits of a series of successful property deals.

'He's very nice, though,' Elías said hastily, 'despite it.'

I knew that Elías viewed Communists rather as César did the French.

'And his wife is very hospitable. Then the boys don't do much. Carlos was at university in Moscow, but I heard that he was chucked out for being lazy and chasing skirts; and then the middle one is very musical, I know him a bit, he's good at parties, and then the little one is at boarding school here in England.'

'Hmm,' César said disapprovingly, 'and what do they do?'

César believed that people either had to do or be.

'They don't really do anything,' Elías said. 'Carlos was, I think he still is, at the London School of Economics, but I don't think he does any studying.'

'He's not a cyclist?' César asked suspiciously.

'No,' Elías laughed, 'it's not as bad as that.'

César loathed cyclists, that is, the kind that wear fancy socks and bands and have racing bikes and are 'in training'. Whenever he saw one, no matter where, he always had a word of abuse to sling after him, and then, to us, 'If I had my way they would all be carting sugar-cane.' This 'carting sugar-cane' was a remedy that he believed in almost as much as in the power of aspirin and the importance of etiquette.

We had approached the road with the painted wall on the

244

corner where the Ramírezes lived, and César was looking more and more gloomy.

'He must do something,' I said.

'Not really,' Elías said, 'Carlos is a simple man, he likes pretty women and he doesn't like Jews. The only one truly striking factor about Carlos Ramírez Illyich is his ambition.'

We had reached the door, and were about to knock, when César said, 'Ambition for what?'

'Fame, future, limelight, power, you name it, and he wants it.'

'And Jews?' César asked.

'His brother says that the only time that Carlos acts like a human being is when he talks about Jews. He says he hates them.'

Otto had grown impatient with the talk.

'Let's go in and see this robot,' he said.

César's expression hadn't really changed since the morning. As we went in and were ushered downstairs, I realised that it was probably a mistake to have come at all. César loathed parties with people he didn't know. But that night, in particular, when his ship had just burnt, he was in no mood for strangers. He refused a glass of rum and insisted on keeping his fur coat on, and went and stood on his own. He was glowering, like a turkey vulture with an eye for an open sore.

I left him and made friends with Lenin, the youngest, who was bored and glad to find someone to whom he could talk. The kind of jokes that go round a public school don't change much, the E-type carrots were still coming out of the ground at ninety miles an hour, and our stocks of stories about geography mistresses and games masters were very similar. Lenin spoke like any English prep-school boy and but for his black eyes and hair and faintly sallow complexion, he could easily have been one. He introduced me to his brothers, who were both less fluent than he.

César continued to smoulder.

Otto came up to me and said, 'As soon as we can, we should get César away from here, he's really in no mood for a party, and he's spoiling for a row.'

Then, to everyone's surprise, César relaxed and accepted a glass of hot rum toddy and sat down to talk to Mrs Ramírez, with whom he found he had a lot in common, if only geographically. I could hear them discussing the ins and outs of such villages as Betijoque and Niquitao and Escuque. Mrs Ramírez seemed to know all about César's family and she soothed him with praise of his cousin, the ambassador, and his uncle, the general, and general this and cardinal that. I was learning more about his family than ever before, and I kept listening with one ear to them, and the other to Lenin, with his scrapes and trials and exploits out of bounds.

'I should think you miss your avocados then, Don César,' Mrs Ramírez was saying.

'Yes and no,' César said, 'you see Israeli avocados are the best in the world, and I can buy them anywhere.'

The moment of provocation had arrived. Lenin nudged me under the table. 'This should be fun,' he whispered, 'my brother hates Israel.'

Carlos had heard but he pretended not to.

'I like Israeli avocados best,' César insisted. 'Don't you, Carlos?'

Carlos Ramírez looked from Elías to Otto to César.

'I don't really like avocados,' he said.

'What about Israelis?' César said. 'I heard you didn't like Israelis.'

'I support Palestine,' Carlos said, posing a little.

'And what about Jews?' César probed.

'What about them?' Carlos said, smiling uneasily.

'I heard that you hated them.'

'I don't really care,' Carlos said, trying all the while to defuse the tension, 'but I don't like them, César,' he said, appealing to some imaginary common bond. 'I don't like Jews and I don't like avocados. I'm not interested in them, you know.'

'No,' César said slowly, 'I don't know.'

Otto, Elías and I were eyeing the door.

After Carlos's last statement, César's eyes were full of scorn. He loathed signs of intimacy where there was none. I could see him thinking behind his frown, 'I don't remember

playing marbles with this boy, that he should presume to call
me thou.'

'Do you mean', César asked, 'that you are not interested in
the fruit?'

'Fruit!' Carlos said emphatically. 'Trees, flowers, I don't
care if I never see one again, and I am certainly not going to
argue with someone I respect about them.'

'If I had my way,' César said, 'people who don't care would
be tied up against a wall and shot.'

'But you've got me wrong.' (Again the familiar 'tu'.) 'I'm a
terrorist, like you, César old man, anyway,' he said
petulantly, 'you're not Jewish are you?'

'No,' César said, as slowly as before, 'I'm not a Jew or a
terrorist, just an old man. But I have done what I was going to
do and now I champion trees.' He paused, and then added,
'What have you done?'

Carlos treated everyone to another cuba libre and drank
down his own. His mother was relieved, but Lenin was
disappointed, there had been no fight, no broken glass,
nothing.

'What did all that mean?' Lenin asked me.

I shrugged and rose to leave, the others were already saying
good-bye to Mrs Ramírez.

'Promise you'll come back, Lisaveta,' Lenin said.

'I'll try,' I told him.

'Where can I write to you?' he asked quickly.

'I don't know,' I said, 'the poste restante maybe, why?'

'I like you,' he smiled, and then, 'Actually, I'm only
twelve.'

Carlos saw us to the street door, he seemed more uneasy
now that we were leaving. Both he and his next brother were
smooth and overweight, and they stood filling the door-
frame.

'Are we friends?' they called after us.

Elías turned round and shouted diplomatically, 'Nothing
has happened, it's all right.'

Later that night Elías said to César, 'Why were you so mean to
Carlos? He's only a kid, he'll grow up.'

'I didn't like him,' César replied.

'He's young,' Elías argued.

'He's about your age, and I like you,' César said.

'Well,' Elías insisted, 'I still think you were too hard on him, he likes you, and he said he didn't mean it about the Jews, it was probably just a joke.'

'No,' César said, 'he wouldn't know what a joke was if it jumped up and bit him. And I wasn't too hard on him at all, I was too soft, he has prejudice and no principles, and he's just out for a bit of fun, and I don't like him and that is that.'

But it wasn't 'that' because there was Lod airport, and Carlos Ramírez Illyich became known as 'the Jackal', and Entebbe, and his fame as a terrorist grew until he became the world's most wanted man.

But the gulf would always be as wide between the old school of terrorists and the new; the principled and the unprincipled, between honour and ambition and notoriety and fame.

Chapter XXVI

The *Montserrat* was given a new sailing date for 4th June, and once again we waited. Every five days or so we crossed the Channel and spent days in Paris, Boulogne or Le Havre.

'Is it safe?' I asked Elías.

'It's never safe to stay in one place too long. And as to going to France,' he shrugged, 'it staves off the boredom.'

'You could go now,' I suggested.

'No,' he said, 'we'll wait until the end.'

By May our two beagles had been banished by Otto, and they scratched in exile at my mother's flat. César had grown devoted to the dogs, and went into a kind of voluntary exile with them during the hours of daylight, ferrying them to and from Clapham South. I was grateful for my kidney infection which kept me insatiably sleepy. Otto said he was in love again, and Elías was restless. From the poste restante came a trickle of notes from Lenin Ramírez.

Three weeks before we were due to sail, Elías announced, 'I'm getting out, is anyone coming?'

But Otto was in love, and César was tied to the dogs, and I was tied to my own inertia, so Elías left on his own, saying that he would be back for our departure.

During the last week of May Otto spent a lot of time sitting quietly with his head hanging out of the open back window. If

I offered him a cup of tea he would say, 'I wish you weren't going.'

And whatever I said, he would answer, 'I wish you weren't going.'

And then occasionally he would rally from his depression enough to give me tips on how to survive in the Andes. 'Never trust anyone', and 'Friendship doesn't exist there. It's just family', and 'Never go out unarmed, and don't carry a knife until you can use it.' It was an odd mixture of advice, and it always ended up with, 'I wish you weren't going.'

But we had our trunks already stored at Southampton, and our cabin luggage all prepared, and César had his Prescott and his *Lives of Napoleon* ready to read on the deck.

'It will be sixteen days at sea, Veta, a real rest,' he told me, speaking as he always did as a man deprived of his daily sleep. And the wooden travelling crates for the dogs had been delivered from Harrods and sent on to the ship, and with their two names, Ross and Megan, gilded on the top. And we had a reinforced sack of dog biscuits to take on board, and six dozen tins of dog food, in case, César explained, we were shipwrecked.

Elías returned on the day before we were due to sail; he came, as he often did, as though he had never been away. We all went to tea at the Ritz with my mother, and from there we took a taxi to Soho. En route, Otto guided us to a leather shop, where we stopped. 'Just a minute,' he said to the others, and to the taxi-driver, and then he pulled me inside. 'You need a handbag,' he said, 'these Gladstone bags won't do for the hacienda. Choose one,' he added waving his arm around the shop. Then he went back to the taxi.

I chose a beautiful shoulder bag in light tan and then went to find Otto.

'Good,' he said, 'you get in, and I'll meet you further on.'

He rejoined us in the taxi two streets away, looking dishevelled and out of breath.

'I bet you didn't pay for it,' I said, disappointedly. I had hoped, for some reason, that he would, as a sort of symbolic, legal last present.

'What would you like me to do with it then,' he said, 'throw it out of the window?'

But I took the bag, and we had dinner, and then took my mother back to Evelyn Gardens where she was to spend the night with us, and then the rest of us stayed up until half-past three playing one of Otto's silly word games with its usual extravagant forfeits. And then we, too, went to bed.

The next morning I wore my cream silk Edwardian dress with the tucks in the bodice and the high neck and the dozens of buttons on the cuff. I saw that Otto had put my new handbag by my pillow and inside he had written on the leather, 'For Lisaveta so that we meet again, Otto.'

I knew that his name wasn't really Otto, just as Elías wasn't really Elías, they were just names that they had used for so long that they seemed more real than their own.

Elías surpassed himself on the drive to Southampton, reaching that port in what seemed like mere minutes, and the hounds on the floor at the back of the car were so alarmed that they began to bay mournfully at Putney Bridge, and did not cease until we came to Winchester where we stopped for a drink, and where they were both violently sick. My mother, who was also ill at ease with speed, had a similar reaction in the front seat, berating and pinching Elías's ribs in an effort to make him slow down. Notwithstanding, we arrived, located our ship and unloaded ourselves and our luggage and the dogs and the six dozen tins of dog food.

César and I said good-bye rather formally, when the time came. At the last moment, everything seemed to be happening too quickly, there should have been more time, after all the months of waiting, it was too soon to board. But none of us really liked good-byes, so we arranged to see the purser and find our cabins and wave from the lower deck. As we moved with a crush of other passengers up the gangplank, only Otto pulled me back, and whispered, 'I hope César loves you more than I do.'

Again, there was no time to speak, with Megan straining at her lead, dragging me out of earshot and into the ship. Our cabin was easy to find, it was marked on all the deck plans and was one of only two of its size on board. I hardly took in the suite of rooms when we entered them that first time to leave our cabin luggage. A steward was pointing out the advantages of our position, showing us the service bells, and enumerating the cabin services available. And then we went back to the first deck, by the quayside, where the others were waiting. They already looked smaller, and their words were mere mouthings in the general confusion. After a moment of staring at each other from high to low as we had all stood leaning over the metal bridges of the Naviglio Grande, staring down at the dead fish and the bed-ends and the waving hand that was a glove caught in the weeds, we waved to each other, and it seemed as unreal as that one hand in the water, and we stopped abruptly.

Elías took my mother and Otto by the arm, and steered them away, then he turned and shouted, 'Geronimo!', and it carried quite clearly up over the crowd, and we waited on the deck to see if they would turn again, say something more, but they didn't, not even my mother, who would have done in normal circumstances. And when they were out of sight, and we were left on our own, we didn't want to talk, so we walked the dogs around the less crowded upper deck, round and round and round, until César said, 'I have to lie down now' and disappeared, and I went back to the railings on the quayside of the ship and stared down at the concrete and the crates and trolleys, hoping, I suppose, that the others would come back, or a fire sweep over the *Montserrat* again, or that a blockade would stop us in our tracks.

None of these things happened, and we weighed anchor at two o'clock, heading for La Guaira, via La Coruna and Vigo, Tenerife and Trinidad, with the two dogs housed not in their own named crates from Harrods, but in two strange sheep pens: for which the chief steward apologised with a smile, the Spanish Line didn't cater for dogs. I remember that the first-class dining-room was nearly empty, even on full nights, there were only ever six of us, and a fleet of stewards to wait, and the quince jelly with the cheeses was very good, and the fish course, in particular, was always excellent, and even César liked the wines. And I remember fresh flowers in our room, I think they were from the captain; and the dogs were delinquent for the entire voyage, and in Tenerife we bought jewels on the black market and at Trinidad we were both too lazy to go ashore. And on the first night, César made me tear up the names and addresses of all our friends, but I couldn't bring myself to throw them away, so I kept them and jigsawed the scraps until they were beyond piecing together and then I threw them over the railings into the sea in a trail for the flying fish somewhere in the Caribbean, fragments of Oxford and Paris and Milan lost in the foam.

Later, César and I grew avocados for seven years, living feudally on his estates in the Andes, with his retainers and his sugar-cane, and we never travelled with the others again. I saw them sometimes, not for years though at first, and always briefly. The last time was in Paris, at Pierre Goldman's the week before he was murdered. It was just two days, and most of them spent on the train, and then a few hours of paranoia and years of reminiscences. Then I went back to Dunkirk and to Norfolk, while the others went to Spain and Pierre Goldman stayed on in Paris, editing *Les Temps Modernes*, and waiting for the birth of his baby, and was gunned down outside the maternity clinic.

I was very fond of the handbag that Otto gave me as a going-away present, and I used it for years; even when it was scratched and battered, it had a special feeling for me. But last year I left it in a telephone box in Wolverhampton and I didn't notice until I was in Manchester, and the police could not trace it. In fact, when I reported the loss, the constable said, 'What can we do about it?'

'I want it back,' I said.

And he laughed and said, 'You must be joking.'

So maybe we won't meet again, as Otto had written on the leather. Maybe there won't even be half a page in *The Times* or the *Observer* with details of his death or murder. I tell myself that I shall go back to Italy some day (if only to stare into the Naviglio Grande) but I fear that the worn tartan will have become plastic, and the cardboard rolls will be kept as soft as cotton wool in cling-film wrappers, or worst of all, the lines will have become all electric, and the old carriages scrapped and replaced by aluminium flyers, and no one will ever know the love of the slow train to Milan.

MORE ABOUT PENGUINS, PELICANS
AND PUFFINS

For further information about books available from Penguins please write to Dept EP, Penguin Books Ltd, Harmondsworth, Middlesex UB7 ODA.

In the U.S.A.: For a complete list of books available from Penguins in the United States write to Dept DG, Penguin Books, 299 Murray Hill Parkway, East Rutherford, New Jersey 07073.

In Canada: For a complete list of books available from Penguins in Canada write to Penguin Books Canada Ltd, 2801 John Street, Markham, Ontario L3R 1B4.

In Australia: For a complete list of books available from Penguins in Australia write to the Marketing Department, Penguin Books Australia Ltd, P.O. Box 257, Ringwood, Victoria 3134.

In New Zealand: For a complete list of books available from Penguins in New Zealand write to the Marketing Department, Penguin Books (N.Z.) Ltd, P.O. Box 4019, Auckland 10.

In India: For a complete list of books available from Penguins in India write to Penguin Overseas Ltd, 706 Eros Apartments, 56 Nehru Place, New Delhi 110019.